angel wing

angel wing

Books by Linda Hartley

Fiction
the broken line
angel wing

Non-fiction

Wisdom of the Body Moving
Servants of the Sacred Dream
Somatic Psychology: Body, Mind and Meaning
Embodied Spirit, Conscious Earth

Edited collections

Contemporary Body Psychotherapy: The Chiron Approach
The Fluid Nature of Being: Embodied practices for healing and wholeness

angel wing

Linda Hartley

ELMDON

BOOKS

For Brue – dear friend, artist, healer

Act One
1927 - 1939

1

Movement was my first language. I remember running in circles around the small patch of grass in our garden, flapping my arms like a bee. As if I could fly.

I was just three when I ran away for the first time. I took my yellow-haired rag doll in her pram and ran out of the gate, along to the corner, and half way round the crescent. Then I stopped. I didn't know where to go next. And anyway, my father had caught up with me. He took hold of my hand without saying a word and walked me back home.

Years later I remember running over the fields – the sheer joy of it – the lightness in my feet as I skimmed over buttercups, and the sun in my eyes.

I was always running – into something I shouldn't have come across, or away from wherever I was. I wanted to get away. This felt like my whole, big purpose in life.

Movement was my first love. I danced, and when I thought no one could hear me, I sang. That is how words began, the language of words, my second language.

And there the trouble really began, because I could not

see how to match the sounds of words to what I was feeling inside, in my body, through my movement. The language of movement and the language of words made no sense to each other. There was no one who could explain the meaning of one to the other, just as there were none who could interpret the words of Esther and Trevor – the people I called Mammy and Daddy – to each other.

They were strangers, unknown to each other, and I was a foreign land. They would visit me from time to time, but we lived in a world of incomprehension and long silences. The art of messaging in our home was a crackle of broken signals, like the static of a wireless stuck between stations.

If I could speak in my first language, I would describe the push-pull excitement of the swing in our back garden. The great tug of effort as my heels thrust through the air, propelling swing and me up and up, and the great thrill surging through my belly. Then stomach tipping over as the swing arced down again, towards the earth, then back and up – whoosh, whoosh – push and arc and the thrill surging up inside me again. I could almost fling myself up and all the way over the top, like a stone tied to the end of a rope. Up and over, down, round, up and over – whoosh – back, forwards.

'Ellen, that's enough now. You're going too high. You'll fall,' she would call out from the kitchen window.

'No, I won't fall. I'm flying.' But she would never understand that, with her tight tied-up hair and skirt to match, her neat clicking heels and polished nails. She would never fly.

Act Three
1945 – 1955

2

I grip the wheel tighter and straighten my back, coaxing my mind to stay alert as the veil of dusk obscures the margins of the road. The car bumps over holes in the tarmac, rattles louder and judders as I press my foot down on the accelerator. I feel tired. No, weary. I carry the weight of the last two years right down in my bones, like an impossible burden I had never expected, not wished for at this moment in my life. Now I have no choice. I have to make this journey. I must find her.

Through the creeping grey of evening mist, the harsh headlights of an oncoming car pierce into the back of my eyes. I want to look away but the glare draws me to stare right into the centre of the beam. The car flashes past and for a split second I am blind. I have swerved towards the centre of the road. I yank the wheel sharply to the left and straighten up again.

The light is fading and still I have forty miles to go. I have driven all day but tonight I will be in Liverpool. In the morning I will catch the ferry, and be in Belfast by lunchtime.

A tune is playing relentlessly in my mind. I begin to sing, quietly under my breath at first, then at the top of my voice, belting it out, just to keep awake.

'My Bonnie lies over the ocean, my Bonnie lies over the sea…oh, bring back my Bonnie to me, to me…' Just thirty-nine more miles. I must keep going. I'll buy fish and chips for supper then snuggle into a warm bed for the night. I had imagined a stroll around the harbour, watching the sunset over the Irish Sea. Instead I will arrive in the dark, wishing I had set out earlier. But it had been so hard to leave.

At the last minute James was trying, one more time, to persuade me not to go. During his fortnight holiday we could leave the children with his mother and he would come with me. He pleaded with me. He would drive and I could rest. Some rest would be good for me, he said. But more than I needed to rest, I needed to do this alone.

James was angry that I had to make this journey. Angry that a letter falling onto our doormat one spring morning had thrown my life, our life together, into chaos, and plunged me into a hole so deep he could no longer find me. He felt hurt when I would not let him help.

'Ellen, this is crazy. Please — if you must go, at least let me come with you. You can't do this on your own. Not the way you are at the moment.' By this he meant the madness in my brain that kept me sad and empty and sometimes flying into a rage for no reason that he could fathom. The car keys were clenched tightly in his hand, which was dug deep into his trouser pocket.

Resorting in frustration to my first language, I moved my arms in a wide circle and brought my fists together in front of my chest.

'I have to do it by myself. I just have to do it, James,' I managed to articulate after one long moment of staring blankly at him. 'Please give me the keys.'

'Mammy, when will you be back? Will you be away for

long? Will you be back to take me swimming tomorrow?'
Martin came running in from the garden, mud on his knees
and a smear of jam across his pink cheek. I had already said
goodbye to him, but now would have to do it all over again.

Anita toddled in after him a few moments later, her yellow
beach pail in one hand and a blue plastic spade in the other. Her
red curls trembled as she swayed precariously. Her toes fringed
the edges of her soft padding feet like two rows of small pearls.

My heart fell at the sight of them standing in the hallway,
mouths open, identical lost expressions on their faces, a plea in
their wide eyes – Anita's blue as a lake, Martin's deep brown, like
my own. They sensed that this was more serious than just an
outing to the coast or a shopping trip to Newcastle. I faltered
as I looked into their innocent upturned eyes, unsure if I had
the courage to leave them behind.

But I did. James finally gave me the keys – more to avoid a
scene in front of the children than from any skilful persuasion
on my part. Thankfully the car coughed into life after a burst
of choke and two sharp turns of the ignition, saving me from
the indignity of the cranking handle. That would surely have
stalled my flight.

I could not look back as I drove away. I knew their forlorn
faces, and Anita's plump little fist clenching and unclenching a
'goodbye', would break my heart and bring me right back home
again. Tears were brimming in my eyes, but my heart was set.

My life had seemed perfect. After the battles and tumult and
lies of my growing up years I had finally found happiness
with James. But that was before the letter arrived. The truth
that Liza's letter brought seared through my life like a volcano
cracking open the crust of hardened earth. The years of joy
were swept up in the firestorm and burnt to ash. It happened so
quickly – in the time it took to read one solitary page of blue-
inked words, my life with James and Martin was ripped apart.

I was eight months pregnant and looking forward to Anita's birth, but I cannot remember the sweet anticipation now. Only a turmoil of confusion, followed by an anger so strong I thought my swollen belly might explode. Then a moment of stark and cold clarity as I understood all that had happened. A grief so deep burrowed into me, so that when Anita arrived I could not even welcome her. I gave her to James to hold because I couldn't bear to look into her tiny cherub face. There was nothing of a mother in me, just a gaping hole where the fire in the earth had erupted and emptied itself out into my life.

Poor Anita. I had nothing to give her. When she is older I will explain and tell her how sorry I am, but for now she is much too young to understand the dark feelings that came between us.

The night is black now. My shoulders are tight and aching, my breath shallow. I have stopped singing but still hum fragments of the tune softly. The road has narrowed and demands my full attention. Even so, my left hand slips into my cardigan pocket now and then. It's a habit that has grown unconscious and firmly ingrained, like an old olive tree spreading its roots wide and deep into dry earth to find the source of nourishment. I finger the small square of rough paper, like a blind person reading a message in Braille. Just to be sure the words are still there. Just to be sure I know where I'm going.

Of course, I can remember the words, but still…

The Convent of the Sacred Heart

Ormeau Road

Belfast

A simple message. Nine words that I have learnt by heart, like a poem. Like a thread connecting me to another world, tying up ends, making things right. At least that is my hope.

I wriggle my shoulders and try to relax, take a deep breath, and centre both hands near the top of the steering wheel, at ten-to-two, just as James taught me. I can almost feel him sitting next to me in the passenger seat, doing his utmost to teach me how to drive.

'Stop! Put the brakes on. NOW!'

'Oops. Sorry. I didn't see it.' We were tipped, nose-down, into a shallow ditch and a bruise was coming up on his forehead where he had hit the windscreen. The bridge of my nose had met the top of the steering wheel with a sharp crack, and I felt a warm trickle of blood. On the other side of the ditch three sheep were staring at us, too startled to run away, as they ought to if they understood anything about motorcars and learner drivers. We both burst out laughing. At least I had been driving slowly and we weren't seriously hurt.

James climbed out and took a photograph of the three bemused sheep, then one of me leaning over the bonnet, sweeping a Chaplinesque forearm over my brow as I tried to push the car out of the ditch. Laughing, he snapped away with his new Brownie box camera, before coming to my rescue.

Remembering that day, a smile begins to soften my tight face. What a gift James has been in my life, despite all the worry I have caused him. He stands by me, dependable, enduring, bold in the face of every obstacle. Troubles seem to give way in his presence, like water flowing round a boulder. He stands like a rock in the midst of my turbulent life.

As I come round a bend in the road, another set of headlights is veering towards me. I sense a steep drop down through the woods to my left. In the glare of the lights I can barely see the space between the side of the lorry and the edge of the road. There is a very narrow passage. There is barely space for me to squeeze through.

The lorry hurtles out of the mist and is looming towards me before I can take another breath. The rusted chrome of the fender glints in the two beams that my headlights throw out, as if in response to them – a bizarre conversation of signals, as foreign to me as those of Esther and Trevor. The silver-red grate of its mouth is leering at me, as if to bite, chew and swallow me up into its entrails of acrid smoke. Headlights flash brighter, like eyes – startled, threatening, and finally enraged. I am in the way.

Esther's face flashes across my vision. The gloss of sleek blonde hair, the sharp glint in her ice blue eyes – a dart of light, a bright pinprick. I was always in Esther's way. By the time I was five it was clear to me she did not want me there.

A fraction of a second and the image is gone – the time it takes for my feet to brace against the clutch and the brake, but the car speeds on.

The headlights are close now. I should get out of the way, but I don't. Perhaps I could manoeuvre through the narrow passage. But that would take such presence, such skill and great effort.

I can't focus. I can't summon the energy and the will to steer myself through the clear space between falling and being crushed against the metal teeth of the lorry that is bearing down on me.

Oh God, James. I wish you were here now. Just take the wheel from me and steer me through, as you always do. I cannot do this by myself.

My mind feels so jangled by the sleepless nights, the crying of my baby, the torment of the lies that were told. In the sliver of space between this moment and the next I cannot find the will to care whether I scrape my way through or not. It would be easier to simply let go, be done with all the heartache and betrayal, the exhaustion. My failure to nurture my baby girl is a constant knife turning over in my soul. I can barely face myself. Better, then, to let go, to surrender and be done.

With that thought, the urgent need to reach Liza springs up again, and I struggle to summon the effort, to make my hands turn the wheel and steer the car through. But my body has frozen. I am as brittle as ice. For once in my brief life of dancing, running, flying, I am unable to move at all. My fingers grip the wheel, tight, white-knuckled. I hold my breath. My arms and legs protrude like rigid sticks, wedging me against the wheel and the metal body of the old Ford. Movement, my first language, fails me. I am wholly inarticulate.

It is almost on top of me now.

Time slows down. I swerve and feel the long arc of the movement. Far away, a planet orbits in space, around its star. I feel extended, eternal.

The great rusting chrome mouth surges into me, turns me over, splits me into pieces like dry clay soil in the path of the plough. I see a flash of red paint and enormous black tyre. There is a smell of petrol and burning rubber, the screech of brakes, a crescendo of metal drums and glass breaking.

Blood rushes up out of the dry soil.

A tangle of smashed ploughs and twisted furrows spreads across the road.

Thick silence descends.

There is a sensation of being dragged backwards, but a flood of images rush through my mind, pulling me towards them. I am diving through sand dunes and sunlight, then dark rooms thick with the smell of furniture polish. I fall back but find I am leaping forwards to a point of departure. My life is strung out on a thread. It has knots and coloured beads all along its length. The ends are frayed.

Back at the beginning there's a sense of softness – something touches me with tenderness and I am curled up and content.

Then this feeling is broken by hard edges, harsh movements that sound like church bells clanging out of tune. An overpowering smell of disinfectant. I bury myself into the moments of warm contentment. Then I am snapped open again by the clanging bells and harsh smells. I am falling inside out, falling apart, snapping, breaking open. I try with all my will to go back to the memory of tenderness but it's too fleeting to hold onto.

Another image. I am sitting on a cold linoleum floor – brown and yellow squares run diagonally across a narrow kitchen. Esther with her neat, blonde hair is looking down at me. I bang a wooden spoon on the floor, jerking my body up and down and laughing. She frowns. I bang louder and squeal. Her face reddens and some harsh noises come from her mouth. The room turns dark and cold, like clouds gathering, and I feel afraid. I shrink into myself, make myself smaller and harder around my edges. She turns away and I am quiet now.

I am falling. The metal box of the Ford is tumbling through trees, splitting them into spikes. There is a crashing sound of metal against tree and the sharp loud snapping of wood. I feel nothing. Time stretches out all around me. Tree branches glow eerily in the tunnel of light that is turning and turning.

Dark branches crack and snap, releasing showers of amber leaves – bright jewels, flecks of light that tumble around me, fluttering up and down like snowflakes unsure where earth is, where to land.

My head feels dense, throbbing, my hands and feet numb. Somewhere in the centre of me I am torn open and my heart bursts out. The breath cannot find a way in and my lungs constrict, wanting to scream, but pain sears up instead. There – a feeling. I am still alive.

I am tumbling in my black box down a cliff. I roll over and over.

Act One

3

I am rolling down a sand dune. It's long and steep. The sand is soft and warm, and gets into my hair, my eyes, between my teeth as I open my mouth and scream with delight as I roll.

At the bottom of the dune stands my father, tracing circles in the sand with his bare foot. He smokes a cigarette and casually leans on a stick he picked up on the beach earlier. He looks down, studying his circling foot. As my body whips over again, I glimpse the balding patch on the top of his head, turning pink in the sun. He doesn't seem to see me, but I'm sure he must hear me.

I land with a bump just a few feet in front of him, hoping he will be glad to see me there. He looks bored as he glances at me and pulls his lips into a paper-thin smile. I sit with my legs splayed out in the sand and catch my breath.

'I rolled all the way from the top! Did you see me, Daddy?'

'Yes, I saw you. Well done, Ellen,' he replies in a flat voice. 'Now let's be getting back. Your mother'll be wondering where we are.'

'But I want to do it again – just one more time. Please, Daddy.'

He turns away from me and begins to walk towards the

opening in the dunes, which will lead to the car and my mother, his wife, Esther. My heart sinks.

I follow slowly, dragging the tops of my toes through the warm sand. My skin is hot and a little red. As evening approaches it will send back out all the heat it has gathered during the day, glowing like a radiator, but it won't make the atmosphere at home any warmer.

Esther is sitting in the car with a magazine lying open on her lap. Her eyes are closed and she seems to be sleeping, but when Trevor approaches she hears him and says, without opening her eyes or turning towards him, 'Where have you two been? I've been waiting over half an hour. I thought we agreed to be back here at four?'

'Sorry, Esther. Took longer to walk back from the castle than I thought.' The truth was, he had lingered over every dreary relic on display, while I yearned for the sunlit beach outside. I trudged some feet ahead of him, along endless corridors, nudging my sandaled feet against the hard stone walls each time he stopped to study yet another rusted piece of very old metal in a glass case.

He goes round to the driver's door, climbs in, and starts the engine. I have to run to the car and jump in quickly so as not to be left behind. I sometimes wonder if they forget I'm here at all. I see how preoccupied they are with themselves, with whatever argument is currently brewing between them.

When we reach the cottage Esther asks what we would like for tea.

'The shepherd's pie would be nice, dear,' says Trevor.

'Ellen?'

I don't answer. I never do. I stand with my hands clasped behind my back and my head on one side, as if thinking deeply about some important but secret thing. My tongue presses sideways into the gap between my two front teeth. One of them wobbles, nearly ready to fall out.

'Jesus, what is wrong with this child? Ellen, answer me. What do you want for tea?'

I am mute. My lips are sealed. I bite my upper lip and clasp my hands tighter. I want sausages and peas, but I won't tell her that. Sometimes I wish I could speak, but since she took me to see the special doctor in his shiny office, to find out what was wrong with me, it had felt impossible to simply start talking again. How can I speak when I've been labelled with a rare and special disorder.

'Elective mutism.' The doctor, in his starched white jacket and silver spectacles, spoke in a hushed voice, as if it was a curse and not a diagnosis he was casting upon me. He looked at me over the rim of his glasses with a quizzical expression that suggested he had no more idea than Esther had why I wouldn't speak to her. 'There's nothing obviously wrong with her vocal mechanism, I'm glad to say. I'm sure she'll grow out of it in time. Try not to worry.' Esther had sighed and I had felt oddly trapped in a sticky web of my own creation.

I pretend I'm going to bed early, but instead of sleeping I hide under the blankets with a torch and *Alice in Wonderland*, daring the pictures in the book to scare me. I hear their voices in the room below, muffled by the blankets and floorboards that lie between us. The cottage we've rented for the holiday has thin walls and floors.

'You never think about what I want. You're so self-centred, Trevor. You just go blindly on pleasing yourself, regardless of everyone else.'

'That's not true. I'm always trying to guess what you want, but whatever I do, you just complain and criticise. Nothing's ever good enough for you.'

'Oh yes, blame me. Make it my fault, as you always do.' I can imagine her tossing her hair back and jutting her chin out, looking at him down her perfectly straight nose, even though he's a good six inches taller than she is. 'You get it wrong and it's my fault. That's clever. That's your problem Trevor – you're just too clever.'

'Look, Esther, I don't want to spend the whole holiday arguing. Can't we, just for once, try to have a normal family holiday?'

'Family! You call this a family?' Her voice is louder now. I hear it clearly.

'It's what you wanted.'

'It's what YOU wanted! You didn't ask me. As usual you just *guessed* what I wanted, and went off and bought me a baby – as if it were a Christmas present! Christ Trevor, have you no idea?'

'She.'

'What?'

'Not it – she! She's a girl, not a thing.'

They're talking about me now, I'm sure. And yet I feel as if I'm very far away and hearing them talk about someone else altogether. It feels safer to listen this way.

'Whatever.'

I think they're going to stop there, but after a long silence she goes on. She's quieter now, I don't hear so clearly, but I sense it's becoming more serious. 'I can't believe you would bring home a baby, without even discussing it properly with me, Trevor.'

'But we did discuss it. We'd been talking forever about having a baby – about trying again – '

'Yes – our baby! Not someone else's.' I'm not sure what she means by this. Did I hear it properly?

'Do we have to go over all this again?' I can feel the sigh in Trevor's voice.

'No, we're not going over it all again. We both know we couldn't have a child of our own after … well, that's history now.' I hear a crack in her voice and wonder if she's about to cry.

'We talked about the other option too.' Trevor sounds very defensive now. She has got him pinned in a corner, feeling his guilt, his wrongness. She's very good at doing that to a person. She does it to me, but I don't let the guilt get into me like Trevor does. I've learnt to protect myself by not speaking to her. It seems to be working so far.

'Trevor, we talked about it, but I never agreed to actually do it.' Now I hear that mix of outrage and exasperation that's so hard for anyone to resist. Even I can come a little undone when that's directed at me.

'I'm sorry, Esther. I thought you had. It sounded as if you wanted to. I thought it would make you happy.'

'So you thought you would buy me a baby to console me – a peace offering!'

Again I'm not sure what she means. I often don't understand what Esther means, though I try to listen carefully. I listen all the time. And watch.

There's a long silence. I imagine Trevor feeling defeated now, dropping his head, sticking his nose back into his newspaper perhaps, or pouring himself a whisky. Esther will be tight-lipped and pretending to read her magazine.

'I'm going for a walk,' he says, finally. There's no reply. A moment later the front door opens and closes again.

Act Three

4

I'm startled back to my metal coffin (did I not die?) as the darkened branch of a tree pierces the windscreen, reaches in and grazes my face. I am lying crumpled in a corner, near to the roof, and maybe upside down (I can't tell) like a baby preparing to burst into the world from its bloody confines. My body feels tight, compressed, a dense weight. Blood throbs inside my skull like a drumbeat. My mind feels constricted by this density of body, and there is no space for thought, but I feel the feathery touch, like a hand stroking my cheek. There is the tender feeling again – something in the beginning about warm contentment and soft, curled up shapes folding into each other.

A fountain of sparks erupts out of the glass where the tree hand reaches through – a shower of silver petals dancing all around me. So much beauty. So much light.

An explosion of creaking, groaning sounds, and I am unexpectedly freed from the metal box and flying. Like a feather from a swan's wing. Or an angel's.

Ah, the angel wing. It flickers across my vision for a moment, then vanishes. Images are fleeting by – my life unwinding before me. My whole life in three acts, like a play that was choreographed from the very beginning to end like this. Act One – life with Esther and Trevor. Act Three – life with James, and then Martin – until the letter came and caused the whole set to collapse – Anita arriving just as it all tumbled down onto a broken stage. Act Two.

The world becomes still, hovering in delicate balance. Then the hard earth meets my cracking bones. I feel the many angles of me twisting apart, straining to disentangle as spaces open up inside. Panic surges in me then dies. There is pain, arriving in waves that pierce and pummel, but I cannot tell where it's coming from. The waves of pain freeze up and ice over. I am still again and thoughts return, unravelling out of me like long ribbons of green and blue and silver, weaving a story.

I haven't spoken to a soul, not even James, about Act Two. I was too ashamed of my betrayal, but one betrayal leads to another and perhaps I am not wholly responsible for what I did during the war. I'll tell him one day, and Liza too – when I find her. I want them to know who I really am, to understand how it was my desperate longing for a mother, and my anger at Esther and Trevor, that drove me to such a crime.

I was twenty-six when Liza's letter arrived. They had let me live under their lie for that many years and were never going to tell me the truth. Only my mother's letter did that.

So now I am on my way to find her. Soon I will be with my own mother, my Irish mother, in Belfast city. I can feel her there, calling to me, drawing me towards her along an invisible thread that links us together. And when I arrive she will hug and kiss me, and I will feel warm and safe at last.

I call back to her – Mammy, I'm coming. A thrill of excitement, of longing, of fear ripples through me as I voice these words.

Amber leaves glow and tumble in the light, casting tiny

shadows. Shards of broken glass, bright sprays of light in the dark night wood, are falling all around me.

I saw it arrive. As the letterbox flap clanged back into place, it fluttered to the floor, a pale lilac envelope, floating like a leaf back to the earth. The faintest scent of old roses drifted through the sunlit hallway.

I held my big belly as I stooped to pick up the fallen leaf from the doormat. Eight months pregnant, I was lumbering around with the weight of a whole world inside of me, and stooping was hard to do.

On the envelope, a name – Eleanor – was written in large and childishly round letters. Was it meant for me? The address was mine, written in a different shade of blue ink, in a style that was graceful and flowing with elongated curling tails that looped one letter into the next. I didn't recognise either script. The hands that wrote these words were the hands of strangers.

The postmark indicated that the letter had been posted in Belfast, but I didn't know anyone from that part of the world. I began to slit the top of the envelope open, but something stopped me, a prick of fear that seized my fingertip as it slid into the gap at the top, then rippled along my arm and right into the chambers of my heart. For a moment I was like a butterfly pinned to a board, my wings still flapping in futile bursts, but my heart frozen by the cold steel pin that pierced through it.

I felt a small twinge from my belly. Just the baby stretching and pushing against my diaphragm so that my breath was interrupted for a moment. I went back to the kitchen and sat down. Breakfast dishes were piled in the sink and the empty cornflake box lay in a corner, on the pale green and grey linoleum floor where Martin had thrown it earlier. I would tidy up soon, now that he and James had left the house.

I opened the envelope and took out a single sheet of white paper. At the top was an address in Belfast and the date,

December 26th, 1948. It had taken nearly four and a half years
for the letter to get here. Where had it been in all this time?
I began to read:

My dear Eleanor, my darling daughter –

*I don't know how to write this letter. There is so much I
want to say, and yet now that I come to write, to reach
out to you at long last, I don't know how to say it.*

*Yes, you are my daughter – I am your mother. They may
have told you that I was dead, but I'm not. I'm here,
alive and quite well, considering.*

I stopped reading, startled. Another twinge in my belly,
more urgent this time, sharper, a kick. I looked to the bottom
of the letter:

*Take care dear daughter. I hope and pray that you are
happy and well.*

May the Sacred Heart be with you, always.

> *Your loving mother,*
> *Liza (Elizabeth)*

Liza! She claimed to be my mother. My heart turned over.
I reached for the sink and threw up over the dirty breakfast
dishes. I sat down again, feeling dizzy and confused.

I had another mother, a real mother, just as I had always prayed
I might. She was not dead, as they had told me. My prayers had
been answered. I had a mother who was not Esther and she was
still alive. Could this be true? I gripped the edge of the table and
stared at the grains in the wood. My knuckles turned white. My
face was falling, my heart hammering inside my chest.

What if it was true, and Esther and Trevor had lied to me all my life? A white-hot fire leapt into my throat. What if they had made me suffer a mother who hated me when my real mother was alive in Belfast?

I tried to stand up – I needed to move – but strength was draining from my arms and legs and I felt giddy. I dropped my head into my hands. Grief at what had not been, could now never be – growing up with Liza, being loved by her – dropped like lead into my soul. All that might have been, swept away into the past.

After my tears subsided I began to imagine my mother – sweet, kind, gentle, generous, pretty – but not in the cool and detached way that Esther was. I hoped she was funny and warm-hearted and tolerant. I knew she would be everything that Esther was not. These thoughts began to calm me, as if I knew her, somewhere inside of me I knew her and she was singing to me and stroking my hair to soothe me.

I picked up the letter and read on:

I have thought about you every single day since you came into this harsh world. I can imagine this will be a shock to you. But I can't imagine how it must have been for you, my baby girl, snatched away from your mother at birth and brought up by strangers.

Can you ever forgive me for not being there for you? It wasn't my wish, truly it wasn't, but I had no power to change the cruel course of events that conspired to take you away from me.

I could read no more. Clutching heavily onto the banister I pulled myself upstairs and lay down on the bed.

Sinking into the soft mattress, I let myself dream for a moment of motherly caresses and heart-to-heart talks at bedtime, of being taught to bake scones over the griddle, and walks in the park with our pet dog – she would be a spaniel with floppy golden ears and big brown eyes. I would call her Pip.

And then the heartbreak came, welling up in a flood of accusation, grief, and fury at Esther and Trevor. Not since I was thirteen, and Trevor had told me that I was adopted when my mother died, had I felt so angry. Now, for the second time in my life, I felt justified in an absolute and righteous hatred. I saw it all clearly – Trevor was someone who had bought me to make Esther love him, and Esther hated me for not being her own child. And my real mother was still alive, not dead, as they had told me she was.

It was some time before I felt able to continue reading my mother's letter:

> *My dear Eleanor – did they keep your name? I told them you were called Eleanor, but they may have had other ideas for you. Do you mind if I call you this?*

Eleanor. My name is Eleanor, not Ellen. My mother called me Eleanor – a real name, a whole name. Something welled up inside me – a rippling excitement and along with it a feeling of growing, of expanding into a woman who was strong and full and brave.

> *You were such a sweet girl, so beautiful. Whatever else I have done in my life, I have always loved you. I want you to know this, at least.*

> *If you receive this letter, I hope there will be a way for you to find me one day, if you want to. I don't know where to look for you. I have no address of my own to give you. I must leave it in the hands of fate. What is meant, will be.*

> *Take care dear daughter. I hope and pray that you are happy and well.*

The feathery hand strokes my cheek, and there is the tender feeling again.

Silver petals dance above me. So much beauty, so much light. I am floating upwards, like a feather from an angel's wing.

Images are flying by so fast they catch my breath and stop my heart. I see each one in exquisite detail as it unfolds before my eyes, before dissolving into light that expands all around me.

Act Two. I see it clearly now.

Somewhere there is an angel's wing. My fingertips reach out to touch it.

Act Two
1939 – 1945

5

Trevor rested a hand on my shoulder – the shoulder closest to him, as he would do to a boy, not his arm wrapped around me as if he might hug me – an embrace meant for a girl. But I know it was his way of showing a fatherly feeling. His way of trying to reassure me.

'War is coming, Ellen – you must be brave. We must all try to be brave.'

'What'll happen in the war?'

'The young men will go away to fight – abroad. Hopefully there won't be any fighting here and we'll be safe. But Mr Chamberlain says all the children should be evacuated from the cities – just in case.'

'Evacuated – what does that mean?' I had an image in my mind of endless rows of children filing into a long narrow tunnel, to be squeezed out of the other end like toothpaste from a tube. I imagined them flying through the air like cannon balls, then landing on the ground and exploding in sprays of bright red. Were we to be cannon fodder, grizzly weapons of blood and flesh sent to frighten off the enemy with our screaming faces and slippery wet stomachs burst wide open and red raw?

'It means you'll be sent to stay at a home in the countryside where there'll be no bombs. You'll be safe there. You'll be looked after by a nice family until the war is over.'

'But I'm not a child anymore. I'm twelve now.' Had he forgotten that I had grown up so much? He couldn't see it yet, but I could. I knew that my breasts were preparing themselves to fill out, like Doreen Brown's had already done. I felt the secret signs. That made me very nearly grown up.

Trevor hated to argue. He was very tired of it. He said so nearly every day – 'Let's not argue about it Esther.' So he just said, 'Well, we'll see,' and strode out along the pavement. I had to half-run to keep up, two of my footsteps for every one of his. I tried to keep in time. We were like a small army, my father and me, marching, always marching from one battle to another. I counted the paving stones as I skipped over them – two steps to a slab, then every fourth slab I managed in one long stride. To make sure I didn't step on a crack, I lengthened or shortened my step now and then. I mustn't step on a crack.

When we arrived home from the football match she was sitting at the kitchen table crying. I felt a bit sorry for her, but not too much. She never felt sorry for me when I was little and very upset, so I wouldn't waste too much pity on her now. But still, it wasn't nice to see an adult cry, especially the one who was my mother. So I put one of the Milkybars that Trevor had bought me on the table by her elbow, and ran into the garden to play on my swing. I had a feeling the war would change everything.

'The war's starting soon – probably tomorrow, Mrs Armstrong told us. So we're going to be evacuated.' I looked into the eyes of Humphrey, my brown knitted camel, and his deep black eyes spoke back to me – 'It'll be alright, it'll be over soon,' he whispered. I squeezed him to my chest, next to my heart, and took a deep breath. Outside the window, leaves on the apple tree were past their best, already turning crinkled and brown around the edges.

'Ellen, what are you doing up there? Have you finished packing yet?' The kitchen door banged shut but Esther's voice still hung in the air, crisp as snow.

I placed Humphrey on the pillow while I stuffed my spare set of clothes into the small leather suitcase that she had left in the corner of my room. On top went the towel, my toothbrush in its little box, a cake of soap and my hairbrush. We were allowed only one toy each, so of course I chose Humphrey. I laid him carefully in the case and fastened the straps.

At the bottom of the stairs Trevor was waiting for me, holding up my gas mask in its black serge bag.

'Now, d'you remember how to put this on?'

I nodded. He had already shown me three times how to fit the horrid-smelling thing over my head. I had sneaked a look in the mirror and terrified myself, but we had to be ready to put the gas masks on the moment the war began – as soon as the sirens blared out across the country. We must carry them everywhere. They would protect us, save our lives when the bombs came. Or so my teacher, Mrs Armstrong had said.

When all three of us had our coats and shoes on, Trevor hung the gas mask over my shoulder and off we marched, out of the house and down the road to my school. I clutched the small suitcase in one hand and Trevor held the other, the gas mask banging between us. I half-ran to keep up with his long stride. Esther walked behind us, her high heels clicking on the pavement.

As we entered the playground I spotted Vera, my best friend, and headed towards her through the tight huddled groups of children. There was none of the usual running and shouting, just whispered conversations, some children standing alone and silent or clutching a mother's hand for the last time. A small boy bumped right into me and looked startled, as if he hadn't seen me there. I saw terror in his eyes and my stomach lurched. A war was about to begin and we were being sent far from home. The boy and I stood frozen for a moment, caught in the shadow of each other's fear.

A shrill whistle pulled me back to the schoolyard.

'Now line up children, quickly. No more talking.' The headmistress's voice cut through the chilly morning air and we immediately fell silent and shuffled into lines. Parents retreated to the edges of the playground and fell silent too – mostly mothers were there, but a few fathers had taken the morning off work to help evacuate their children. I was glad Trevor was there. 'Your class teachers will give you your nametags. Please keep in line, nice and quiet, while they do this.'

I stood close to Vera and reached out to take her hand. She gripped mine tightly and I could feel that she was shaking – or was it my hand that was shaking? I felt cold even though I wore my new winter coat – 'It'll have to last you through the war,' Esther had told me, 'so mind you look after it'.

'Are you scared?' I asked Vera.

She nodded and looked down at her shiny polished shoes.

'Are you?'

I nodded.

'We'll remember this day for the rest of our lives. That's what my dad said.'

'I suppose so.' September the first, 1939. I carved it into my memory, just to make sure I wouldn't forget.

Mrs Armstrong was making her way down the line, speaking to each of us and handing out labels.

'Here, Ellen. This is your nametag. You must wear it till you reach your new home. This is the place you'll be staying.' She gave me a piece of soft card with string attached at one end, like a parcel label. 'Tie it into your buttonhole – that's it, nice and tight so it won't fall out. You mustn't lose it.' We were all to be labelled up, like parcels, and transported to a new and safer life.

She turned to Vera as I fumbled with my label. I dropped it and the wind caught it up like an autumn leaf and swept it across the grey tarmac. I darted out of line and chased it to the railings. A woman, someone else's mother, standing nearby caught it before it flew out onto the street. Other children were running after dropped labels. The neat lines began to disintegrate as a frenzy of pent-up tension boiled over. The headmistress blew her whistle again.

'Children, get back into line! This minute!'

Parents came to help and in no time there was hugging and crying and shouting and general chaos, despite the re-formed lines that ran from the school building across the playground, right to the tall railings that kept us off the street.

I glanced at Vera's label. Hexham, it said. I looked again at mine. Bellingham.

'Are you not coming with us to Hexham?' asked Vera, her brow furrowing as she peered at my label.

'My dad said I have to go somewhere else. He said it'll be safer. Hexham is near the airfields and they'll be the first places to be bombed.' I felt ashamed as I said this. Vera, my best friend, was being sent somewhere unsafe. And I felt sad – I wouldn't be with her and the rest of my class.

'No they won't. Newcastle will – that's why we have to go away.' Vera gave me a sharp look and I dropped my head.

As well as being a businessman, Trevor was on the City Council and knew how to 'pull strings', as he called it. Most of my class were going to Hexham, but Trevor had arranged that I would be evacuated to my own village in the heart of Northumbria, hidden deep in the hills and dark green valleys. My parents always had to do things differently.

'Anyway, since we won't be in the same place for the war, take this – so you'll remember me.' She pulled off her bracelet of coloured plastic beads, all held together with elastic, and gave it to me. They were pink and blue and lilac – pretty, like a sunset.

'Thank you. And you have mine.' I took off my string of bright red and orange beads and offered it to her. I thought I might cry but the whistle blew again and we were ordered to stop talking and begin marching, in line, two by two, behind our teacher. Ten lines of children – off on an adventure, to safety, away from home and everything we knew – began to snake across the playground, out of the school gates, and onto the old green buses that waited for us on the street.

At the Haymarket we scrambled off the bus and marched in double file all the way to Newcastle station, our parents straggling behind. Vera and I held hands, looking out for signs of war along the busy streets. A few of the older boys whistled and swung their arms like soldiers, but most of us were anxious about what lay ahead and walked quietly. At the station we were separated into groups, according to where we would be sent.

I said goodbye to Vera as the evacuation officer led me to my place amongst a gaggle of children of all ages – the misfits, the ones who got left out, I thought. Some looked rich – some looked very poor. I knew none of them.

Esther, Trevor and I stood in a small huddle amongst the other huddled families clustered along the length of the platform. The air felt dark and dense. It smelt of coal dust and cheap perfume and fresh cigarette smoke. Mothers and small children were crying. Fathers were alternately looking at their silver watches then staring down the track for signs of a train, sighing and tutting at the delay. As if they were each personally responsible for the success of this mission, their first battle of the war – prizing young children out of mothers' clinging arms, and depositing them safely onto a train.

A sea of grey caps and grey school jackets began to coalesce near the platform edge as the older boys, eager to escape this clutch, prepared to jump on board and secure the best seats. Ready for an adventure.

Finally the whistling, steaming train rumbled into view, curved along the track into the station and came to rest alongside all of us with a great complaining belch and bellow of steam. Our army of evacuating children were hidden momentarily in a thick grey cloud. There was chaos as children darted away from parents, and parents called after them. Some found a step up onto the train. Some ran in circles and bumped into the adults again, as if unsure whether to go or not.

The train whistled and belched once more, keen to be moving on quickly now that it had finally arrived. Impatient with us for the delay, even though it was not us who were late.

'Goodbye Ellen, dear. Take care of yourself, and be very good for Mr and Mrs Grainger, won't you,' said Trevor, looking anxiously at me, then at Esther. 'Now say goodbye to your mother, there's a good girl,' he added, after kissing me lightly on my forehead. There was neither hope nor expectation in his voice, just the stubborn monotony of habit.

I looked up at Esther, who looked down at me, her pale and sleek face drawn and expressionless as a peeled hard-boiled egg. I had no idea what she was thinking or feeling about all of this.

'Goodbye Mother,' I said.

She looked startled, so did Trevor. It was the first thing I had said directly to her for years.

I picked up my bag and my gas mask, my hands trembling with fear, with the shock of saying goodbye to everything I knew, with a flicker of excitement that I was finally escaping Esther's world. Now I was running away in earnest and they willingly let me go. I turned from them and climbed up onto the train. And that was it. I was evacuated. Act Two of my life began.

The countryside was thickening as the train sped deeper into its soft folds – green fields and pink heather and the gold of bracken-clad hillsides flew past. Even the long trail of sooty steam looked cleaner, whiter against this background of green and gold. I sat alone with my nose pressed against the dirt-streaked window, letting the details of the landscape fill my mind so I might forget the sadness I felt at leaving my friends, the fear of what lay ahead, of the war, of stepping out into the world truly alone for the first time in my life.

My fingers counted the plastic beads of Vera's bracelet, worrying the coloured beads along in time with the rhythm of the train's k-lunk k-chang k-lunk. I was sure the war would be over soon, but even a week apart from your best friend could feel like a long time.

When the train stopped at a small country station, my ragged group was bundled off. Vera stayed on the train that was going on to Hexham. From the platform, I saw her huddled inside the lamp-lit carriage with the girls from my class, talking and laughing together. I waved but they didn't see me. Looking in from the outside, I felt invisible. Perhaps already forgotten.

As we climbed onto the new train I fell into a deeper silence, trying to ignore two groups of noisy boys from Wallsend and Byker who were throwing insults at each other and fighting for the window seats. The journey was long. We changed trains again then waited ages for a bus to take us on the last stretch, going further up into the hills along a river valley and through forests of tall pine trees until the old world felt very far away.

But when we finally arrived in Bellingham I was surprised at how easily I could forget to think about what I had left behind. I wasn't thinking about Esther and Trevor, or even Vera, as I stumbled from the creaking bus and stood on the edge of the weary group of city children, each of us staring blankly along a wide village street in the smoky light of late afternoon. Lost, dis-located, and unsure of how to step into the newness of it all. Some of the twenty or so vacees had probably never been out of the city before. They would miss the noise and soot.

We were ushered into a dark wooden-floored hall with a stage at one end. Frayed red velvet curtains hung at each side of the stage. People were milling about, women in headscarves and cotton dresses calling out, trying to jolly us along. Some children were crying, others were quiet, like me. A lady in a flowery wrap-around pinny, her hair neatly waved and clipped back, gave me a cup of milk. Standing alone near the doorway, I began to count the wooden boards that ran across the hall. The dark wood varnish had peeled off around the edges of each plank so that the parallel gaps showed up clearly in the gloom. This made them easy to count. I got to eighteen before a voice called my name from across the hall.

'Ellen! Is that Ellen Rushton? Me dear child, A was so worried. We expected y'all ages ago. Are y'aalreet, pet?' A broad-hipped, round woman, with a smile like a sunflower opening up, was waddling towards me. I dropped my bag and took her in. My new mother, my war mother. I liked her immediately. She was not Esther.

Mrs Grainger came right up and hugged me, enveloping me in rolls of soft arms and breast. She smelt of flour and carbolic soap and salted butter. Something inside me fell away, like a safety pin coming loose.

'Welcome, Ellen. Ye'r very welcome pet. A'm Mrs Grainger and ye'r to be living with us. Ye must make yasel at home for as long as ye'r he-er. Me husband, Mr Grainger, will be home from his work soon, and then the three of us will have wor first tea together. A've made mince and dumplings. A hope ye like that.'

She chatted away as we walked to her house. It was the last in a terrace, down at the very end of a muddy lane, right on the edge of the village. The walls were made of thick, warm grey stones, so large and solid looking that I immediately felt safe. No German bombs could knock these houses down, I was sure.

'Come on in dear, and let's have a cup uv tea. D'ye like tea, or would ye prefer milk? Now tell me about yer journey. Was the train late? Are ye tired pet?' She bustled about, preparing a pot of tea, pouring a jug of frothing milk, and toasting crumpets over the fire. I watched her brown-stockinged feet, spilling out in soft folds over the bars that criss-crossed her scuffed brown shoes. They shifted this way and that between sink and range and table – the dainty steps of a dance she had rehearsed many times and knew by heart. A pattern worn into the grey flagstones of the floor.

'Yes, the train was late, and we had to change twice. Then we had to wait for the bus. But I'm not too tired. Thank you, Mrs Grainger.' That felt like a lot to say to my war mother all in one go. I settled back into my habit of silence, but she didn't seem to mind. She placed a big blue-and-white striped mug of milky tea in front of me. In the centre of the table she put a plate of warm crumpets, a dish of butter and a pot of plum jam.

'This'll be a rare treat once the war begins, pet. Wor food'll be rationed, A guess, so let's enjoy it while we can.' The lilting notes of her speech sounded like a song, and song was a language I felt at home with. She began to butter a crumpet and gestured for me to do the same. We sank our teeth through the melting butter and exchanged a sly smile. I thought I would grow quite plump in Mrs Grainger's kitchen, but I didn't mind.

The room that was to be my bedroom was at the back of the cottage, big enough for a narrow bed with an iron bedstead, a large oak wardrobe, a small chest of drawers painted with sprays of roses in pink and green, and me. It looked out over the back garden and beyond to the fields and the edge of a wood that ran along one side of the village. The sun was low in the sky, a deep pink-orange colour. The sky was clear of clouds and blue, turning gradually to purple.

'This is Kevin's room. He's me eldest son. He's joined the army and gone off to fight. Me youngest too – Stephen – he left just two weeks ago,' she told me proudly. 'So A'm very glad ye've come, Ellen pet – to fill the house with childish things again.'

I smiled and thanked her as she left me to settle into my room.

I opened my bag and took Humphrey out.

'This is our new home Humphrey. See, it's not so bad. You'll be alright here.' I sat him on one side of the deep windowsill, and sat myself on the other side, my knees hugged up close to my chin. We gazed out at the wide green country. It was all mine to explore. I could feel in my bones that a new life had begun.

Downstairs the front door opened and banged shut, shaking the lamp on the chest of drawers. I heard muffled voices, then Mrs Grainger calling up to me.

'Ellen pet, it's tea-time. Come on down and meet Mr Grainger?'

As I entered the kitchen she gestured to a chair. She was sitting near the range, he sat at the head of the table, near the door. 'That was Kevin's seat,' Mrs Grainger told me fondly. I knew, by the way she said it, that Kevin would have liked me to sit there. I knew that I had a place here.

'Are ye hungry, dear?' She was addressing her husband now.

'Wey aye, hinny. A've had nowt all dey.'

Growing up in one of the nicer suburbs of Newcastle, as I had, I struggled to understand him, but I got the general gist of their talk as they discussed their day, the war, me and what a nice time I would have with them until the war was over.

For a moment I wondered what Esther and Trevor were doing, if they were missing me as they sat down to their first tea without me, or if they were relieved that I was gone. Surely Esther would be glad. I felt both happy and sad to be so far from the familiar spotless kitchen with its linoleum floor and cream-coloured cupboards on the wall, but soon the intricacies of Mr and Mrs Grainger's daily tasks, of village life and the challenge of understanding his particular way of using the English language drew my thoughts right back to Bellingham.

6

I came down stairs next morning to an empty kitchen, the back door open and swinging on its hinge. A soft breeze had swept some leaves in across the floor. I went to the door and rubbed my sleepy eyes in the bright sunlight.

'Ah, Ellen pet, ye must have been tired. It's past breakfast time, but never mind, A'll put on an egg for ye – just let me finish this.' Mrs Grainger was pegging sheets onto a washing line strung across half the length of the back garden. A path ran down the centre of the garden and on one side of it was a vegetable patch overflowing with carrot and potato tops, cabbages, beans and weeds. On the other side, beneath the washing line, half a dozen chickens were scratching in the dry grass for seeds.

'I'm sorry I'm up late.'

'Don't ye worry, pet. Ye had a long journey.'

I stepped into the sunshine and felt the clean air fill my lungs. I stretched my arms up and yawned, then twirled around as they came down again. I wanted to dance but I could feel her eyes on me so I clasped my hands together and asked, 'Can I help you?'

'Thanks, pet. Just take the end of this sheet and pull it tight. That's it. There, we're done.' She bent down to pick up the empty washing basket and waddled back to the kitchen to boil me an egg.

'Mr Grainger's gone to his workshop down the other end of

the village. He's a carpenter ye know, makes tables, cupboards, carts for the farmers – whatever people need.' She said this with pride, and I guessed he was an important person in the village. As she set my breakfast on the table, then turned to the sink to wash up, she continued to recount some of the things he had made, who he had made them for, and how beautiful they looked. 'Now the war is starting he'll be helping out on the farm too, so he won't be home much. Most evenings, after tea, he goes to the pub for a 'neet-cap', as he calls it.' She winked at me. 'He works hard, so he deserves his bit of pleasure, poor dear.'

I finished my egg and toast, gulped down the mug of tea she had placed on the table, and rinsed my mug and plate under the tap. I wasn't sure what I should do next, what was expected of me. 'Shall I help you Mrs Grainger?' I ventured.

'Well, that would be nice pet, but for today, being as its yer first day he-er, why don't ye go out and play, explore the place a bit. Me boys were aalways out in the fields, the woods, aal over the place. Ye can help me tomorrow if ye like. There's aalways plenty to do.' She gestured to the kitchen in general. 'Now, A'm going to the shops, and we'll have wor dinner at half past twelve. Can ye be back by then, pet?'

I was to discover that Mrs Grainger's life took place in the kitchen and the vegetable patch out back. Her routine was broken by a daily walk to the village grocer, the baker, the butcher when there was money to buy meat, and her friend Daisy who lived in the cottage at the other end of the terrace. If I wanted company I knew where to find her. If I didn't, she left me to get on with my life as I chose. Because I enjoyed helping her, each morning I would peel potatoes, chop carrots, pod peas or scrub pans for an hour or two. She always found me a different job to do so I wouldn't get bored. We would stop for a milky coffee and biscuit as we listened to news of the war on the wireless. Everyone was obsessed with it, but if it weren't for the wireless we wouldn't know there was a war going on at all. Apart from being evacuated, of course. And the blackout every night.

She was all 'pet and dear'. He was all 'hinny and luv'. Words like that were rarely used in our home – except when Trevor was trying to pacify Esther, or get her to see his point of view, or subtly put her down in front of guests, he would call her 'dear'. I didn't say it out loud, but to myself I called her Pet-dear and I called him Hinny-luv. I grew fond of them both, and even fonder of the freedom they gave me to do just as I pleased.

The green fields were mine to roam in. I could run and run for miles with the wind flying in my hair. I picked wildflowers to press between the pages of old newspapers and lay for hours in the tall grasses, dry and straw-coloured after the long hot days of summer, watching them dance across the sky above me. The scent of red clover filled the warm air and trickled through me with the sound of buzzing insects. The dark woods were for hiding in and burying secrets. I learnt to sit so still that the little animals of the woods came out and sniffed around right in front of me, letting me be in their world for a while. The stream was for paddling in on warm days and catching minnows in a net, putting them in a jar, then throwing them all back to freedom at the end of the day. This was the best part of all. I loved to see them flick their spines and dart away along meandering pathways through the green water when I released them.

The days stretched out around me like whispers in my ear, inviting me into them. I could lose myself – my old solemn, stubborn, sad self – in the secrets of these late summer days. I could dance in the fields and climb into the high branches of the trees.

When all the upheaval of moving children out of the homes they knew into the homes of strangers had settled down, of course they had to think about schooling us. That was a pity. I had thought we would be let off school for the war – a kind of extended playtime. But that dream was not to be. One morning, as Pet-dear and I were in the scullery shoving and pulling wet sheets through the mangle, a middle-aged lady with a small grey hat and greenish tweed coat knocked on the door.

'Good morning, Mrs Grainger. I am Miss Parker, the schoolmistress.' Of course Pet-dear knew this already, as both her sons had been schooled by Miss Parker, but she just nodded and let the schoolmistress go on. 'And this must be Ellen.'

Pet-dear and I peered out of the dimness of the front doorway into a bright early autumn day. She examined me up and down, from tangled hair to scuffed shoes, then returned her gaze to Mrs Grainger and kept it steadfastly there.

'Yes, this is wor Ellen, luvly lass she is. Settled in reet well, as if she'd been born and bred he-er aal her life,' said my war mother, patting my head and smiling at the thin-lipped stranger. Her cheeks were rosy with the effort of the mangle and her cardigan sleeves were rolled up and wet.

'I'm very glad to hear that.' The lady returned a dry crack of a smile. I thought of Ellen and bit my upper lip. 'I've come to talk about her schooling while she's here in Bellingham. Of course all the children must resume their studies as soon as possible.' I didn't like the way she spoke about me to Mrs Grainger, over my head, as if I wasn't there. I was not invisible, but I became mute again.

'Yes, uv course. She must go to school while she's he-er. She's a bright young thing, aren't ye pet.' I wanted to throw my arms around Pet-dear's big wide waist and lose myself in her for a moment. I was happy, for the first time in my life I was happy, and I didn't want anything to change. Besides, I was nearly grown up, which meant nearly too old for school. I was twelve, after all. I wanted to tell the tweed-clad lady all of this, but I didn't.

'Because there isn't room for all the new children to join

the village children in our one classroom, the plan is to send the village children to school in the mornings, and the city children in the afternoons. So they will all have half a day of school and be expected to work at home by themselves for the rest of the day. I will set them homework to keep them occupied and out of trouble.'

A canny plan, I thought. All nicely squared off and parcelled up. A plan to keep city children out of trouble and stop the two groups mixing. We might have a bad influence on the morals of nice country children. I could read these unspoken thoughts as the tweed lady wrote something in a large notebook, tore out the sheet and handed it to Mrs Grainger.

'This tells you everything you need to know – where to go, when she begins, what she should bring to school.' Still she didn't look at me, as if she was passing a sentence, about to chop off my head or send me to the ducking chair, but daren't look me in the eye because she knew I was innocent of any crime. Everyone knows that if an innocent person meets the eye of their executioner they will curse and haunt him – or her – forever.

Miss Parker left and we went back inside the house. I was quiet now. Pet-dear didn't know me in my silent moods. With her I was free to speak when I wanted to, and be quiet when I didn't. It was never a problem. Now the words had frozen up again.

'It'll be fine, Ellen. Just a few hours of school in the afternoons, and ye'll be free to please yasel the rest uv the day. Come on pet, cheer up now.' When I didn't respond, she continued. 'The school's not so bad, ye know. Both me boys went there, and they managed aalreet.' She laughed her warm honey laugh as she remembered them in their school uniforms, the jackets and trousers always too big or too small, trudging home in rain and snow and sun. There was mud on their knees, whatever the weather.

'Come on pet, let's have a nice cup uv sweet tea and a ginger biscuit, and A'm shuwer ye'll soon feel better.'

How did she manage it, always so kind to everyone? My heart broke open a little and I relented. I yielded into the arm that enveloped my shoulders, accepting the hug and the offer of tea and ginger biscuits. I had watched her bake them earlier, as I podded a basket of broad beans from the garden. She didn't know that it was not the idea of school itself so much as the manner of the schoolmistress that had dampened my mood. I would not tell Pet-dear this. I feared that my own dark thoughts might poison the kindness she had wrapped me in if I shared them.

The next week school would begin and I would be condemned to spend my afternoons crammed into a small classroom with Miss Parker while the magic of autumn was unfolding all around the village.

Act One

7

My first day of school. Esther is tall in her high-heeled patent leather shoes and cream pin skirt. Why does she have to dress up like this when all the others are wearing old cotton dresses or slacks and flat working shoes? We stand out like two shiny buttons in a tin of well-used bobbins, me in a smart school uniform that actually fits, and my wavy auburn hair pulled back into a tight ponytail. The other women are chatting in small groups while their children run about the playground squealing and shouting. They seem to know each other. Did I miss something?

As the crowd of mothers and their children drift towards the school hall, we stand slightly apart, Esther holding my hand firmly. That's so that I don't run away, as I had threatened to do last night when Trevor reminded me that I would be starting school in the morning. Eventually the teacher comes up to us and introduces herself.

'Hello, Mrs Rushton. So this is young Ellen. Hello Ellen. I'm Mrs Ward and I'll be your class teacher this year.' I look up at her smiling face, haloed by greying frizzy hair. Her eyes are a watery blue and she seems friendly. I feel like saying hello to her, but Esther is there and she says it first.

'Hello Mrs Ward.'

'Now tell me, Ellen, what do you like doing best? Do you like dancing, or singing, or books, or making things?' I'm about to reply when Esther answers for me.

'She likes moving – she's always moving. Sometimes she sings. She doesn't like talking though. I hope she won't be any trouble for you.' I see Esther's lips tighten and stretch, as if she wanted to smile but couldn't quite manage it. A muscle at the side of her jaw twitches. I feel small. My voice has gone again, and I hide behind her cream skirt and peek out at Mrs Ward.

'I'm sure she won't be any trouble,' says Mrs Ward, smiling at me. 'There's no need to be shy, Ellen. All of the children are a bit shy on the first day, but I'm sure you'll soon get used to it all.'

I do, and I learn to talk to Mrs Ward when Esther isn't there to interrupt me. She is kind and encourages me to dance and to sing. School becomes a refuge, a place to run away to.

Act Two

8

Each day at exactly twelve-thirty Miss Parker rang the school bell, which signalled the moment to stop our running about and line up nicely outside the Girls' entrance to the single-storeyed, grey-stone building that was the Bellingham Village School.

We waited, subdued and shuffling. Now and then a boy would prod a neighbour, making them laugh or squeal out loud, or lose their balance and stumble out of line. We girls would wriggle and fidget. We watched as 'that lot' filed out of the Boys' entrance in silence then erupted into whoops and cries and strange gyrations, as if rehearsing for a part in the circus, the moment their feet passed over the line that crossed the width of the small tarmac-covered playground. This white line marked the edge of a magic circle beyond which all human form was shed and something more bizarre and animal-like emerged. The 'nice' village children became knobbly-kneed demons as they escaped the restrictions of three and a half hours of penance in the classroom under the strict eye of Miss Parker.

We were luckier. Some days she left us to the devices of Mr Paterson, her young assistant, who had not yet been moulded into the stultifying guise of schoolmaster. He could still be shaped by cunning young minds into something more flexible and amenable. Mr Paterson wore thick dark-rimmed glasses, and he walked with a limp because his feet turned the wrong way round, or so the older boys said. I suppose this was why he had not been sent off to fight. There was no use being a soldier if you couldn't see and couldn't run away from the enemy.

Each day we watched the 'scruffy, smelly village kids' leave in a state of disgraceful abandon. They in turn scornfully eyed the 'snotty-nosed vacees' as we stood dutifully in line, waiting our turn, more grist for the mill. Two motley groups of vagabonds with nothing but a world war to bring us together.

It was the second week of school, and we all filed wearily out of the school gates after a long afternoon of reading, writing and 'rithmetic with Miss Parker. We each began to wander off towards our own homes, half of us going left and half going right along School Road. I was with the left group but I kept to myself, trailing behind as I tried to remember how to spell 'occurred'. I didn't want to get the ruler again the next day. Already I'd forgotten whether it had one 'r' or two, and soon I would be confused about how many 'c's there were as well. I had to be careful, keep it in mind.

At the place where the road curved to the left there was a big rhododendron bush. It blocked the view of the rest of the road, and cars and tractors had to slow down so as not to crash into each other if they were coming from opposite directions. Just as the boys at the front of our lot reached the bush, there was an uproar of screaming and hollering, and about a dozen of the village boys – some girls too – leapt out from behind the greenery, waving sticks and stones that they gripped in their hands. They began to hurl the stones in the vague direction of us.

They were quick, the boys from Wallsend and Byker. Before I had time to stop worrying about 'occurred', they had thrown themselves in the direction of the village boys – and girls – and were punching into the air. Some fists landed on a chest or chin. Some stones and sticks hit their mark. In seconds they were all on the dusty ground wrestling, punching and kicking. Yells from the ones fighting. Screams from the girls who had not joined in but stood around the scrum, jumping up and down, their fists waving and cheeks pink with excitement.

I didn't know what to do. I had never seen an ambush before but I guessed this was one, and I imagined this was what the soldiers were doing in the war. As I was wondering, a stick hit the side of my head. It hurt. I picked up the stick and charged at the boy who had thrown it. He was taller than me but I wasn't scared. I threw myself at him and jumped onto his back. I was clinging on with my legs and my left hand, and pounding his shoulder with the stick I held in my right hand. My heels jabbed into his thighs. He yelped as I bit the hand that was reaching up to pull me off. He bucked like a horse and I was slipping down his back, but I grabbed his hair and pulled him to the ground as I fell. We ended up in a heap, him lying over my right knee and my two hands tugging at his hair.

He rolled over and looked me straight in the eye. I thought he would put his hands around my throat but instead he brushed back his hair and looked around. I glanced up and saw that the two groups had stopped fighting and stood in a circle around us, clapping and shouting. The boy disentangled himself from me and stood up, brushed himself down, and sauntered off as if nothing had happened. As he walked away I saw that his ears were bright red, sticking out from under his pudding basin hair, and guessed that somehow I had won the fight. No one bothered me like that again, though the two groups of boys often had scraps after school. I suppose they felt part of the war that way. Maybe they were practising for it.

Bellingham in the autumn was full of wood smoke and golden leaves, haystacks and red apples to pick. The hills surrounding the village were an exciting world to ramble over and explore. I felt glad to be out of the city and spent every moment I could outdoors. Apart from those dreary hours in the classroom, the days slipped easily and gently by as I waited for the war to end. I didn't expect to meet someone like Ash, but I was to learn that the war would bring many surprises.

It was Tuesday, late October. Fallen leaves eddied and the high winds blew steely clouds across the sky. Dusk was already creeping in but still I walked the long way home from school, down to the stream and round the back of the houses that lay in the shadow of the meat processing shed. The smell was always strong at this time of day – the smell of fear that was carried in the blood of the sheep taken from the hills and soon to be laid out grandly – roasted or stewed – on our kitchen tables. No coffins – just a pot or a baking tray.

I was crossing the field. The light was so dim that at first I couldn't be sure if I really saw her, or if she was just a shadow, something remembered from a dream. What I recall now is a large muddy pool at the edge of the field, and she was sitting there, up to her waist and covered in the grey-brown filth. She was drawing a muddy hand down over her face, pulling strands of wet hair over her eyes.

Even in the fading light I could see that she had been crying. Her eyes were two dark slits drowning in a sea of swollen, wrinkled skin. She wailed faintly as she scooped up another handful of mud and poured it over her head. I wondered if she was human, if she had walked across the field to the pool and sat herself down in it. Or if she was a creature that had risen out of the earth, out of the mud and slime, and momentarily lifted her head up into our world.

Here my habit of silence seemed totally appropriate. There was nothing I could say. I observed her carefully for a few minutes. She eyed me with a sidelong stare then continued with the pouring and the wailing of one gone far beyond distress into some other state of being.

There was nothing else I could do. I put my right foot into the mud. Then my left. I waded in a few steps then crouched down until I was sitting beside her, about a foot away. The cold muddy water came up to my waist. I brought my two hands together and poured mud over my head, just as she was doing. I turned to look at her. She eyed me with suspicion but growing curiosity. Each time she scooped and poured I did the same, until we were both drenched with the wet disgusting stuff.

Some deep-down buried part of me thrilled at the sensation of the cold wet dirt sliding down my face, my neck, through my fingers – down my sleeves and collar, up my school skirt and all around me. I began to laugh. I had never felt so free.

She stopped wailing, turned to stare at me again, then burst out laughing too. We howled with laughter. We lay down in the mud and rolled about and howled until our stomachs ached.

After a while we both knew it was time to stop. The cold was creeping closer to our bones and there would be business ahead for each of us when we arrived home drenched in mud. We slithered and slipped out of the pool and sat on the hard ground, side by side. Like sisters, I thought. The wet trickled down us and made dark pools on the ground all around our two bodies. The earth was gathering herself back in for the night.

'A'm Ash,' she said eventually.

'A'm Ellen.'

'Hmm.'

She turned towards the row of houses that sat squarely across the field behind us, black shapes against the darkening sky, with yellow squares of window signalling evening activity in each home. The windows would be blacked out any moment now, just in case Hitler's men flew by. They never did.

Ash was staring at a figure in the window of the third house along. No more than a dark outline against the yellow glow, a shape hunched over a kitchen sink. She tensed, pulling her knees up close to her chest, and began to cry softly.

'What is it?' I asked.

'Can ye keep a secret?'

'Yes, of course. I'm your friend now.'

She nodded.

'A cannit go home. A cannit eva go back home,' she whispered.

'Oh. Then you must come back with me. There's room at my house.' I didn't give a moment's thought to what Pet-dear and Hinny-luv would think of the two of us turning up all covered head to freezing toes in wet mud.

We walked home side by side, through the village, dripping a wet trail behind us. Luckily the creeping darkness concealed our sorry state from passing eyes. I felt a thrill of excitement. Ash and I shared a secret. We were like partners in crime.

Luckily Hinny-luv was out when we arrived. Pet-dear opened the door and shrieked at the sight of us, looking like creatures from the deep, some underworld nightmare come to haunt her perhaps. She stared into our faces with the mud now caked dry as a mask, not recognising me at first.

'Ellen! Ee neva! What's happened to ye, pet?' she gasped, as she recovered from the shock of seeing us like that.

I muttered something about falling, and she pulled us both through the doorway and into the warmth of her kitchen.

'It's me fault, really – not Ell's.' Ash was standing by the kitchen door, unsure whether to come right in.

'Are ye wor Ellen's friend then?'

'Aye, A'm her friend.' She shifted from one foot to the other as if wanting to pee. We were both shivering from the cold.

'Well, neva mind all that now. Come on in pet, and let's get ye both out those wet things and warmed up.' She tutted, and 'oh-dear-me'ed' as she brought the tin tub in from the scullery and placed it in front of the fire, then ladled hot water from the copper into it. Once I was squeaky clean and wrapped up in a warm towel, she emptied the dirty water out in the back yard and filled the tub again. Ash climbed in and sat up to her waist in the steaming water, just as she had sat a short while ago in the muddy pool. I watched as watery trails of mud dripped from her wet hair and slid over her shoulders and down her back. Her neck was graceful as a swan's, her arms slender and long. Eventually Ash emerged, pink and glowing from the heat of the bath.

Pet-dear gave us dry shirts to wear – Mr Grainger's old ones. After a cup of hot cocoa and a biscuit, she took Ash into the front room for a private talk. She agreed that Ash could stay the night. She would sleep in Stephen's bed.

Next morning Mrs Grainger took Ash to school. There was a big commotion. Ash disappeared for a few days, but when she returned we became the best of friends. Even though she went to school in the morning and I went in the afternoon, we met most evenings and weekends. She came often to our house and Pet-dear was kind to her. Hinny-luv tolerated her presence but became quiet when she was around. I think he disapproved, but he wouldn't say so, as Pet-dear had welcomed Ash into their home.

Ash never invited me to her house. She told me I wouldn't like it there, and besides, it could be dangerous for me. I didn't question her. She was fourteen and very grown up, so I was proud that she wanted to be my friend. Although she was a village girl and I was a city girl, neither of us minded that anymore.

And that's how Ash and I became best friends, war friends.

'Where did you get a name like Ash from?' I asked her one Saturday afternoon as we sat idling our time away by the stream.

We dangled our feet into the icy water until we couldn't bear the cold any longer, then we jumped up and stamped them on the rock in a kind of dance, until they were warm again. We were imitating what Ash said Mr Paterson had told their class the people from far away did when they had a party. Because the boys asked him to show them, he rolled up his trousers, right to the knees even though his feet were turned the wrong way round, and gave a demonstration. At least that's what Ash told me. They were too surprised to laugh at first and he took that as a sign of respect for the customs of the African people that he was teaching them about. We should be grateful to them, he had said, because they were helping us to win the war. When, a few moments later, first one then the whole class began to snigger, then laugh out loud, he thought it was at the joke he had just made.

When Ash told me about this, we both rolled about with laughter. She liked to laugh, loudly, and I always joined in. I wasn't sure I believed her story, that Mr Paterson would have danced like this. The way Ash described it, it felt like making fun of the kind people from Africa who were helping us win the war, but I didn't want to spoil the game.

Ash and I had just finished the third round of our dance and settled to dangling our feet again.

'Me mam says it's 'cos A used to disappear for hours on end, like, and once she found me sitting up in the ash tree at the end of wor garden. Once she knew where me hiding place was though, she let me be.' She kicked her feet against the surface of the stream and a spray of water reached our faces. 'Me dad says it's 'cos me eyes are the colour uv his tab ash.' She was quiet for a moment, reflecting on this. 'They're not, are they?'

'No,' I reassured her quickly. 'They're a lovely silvery–blue colour. They shine like jewels when you smile.'

'Ta, Ell. Ye'r a reel friend.' Ash tossed her dark hair back and tilted her head to show off her best profile. A few wayward strands of hair flopped back over her eyes. She lifted them up with her middle finger and flicked them back again. I thought how beautiful she was.

'Me brother says it's 'cos A made such a hash of everything when A was little that he called me Hash, but A pronounced it Ash. And that's the name that stuck. So take ya pick. It's all the same to us.'

'I like the first one best,' I said. 'Did you have another name before Ash, then?' I was curious about how people's names could change, wondering if this changed the person who had the name.

She looked up and my gaze followed hers. Through the canopy of trees that sheltered the stream, patches of blue sky could be seen where the leaves had already left the branches. If you put your head into just the right place, a shaft of bright autumn sunlight fell over your face. I played for a moment at shifting my head from side to side, letting the light and shadow fill my eyes. Ash considered whether or not she would answer my question.

'Yeah – A was christened Marjorie. Dumb name. A prefer Ash any day,' she finally admitted.

'Me too.'

'C'mon, this water's freezing me toes off,' she suddenly declared. We dried our feet on our handkerchiefs and put on our socks and shoes.

'What shall we do now?' I asked. Ash always had something new to do, somewhere to go.

'Along he-er. A know a secret place.'

I followed her up from the stream and across a bit of scrubby land at the back of the village. No one seemed to take care of it. It was dry and full of stones and rubbish, and nothing would grow there anyway, she told me. So in the day the young children used it as their playground, and at night the older ones came out and skulked around in the dark corners between bushes and piles of junk that had been thrown there and left for years.

We skirted around a group of boys who were playing football with an old tin can. It was the vacees versus the village boys these days. There was too much shouting and running about, not enough tackling and kicking – even I could tell that – so the game went on forever and nobody ever really won or lost. Ash led as we ducked between bushes then squirmed under a wooden fence, broken at the place where a narrow path had been worn into the hard earth. We followed it through a piece of scrubland dotted with clumps of grass and hardy weeds that were defying the onset of winter.

'In summer ye can hardly get past he-er 'cos of the nettles,' she told me.

We came to a hedge, a thorny barrier, but Ash knew the way through. We crawled on all fours and emerged with knees scratched, clothes and hair covered with the dried out crumbs of last year's leaves. I raised my eyes from the brown earth onto a small field with a wooden hut standing close to the hedge. She was already walking towards it.

We pushed the rickety door. It hung loose from one of its hinges and scraped the floor as it opened. There was a small scurrying sound – probably a mouse. As my eyes became used to the dimness I could make out an upturned crate in the middle of the room, with a tin mug and a box of matches defining it as a table. A very broken wooden chair sat in one corner, and a mess of dirty blankets on the floor by one wall suggested that someone might actually live here.

'My God, is this somebody's home? Should we be in here Ash?' A chill ran up the back of my neck, as if someone had blown cold breath at me from behind.

'Divint knaa 'bout that. Looks like it.' Ash nudged the pile of old and rank smelling blankets with her toe, and jumped back as a mouse darted out from under them. 'Flippin heck! A hate vermin,' she yelped. She stamped her foot as if to squash the fleeing grey streak of fur but it had gone. 'A neva seen anyone here before, like, but A guess someone might av moved in for the winter.'

Ash was poking around in corners, sniffing at odd utensils she found – a bent fork, a tin plate, an empty baked bean tin full of rusty nails. 'Phah. What a stink. Looks like someone's had a reet old feast he-er,' she said.

I picked some paper up from the floor under the chair.

'Look, Ash, a magazine.' I opened the stained and torn copy of *Woman's Own*, the pages that were left of it, and we both stared at the photographs of pretty young women wearing bright coloured summer dresses. Further in, drawings of well-endowed women in lace underwear adorned an advertisement feature.

'That's weird!' I said, a note of contempt in my voice disguising the fact that I was stranded somewhere between disgust and fascination.

'Shh. Listen.' Ash grabbed my arm, but we were too late to hide. The light streaming in through the doorway was suddenly blocked out and the large shape of a man was standing there.

'An' what ye two doin in he-er?' he asked, a hint of annoyance in his voice. 'Pokin around in me things, war ye?' He stepped closer and glimpsed what we were looking at just before Ash hid it behind her back.

'No, sorry – I mean, we didn't know they were your things,' I mumbled by way of pleading innocence rather than offering an apology for intruding.

He ignored me and stepped closer to Ash. 'Like the pictures, do ye, missy?'

'Na, not really. A bit boring, like,' she answered boldly, sticking her chin out to show her best profile again. She dropped the magazine onto the dusty floor between them, like throwing down the gauntlet, and he picked it up.

'A see. Ye want summit a bit more – then, do ye?' he sneered. I didn't know what was happening but I sensed danger.

'Ash, let's go,' I whispered, tugging at her arm.

'Ah, the scraggy littl'un want's to go home to mammy, does she? Go on then missy, we divint need ye he-er. Do wuh?' He stepped right up to Ash, sticking out his chin to meet hers. She stepped back and smiled such a wicked smile, raised her eyebrows, and looked the ragged man up and down.

'Cannit see as how A'd be needin yasel, either,' she taunted, seeming fearless.

'Ash, come on.' I grabbed her arm tightly and dragged her

sideways and towards the door. There was just room to barge the weight of the both of us past him and out into the cold sunlight again. He didn't try to stop us. Not really interested enough.

'Just thought he'd try it on, like, but he's not up t' owt.' She pulled her arm free of my grip and brushed her skirt down.

'What were you doing, talking to him like that Ash? He could have done anything to us. He could have killed us,' I gasped in a high-pitched voice that I didn't recognise as my own, as we began to run back towards the opening in the hedge.

'Murder's not what he was about, Ell. D'ye know nowt yet?' she retorted, as we struggled free of the hawthorn hedge. 'A tell ye, he was'na up t' owt in that state. Drunk as a skunk. A can tell.' Her tone of voice made it clear that she was the expert on the subject and the conversation was now closed.

We walked back over the scrubby field in silence and I was glad to get back to the football game, where there was still too much flailing about and not enough skill to score a decent victory. I knew a bit about football because Trevor used to take me to the match at St. James's every Saturday afternoon. I felt a pang of sadness as I remembered that, but it didn't last long. Being in Bellingham with Ash was much more interesting.

9

The posh man's voice on Mrs Grainger's wireless told us that the war was going on in earnest now. He spoke in a sharp and mechanical way that was meant to make us forget that he was talking about people dying somewhere in the world. The bombs had not yet come our way. We were still waiting. Meanwhile, food was becoming scarce, so we were sent out to the farm in the mornings when we weren't at school, to help grow more. We were all part of the war effort. Even the smallest children could help to feed the pigs, or pick up the small misshapen potatoes the rest of us had missed.

I loved the mornings. I loved being out in the fields raking hay in the sunshine, or in the sweet-smelling barn searching for eggs the hens had hidden in dark corners, or swilling out the farmyard once the cows had left for the fields after milking. We picked cabbages and onions and carrots. Sometimes we were up early to collect sphagnum moss, crouching in the dew-laid grass as the early mists rose from the fields.

We had all stopped carrying our gas masks with us. There didn't seem much point and they just got in the way, banging against your back when you were running.

When the first Christmas of the war approached, many children went back to the city, but I had no plans to go home. I felt happy in my new life.

'Are ye shuwer ye don't want to go home for a bit, Ellen pet?' Mrs Grainger asked. 'A bet yer parents will be missing ye by now.'

'No thank you, Mrs Grainger. I'd like to stay here, if that's alright with you.' I didn't really consider whether it was alright with them, or if they would have liked me to go away for a while. I couldn't think about that. 'My father says they'll be with his parents anyway, so I'd just be in the way. Their house is very small, you see.' This wasn't strictly true, but not entirely a lie either. Yes, my grandparents' house in Cullercoats was small, but they would come to stay with Trevor in Newcastle for Christmas.

For a brief moment I had considered accepting Esther and Trevor's invitation to join them for the week, but then thought better of it, fearing it could be a trap. Expecting that I wouldn't be allowed to return to Bellingham. And I was right, for many vacees didn't come back after the Christmas holiday.

Mr and Mrs Grainger did their very best to make a nice Christmas for me. In the front room we put up a small fir tree and hung stars we had made out of painted cardboard on the branches. She roasted a chicken for dinner and made plum pudding with bright yellow custard. They gave me a ragdoll with brown hair made of wool. Not something I needed, but I was grateful for the thought. Esther and Trevor had sent me a copy of *Little Women*, a new cardigan (knit by Aunt Mavis), and some green ribbon for my hair. A rare note from Esther told me, 'We will miss you at Christmas-time, dear Ellen. I hope you like the book. We are sorry we could not send more presents but with rationing, you know ...' I felt a touch of sadness behind her words, and wondered if she regretted sending me away after all.

We all tried to have a jolly Christmas Day but I could see that the Graingers were missing their two boys, and to my surprise I found that I was missing the familiarity of Christmas at home with Esther, Trevor, and whichever grandparent's, aunt's or uncle's turn it was to come. So we sat quietly by the fire into the evening, and I read *Little Women* until it was time for bed.

Soon after that Daniel arrived, and nothing was ever so peaceful again.

★

The three of us, Mr and Mrs Grainger and me, were sitting around the table, just finishing our potato stew and quietly minding our own business. I liked these times, when we were all talked out and comfortable to sit together with just the hiss of the kettle on the range and the spit and crackle of the fire to fill the silence. At home – Esther and Trevor's home, that is – silences were awkward and prickly. I would wriggle about in my chair as if I had an itch, and couldn't wait to be excused – 'please may I leave the table' I would chant in my head, but I couldn't say it out loud because I didn't speak to Esther. Here there was a warm feeling, like the treacle suet pudding Pet-dear sometimes made for us on Sundays.

'Ellen pet, we're having another child to stay for a bit,' she told me as I finished my tea. 'A lad called Daniel will be coming. He needs a home, just for the war. Ye won't mind that now, will ye, dear?'

I thought how kind it was of her to ask me, and said so.

'That's aalreet pet. A know it'll be different for ye with someone else he-er. But the two of ye can be friends for each other. Not so lonely, out he-er in the back uv beyond.'

'I suppose so,' I answered. I had a friend of my own now, and didn't really need another one. 'When will he come?'

'D'ye know when he arrives, dear?' she asked Mr Grainger, who was scraping the last scraps of potato from his bowl.

'A divint knaa, hinny. Isn't it this weekend?' He reached over to the dresser and picked up a letter. 'Sez he-er Satadey, 'boot twelve, like.' I loved the way the notes of his words went up at the end of a sentence. As if everything was a question, and life forever open to endless possibilities. It gave me a hopeful feeling.

'He'll arrive on Saturday at twelve, Ellen pet,' she translated for me. 'Can ye be he-er to greet him with us? He'd like that, A'm shuwer.' Actually, I had learnt to understand Mr Grainger's language very well now, and started to try it out myself.

'Aalreet pet. A'll make shuwer A'm he-er, then,' I replied.
They both laughed.

'Puwer lad. He willna knaa oot any uv us are sayin to 'im,'
said Hinny-luv. I smiled. I probably could help there.

It was all a bit of a disaster. Daniel turned out to be eight
years old, a small and skinny-legged boy from Germany with
a mop of black curly hair and large metal-rimmed glasses that
magnified his eyes and made him look much dimmer than
he actually was. It didn't help that he couldn't speak proper
English, let alone Geordie.

The silence around the tea table was not so cosy that
evening.

'Ye can have Stephen's chair, Daniel pet. He-er, sit down
he-er, and make yasel at home,' said Mrs Grainger.

The strange boy continued to stand in the doorway,
clutching a black felt hat with a knot of battered pheasant's
feathers along its rim. He didn't move.

'He-er, Dan-iel. Sit he-er,' she encouraged him, pointing to
the empty chair and speaking very slowly. Eventually Daniel
climbed up and perched on the edge of the chair, ready to
climb quickly back down if needed. His legs dangled in mid-
air. She ladled out a portion of meat stew – although there
was more stew than meat these days. Daniel began to cry and
wouldn't eat the stew.

That night I was woken in the early hours by a scream that
could curdle the milk in farmer Bill's big churn. I clutched my
blankets up to my chin and peered out over the top of them,
waiting for a monster or a burglar, or even a murderer to burst
into my room. Maybe Hitler himself had followed this little boy
all the way from Berlin to our quiet Northumbrian village. My
mind spun with fantasies of the boy and his strange German life.

Pet-dear and Hinny-luv went to Daniel's room and there
was whispering from them and crying from Daniel. Eventually

a hush settled into the cold night air again. I slept restlessly, and dreamt of dark tunnels and a large black bear. It climbed onto my bed and was reaching a clawed paw towards me. The glistening black jewels of its eyes were small and sharp. I woke with a hard bump on the floor beside my bed, and the image of the bear tumbling down on top of me. I didn't scream out. I climbed back into my bed and thought about how everything had changed again.

The next morning as I went down to the kitchen I noticed the door to the parlour was ajar. Usually it was closed tight. Nobody went in there except on Christmas day, and when we had an occasional visit from someone important like the vicar or the doctor. I peeped round the door and there in the dim light of early morning – it was always dark in this room except in the morning when a thin sliver of sunlight might briefly skirt up the wall and across the ceiling – Daniel was standing in the very centre of the room with his head hanging down. I held my breath so as not to disturb the still air, not to alert him to my presence behind the door, and watched as he turned to face the wall opposite the door, paused for a long moment, then turned clockwise to face the window and paused again. I ducked behind the door as he began to turn towards me. I counted the seconds until I estimated he would have turned away from my wall, then peeped around the door again. Daniel was staring directly at me, his dark eyes wide and angry. Then he turned away from me to the fourth wall and stood dead still, not even blinking, as if he would stand there for eternity. Confused and embarrassed, I slipped away to the kitchen and noisily busied myself with preparing breakfast.

I decided the best thing to do would be to ignore the strange boy who had intruded into my life and my home. I hoped he would not like it here and would soon go somewhere else. Then I felt guilty for these thoughts as I could see that he was very young and upset about things, and probably didn't want to be here with us either.

Out of respect for Daniel being a Jew, and with all the commotion of the night, none of us would go to church that Sunday. So after breakfast I left the house to search for Ash down by the stream, our usual meeting place. It was cold. Frost sparkled on the ground, highlighting the rutted crust of earth where the wheels of Hinny-luv's cart had made deep trenches after last week's rain. I stepped out briskly to keep warm, and to shed the gloom that Daniel's presence had brought to the house. Then I heard the door open and close behind me. The crunch of small feet on the frosty lane, quick, urgent. I knew without looking that it was Daniel, and I knew I didn't want him following me, so I began to run. Faster, down the lane, into the main street, over to the wasteland and on down to the stream. I didn't stop till I was there, breathless and pink from the meeting on my skin of the cold air with the heat inside me.

Ash wasn't there so I kept on walking, quickly, purposefully, though I didn't know where else to go. I just walked, around the village, into the woods, across fields, until I was a little lost. I remembered running away when I was three, the feeling of needing to get away but having nowhere to go to. I was angry with Daniel for stirring this old feeling up in me again. The day had become colder and greyer, and in my mind everything that was wrong with the world was Daniel's fault.

When I arrived home a little later, damp from a brief snow flurry that had whipped through, the parlour door was still open but now the light was on. I peeped in again and saw Daniel curled into the corner of the settee with his nose quite literally buried in the pages of a book. This time he didn't notice me there. I understood that books were the place he ran away to, and felt a little hope that we might more peacefully inhabit our different worlds, even if we had to do it alongside each other. I could always outrun him, I knew, and there were endless places to hide.

★

'Ellen pet, watch out for Daniel, won't ye. It's aal so new for him, and he gets scared so easy, poor lamb,' Mrs Grainger begged me, knowing it was a lot to ask. It would be Daniel's first day at school. The general view was that he should start straight away, to stop him dwelling too much on his unhappy situation. We all felt nervous on his behalf. All morning he had been shuffling around the cottage in his bare feet, despite the cold, humming one line of a German song. He would not get dressed.

Pet-dear first tried coaxing, then gentle scolding, and in the end she dressed him herself as if he was still three years old. He stood by the range, feet planted wide apart, picking at the feathers on the black hat and humming his song while she tugged at trousers and pullover and shoes. Finally he was ready and we were on our way. I had no choice but to take him to school.

As we approached the school gate Daniel slipped his cold, brittle fingers into mine. It felt odd to have his small hand there. Up to now he had kept his distance from me, despite trying to follow me that first morning. He would just look at me through his ghastly magnifying glasses and pout his embarrassingly soft and plump lips, as if about to cry. But I knew that, like me, in his silence he was listening to everything, and learning.

His English was improving quickly, and I could see he was bright in the academic kind of way – though not in the way that Ash was bright, of course. I couldn't see how much use all that cleverness would be for him here at Bellingham Village School. I thought the boys from Byker would pull streaks off him.

Lambs to the slaughter, I thought, as we entered the hall, the two of us hand in hand.

We were late and the other vacees were already seated along the tressle table, eating their lunch of mashed potato, peas, corned beef and gravy. The starchy smell of mash and bisto pervaded the room. One by one they stopped talking and turned to stare at us. It was like watching Christmas lights go on in the city – a ripple of awe running through the two rows of children as the lights popped on in sequence. I prodded Daniel over to the two empty places at the far end of the table, heads turning to stare as we passed. The dinner lady came over with two plates of food and the spell was broken. The famished children returned to attacking their meal.

Fortunately they knew that I would be bringing the new boy, the Jewish boy, to school that day. I didn't have to explain, and could eat my meal in silence. At least Daniel knew how to eat with a knife and fork. Some of them had no idea, shovelled the food in with their hands. Daniel ate ravenously, as if this meal might be his last.

Finally I found Ash, sauntering down the main street, but not till Thursday afternoon and I wondered where she had been.

'He-er and there. Nowhere special.' She kept walking, her head down and a scowl on her face.

'I've been looking for you. Something happened.'

'What like?' Now she stopped and looked at me, a startled expression on her face.

'This boy who's come to stay with us – he's a nightmare. I think I'll go mad.'

'Oh – A thought you meant summit else.' She continued walking, hitching the shopping bag she was carrying over her shoulder. 'What's he like then?'

'He's really annoying, you wouldn't believe it. He's stubborn, he argues all the time, or just buries his nose in a book. Sometimes he starts screaming in the middle of the night. He's German, you know. A Jew. And only eight years old.'

'Is he, like? Can A see him?'

'You won't like him. He wears big glasses that make him look stupid.'

'Never mind, A'm curious to see him. A'll sort him out for ye, if ye like.'

'How?'

'A'll see.'

'Okay then, but I've warned you.'

We turned around and headed towards the cottage. I took Ash into the kitchen where Pet-dear was preparing tea.

'D'ye want to stay for a cup uv tea, pet?' she asked Ash.

'No ta, Mrs Grainger. A won't be stopping.'

'Please yasel then.'

We found Daniel in the parlour, sitting in the dim light with a book glued to his face. We edged in and sat side by side on the sofa. Ash nudged me and I giggled.

'Hello, Jew-boy,' she said.

Daniel looked up, glared at Ash, put down his book and clenched his fists. He moved as if to stand up but thought better of it. Instead he retreated further into the armchair and glowered at Ash, not saying a word.

'What ye reading then?'

He held up the book to show her the cover. She screwed up her nose and frowned – Ash couldn't read properly and there were no pictures on the cover to show what the book might be about.

'Looks a bit boring to us,' she ventured. I was unsure if she meant the book or Daniel. He was pretending to ignore her and continue reading, but I could tell he was curious about Ash.

After a while he turned to me and demanded, 'Who is that?'

My friend, Ash. Can you be nice to her?'

'No. She not nice to me.'

Ash laughed. 'No, A'm not nice. Never mind little boy, A won't be bothering ye, if ye divint bother us.'

And that was that – Ash had laid down the rules and he was expected to obey them. She got up and left the room. I jumped up after her and we stood for a moment on the doorstep of the cottage, whispering.

'Jesus Ell, just divint bring him along with ye. Ye'r right, A don't like him much, and he's so small!' She threw up her arms in a gesture of despair, and turned away down the lane. I sighed, and hoped I could keep Daniel away from Ash.

It was Saturday – our free day. He had followed me down the farm track and was irritatingly kicking up stones that had been sitting quite happily in the dirt for a very long time, unbothered by the heavy tyres of the tractor or the muddy hooves of cows that passed that way each day. A sharp edged stone hit the back of my leg.

'Stop that Daniel,' I snapped, and turned, as if to chase him. I couldn't be bothered though, and continued on to the big five-bar gate at the end of the track. I leant against it and stared out over the field, my arms hooked over the top bar and my chin sitting heavy in my hands. I wanted to be on my own. I had a lot to think about today – grown up things that were no business of Daniel's. I was thinking about all those years I had spent in our house with Esther, how unhappy I was, and how much better it was here in Bellingham with Mrs Grainger. I needed to make plans for my future and wondered how I could stay here forever.

The far off whistle of a train pierced the air, for a moment drawing my attention away from the bleet of the first new lambs in the field, and the chirp of two blackbirds poking about under a strangled hawthorn bush. The air was full of the scent of cut grass. Bill had just been out with his scythe and the edges of the track had been shorn as bare as a pig's backside, as Ash would say.

'I hate the sound of trains,' declared Daniel, as he caught up with me. 'Everyone hates the sound of trains.'

'No they don't. I don't.' I was feeling cross with him for following me, and irritable.

'I hate trains. I don't ever want to see a train again,' he continued doggedly. I was sure he did it just to annoy me.

'I like trains.'

'Trains take you away from home and then you are left somewhere – some place.' He was struggling to find words for this difficult feeling. 'How could anyone love trains? They are monsters, tearing through the country with their black smoke and noise. Trains are bad.'

Oh no, where was he going with this? The boy had too dark an imagination. I wanted to ignore him but felt drawn into the argument.

'Trains are good. They take you out of boring places into new adventures,' I retorted. I pushed myself off the gate and began to stomp back down the lane. Daniel came tripping after me, determined to make his point clear and, more than that, to have it agreed with. It was important to Daniel that everyone agreed with him, that he was considered to be right – all the time. Pet-dear humoured him, but his dogged insistence on being right only led me to argue with him even more.

Daniel kicked a large stone and it hit the back of my knee with a painful wallop. I stopped and turned to face him. Now I was angry. 'Stop kicking stones at me, or I'll tell Mrs Grainger and you'll get no tea.' I sat down on the bottom step of the sty at the edge of the track and picked up a stone of my own. I made as if to throw it at him, but tossed it into the field instead.

Daniel frowned and scuffed his worn shoes in the dirt, digging a small hole there. 'Trains are bad things. I hate them.' His persistence was remarkable, his stubbornness extreme. He took off his dark navy cap with the thick peak at the front and ruffled his hair, then put the cap back on, still frowning. He thought me cold, hard to please, argumentative, no doubt. But he was so infuriating.

'Well I don't care. I love trains, and I love the sound they make, rumbling through the countryside. So there.' I jumped up onto the top step of the sty and peered down at Daniel. If all little boys were like him, thank God (if there was a God, and I wasn't sure about this anymore) I didn't have to suffer growing up with a younger brother. At least I was spared that particular torment.

'Daniel, when will you be going back home?' I asked, bored and irritated beyond words with the stupid argument about trains.

Now it was Daniel's turn to be angry. I was not supposed to talk to him about home. Home did not exist anymore. He was scowling at me, the furrows in his brow as dark as the curly hair that sprung out from under his cap.

'I do not want to talk about that,' he said, in his square and solid German accent. He stamped his foot on a beetle that had been rummaging between the stones. The beetle expired with no more than a bleak crunch. Daniel began to stomp away.

'Danny, where are you going?' I called after him for some unknown reason. I could have let him go.

'Do not call me Danny! My name is Daniel,' he shouted back at me.

'Daniel, my name is Daniel.' I mimicked his stilted English. I just couldn't help myself.

Daniel turned back, picked up a large pebble and threw it in my general direction. It landed in a cowpat by the fence.

'Crikey, you can't even throw a stone straight.' I tossed my head disdainfully. Then I relented a little. I knew I was being too harsh on him. 'Oh, come on, I'll teach you to throw properly.' If we were to be stuck with each other for the rest of the war, which is what I now feared, we would have to find a way to get along.

With that reluctant thought in mind I slid down from the sty, selected a round polished stone and aimed. It neatly hit the trunk of an oak tree that stood some distance away in the middle of the field.

'C'mon, Daniel. You try.'

Still scowling, he picked up a large stone and let me place all the parts of his body into the best position for a throw.

'Now take a deep breath in – no, slowly, like this.' I demonstrated. 'Look at the target. Pull back, then forward, breathe out – light fingers – release your wrist.'

The stone hit the earth a few yards away with a thud. I could see the lesson would take some time and searched inside myself for the patience I had learnt when refusing to speak to Esther. I would need this if I was to control my impulse to argue constantly with Daniel. I momentarily thanked Esther for teaching me at least this one skill.

10

Saturday afternoon again. I was free to do what I pleased, but still I tiptoed out of the house. I longed to bound down the stairs, two at a time, and run down the lane, but Daniel was in the front room reading his book and he mustn't hear me leave. I was tired of him tagging along, getting in the way when Ash and I wanted to talk about grown-up things, now that he had discovered our meeting place. I pulled the door shut with just the softest of clicks, and hurried down the lane with my shoulders hunched up and my sides pulled in – as if making myself feel smaller could make me invisible. It was a skill I had practised as a child and it seemed to work with Esther, but then she would rather not see me, so it was easy to be invisible to her. Daniel, on the other hand, was watching out for me constantly and had an uncanny knack of following me when I thought I had slipped out unnoticed.

I found Ash down by the stream, in our once-secret place. Spring had arrived in its fullness, and I could hardly see her – just one bare knee poking up out of the long grass. She was lying on the bank chewing a blade of grass and sunning her face. She wore the same dark green skirt, flaring out to just below her knees, that she had worn all winter. Ash had even less clothes than I had. Her faded and darned blue cardigan was open, and through a thin flowered blouse I could see the outlines of her bra. She had undone the top buttons to feel the sun on her chest, revealing a frayed bra strap and a mole just below her left collarbone. Ash was pretty – prettier than me, I thought.

'What you up to?' I sat down beside her in the grass.

'Just thinking.'

'What about?'

'Things.' She contemplated the chewed blade of grass without opening her eyes. I lay down nearby and closed my eyes too, joining her in a languid world of buzzing bees and gurgling water. The air smelt fresh, of damp earth and green grass. The scent of Ash's unwashed skin was sweet, like oranges and sage.

'A think A'll be leaving home soon,' she said, after a long pause. The words, leaping naked and stark out of the silence like that, startled me.

'But why? Where will you go?' I asked, louder and sharper than I had intended, so it sounded as if I were telling her off.

'Divint knaa yet. A'll think uv summit.' She threw the stripped blade of grass towards the stream, plucked another and resumed chewing.

'But Ash, we're friends now. You can't just go. I mean – I don't want you to go. Can't you be somewhere nearby, even if you have to leave home?'

'Not if he stays around, A can't. A'll have to go to another country. People are going abroad – America and places – to get out uv this blasted war. A could go there.' She waved her hand in a gesture that was meant to convey a casual ease, as if the world were wide open to her and she just had to choose which part of it she would grace with her presence. But what I read was despair.

'Has something happened?'

'Shuwer. Things are always happening. A've had enough. Me mam won't help. Sez A'm making it up if A try to tell her, like.' I turned to look at Ash. A thin tear trickled from the corner of her eye, down her cheek and into the soft furrow at the edge of her nose. Her hand came up to brush it away.

'Is there anything I can do – to help, I mean?'

'Doubt it. He gets raving mad if ye try to say owt to him. There's no point, man. Best thing is for me to go away. A'll finish school soon, and then A can do what A like. Perhaps A'll go to Scotland and join the Lumber Jo's.'

'I don't know what I'll do if you're not here, Ash.'

'Ye'll be aalreet, man. War'll be over soon, and ye can go back home.'

'I'm not going home. I like it better here. Or maybe we could run away together Ash, you and me.' I felt my spirit lift again as this idea found its place in the realm of possible worlds.

'If ye want to, ye can come with us.' She tossed the grass after the first one, stretched her long legs out, then stood up. 'Come on, let's see if owt's going on in the village.' By the village she meant the scrap of wasteland that was the children's playground during the day, and a meeting place for the young folk when it got darker. I felt troubled by her mood but I followed her.

My gaze was fixed firmly on the ground as we approached the wasteland. I was trying to avoid the dry earth cracks and stones that covered it, so I didn't notice three older boys lounging next to the old cow shed at the far end. One shouted over to us. 'Hey, Ash, where ye gannin, man?' I admired the way her hips swayed gently as she walked towards them, how she tipped her head up slightly and cocked it to one side as she called back. 'None of ya business, is it, like.' She always knew how to look her most beautiful when there were boys around.

Ash went right up to them, but I hung back. I felt intimidated by their big muscular bodies, their rough voices, the way they lounged and loped against the cow shed, giving off the message to come close but also not to mess with them. Telling the world they were in charge and we *should* feel intimidated. But she did not. She went right up to the one who had called. He took a last drag on his cigarette then threw it to the ground, stubbed it out with his heel, and grabbed hold of her arm. She let him draw her close and plant a kiss on her cheek, then pretended to wipe it off and turn her head away in disgust, but she was laughing. He took that to mean she was game and pulled her behind the shed. Ash pretended to resist but I think perhaps she was enjoying the game.

I felt scared. I didn't know what to do, whether I was meant to rescue her or let her be. The other two boys threw down their cigarette ends and one took a step towards me. They were both staring at me, piercing me with their eyeballs. I heard Ash giggling from behind the shed, the man speaking to her in a soft voice, some rustling. The one who had stepped towards me laughed, kicked a stone then backed away. The other continued to stare at me, saying nothing. Now I was very scared. I heard banging against the wooden shed, a cry from Ash, then a moaning sound. I desperately wanted to help her, but the boys were blocking my way. When the second one scowled at me and took a few steps towards me, I ran. I thought I heard more giggling from Ash, or was it crying, as I fled the crumbling place.

I ran all the way home. I felt full of shame for not helping her. But I was confused too, unsure whether she had been laughing or crying, wanting my help or not. I felt I didn't know Ash at all and this filled me with pain. She was my only friend now and I needed her to like me. I went up to my room, avoiding the kitchen where Pet-dear would want to draw me into conversation, lay on my bed and buried my head under the pillow. I felt too confused and ashamed even to cry. I just wanted to disappear.

That evening Mr and Mrs Grainger went out. The village people were holding a meeting – about the war effort they said – and they both had to be there. I was put in charge of Daniel.

I was lying in bed, still thinking about Ash, wondering if I had done wrong by not helping her, hoping she would still like me. Another part of my mind was counting the cracks in the plaster on the wall, imagining them into shapes that became animals and trees. Daniel's wheezy breath drifted down the attic stairs, telling me he was sleeping.

I'm not sure if the cracked animals were still on the wall or had entered my dreams. I was pursuing a rabbit shaped creature, big floppy ears bouncing, when a scream burst through the quiet night. I jolted upright in my bed, gasping for breath and my heart pounding. Little pricks of fear ran through my arms to my fingertips. It took a moment to remember where I was, and that the scream would be coming from Daniel. It always was. But tonight Pet-dear was not here to sort out the drama.

I slipped out of bed, the cold wooden floorboards against my warm feet completing the wake-up call. Heart still racing, I tiptoed up the steep and narrow staircase to Daniel's attic room and peeped in, half-expecting to see a monster crouching on his bed. There was nothing on his bed but a pile of tangled sheets and a dark wet stain in the middle of it all.

'Daniel, where've you gone?' I whispered through chattering teeth. I'm not sure if I was shaking from the cold or from fear. I went to the window, which was slightly open, to see if he had escaped that way. I couldn't see him on the ground below, and there was nowhere else to go but down the sheer stone wall of the cottage. The grey slate roof was too steep and slippery to give a foothold.

I was afraid to look under the bed. When I was very young, that's where monsters had always lurked until Trevor came to chase them away.

Then I heard a tiny rumble coming from the wardrobe – a shoe being dislodged from its place perhaps. Oh, why did they have to go out tonight? I could not deal with this.

I cracked open the wardrobe door and Daniel screamed at the top of his voice. I slammed it shut again – just a reflex. I didn't mean to lock him in. It took a moment to steady myself and find the courage to try again. I called to him first – 'Daniel, it's me, Ellen. Don't scream. I'm going to open the door.' I did. 'Please come out, Daniel.'

Big brown eyes stared at me out of a ghostly white face. His dark curly hair was damp with sweat and flattened over his forehead. Daniel tried to lodge himself more deeply into the corner of the wardrobe, half-hidden behind woollen overcoats and thick winter shirts, one arm wrapped tightly around his knees and the other hand up in front of his face to ward me off.

'Daniel, what is it? Don't be afraid – it's just me, Ellen,' I whispered. My heart was softening. I know I had sometimes been unkind to Daniel, but I had never seen anyone so frightened before and I wanted him to feel safe again. I held out my hand, reaching very slowly into the darkness of his hiding place, trying not to startle him further.

It took ages, but I found patience inside myself that I didn't know I had. When his white fingers finally uncurled and hooked limply over my own, I just sat there and waited until he was ready to take hold of my hand. Then I waited some more until he was ready to climb out of the wardrobe. We went over to sit on the edge of the bed together in the near-darkness, avoiding the wet place, me holding his hand and Daniel still trembling. A faint thread of light found its way up the stairs from the fire burning in the kitchen hearth below and the small lamp that sat on a corner table on the landing.

'Tell me what happened, what frightened you?' I finally asked.

'Banging on the stairs – big boots, banging on the stairs – lots of them,' he finally stuttered. I could feel his shoulders tense up and his body become rigid again.

'You can tell me about it, Daniel, if you want to.'

'Took Mutti away, took Vati away.'

'And what happened to you, Daniel?'

'In cupboard, hiding. Very dark. Loud banging.' Then it came, a torrent of tears, an avalanche of deep, wrenching sobs. I didn't know such a small and wiry body could hold so many tears, could cry so furiously and for so long. It seemed to go on for hours, but probably it wasn't that long. Eventually Mr and Mrs Grainger came home and took over. They sent me downstairs to get Daniel and me some warm milk, then back to my own bed. I didn't sleep much after that. I kept hearing noises on the stairs and imagined that Esther was being dragged away. I was not sure if I was glad or sorry about that. More shame and guilt for these thoughts. More confusion.

11

Trevor wrote me a letter on the first day of every month. He never failed in this duty. It would often arrive days, or even weeks later, but he dated each one so I knew exactly when it had been written. There wasn't much of interest in his letters, but I was glad he still thought about me once a month.

He would tell me what he and Esther had been doing, how successful his business was, how the war was affecting them, whether it had been raining or sunny. He would always end with – 'Take care and be good for Mrs Grainger. Yours affectionately, your loving father.' After this there would be a short message from Esther, written in her tight and spiky hand – 'Do take care of the coat we gave you, as with the war on we won't be able to buy another one at the moment.' 'Your father is growing vegetables in the garden now. Do you grow vegetables in Bellingham?' 'There is not much meat and cheese here in the city. I suppose it's better in the countryside?' 'Give my greetings to Mr and Mrs Grainger. I hope you are being good.' I wasn't expected to answer the questions.

It was mid-summer, nearly a whole year since the war had begun, when Trevor's July letter arrived. The content of his letters was quite predictable, so I was in no hurry to read it. I finished chopping cabbage and onions for the soup then went out to the back garden. The sun was bright and cast deep shadows on the grass. I threw a handful of corn for the chickens, my fingers dancing with the long arm of my shadow.

The chickens flapped and flurried then settled back to their pecking and scratching. Four bedraggled skinny birds, but they laid enough eggs for the four of us at least, with a few left over for Daisy.

Our shelter was in Daisy's garden, so if there was ever an air raid everyone from the terrace would run down there and hide from the bombs. The first time we had practised this someone had rung the church bells – just clashing them about, out of tune, so we had known it wasn't for church but for air raid practice.

'C'mon ye two,' Pet-dear had called, as she gathered up her hat and coat. She bustled out of the door as if it was for real. I squeezed through beside her and skipped down the lane, with Daniel running not far behind me. I was hooting like a siren, like the ships' foghorns I had heard out at sea in the night, back at home. Daniel tried to copy my skipping but he tripped over his big shoes and fell flat on his face. He didn't cry though. Just got up and ran after me with his shoe laces undone, which made him take wide slow steps, like a scarecrow might if it could run.

At Daisy's cottage a small crowd was gathering – Mrs Harris from next door, Mrs Dewey and her two little ones, Sam and Ivy, Daisy and us. The men were out at work so probably didn't have an air raid shelter to go to.

Laughing and chattering, pushing the one in front, we all bundled down into the shelter. It smelt of damp earth and was dark, until someone switched on a torch and we could see benches along each side. We four children were first inside and sat along one bench. The women sat along the other side. We looked at each other across the small gap and I wondered how long we would need to stay like this. For a moment no-one spoke, then Mrs Harris nodded.

'I guess that's it then. We can go back now.'

'I suppose so,' Daisy had said, shrugging her shoulders.

'Is that all?' I asked, a little disappointed.

'I want to stay and play,' cried Sam, but his mother had taken him under her arm and hauled him up the steps, back into the daylight. And that had been the end of the air raid practice.

When I was ready, I took Trevor's letter upstairs and curled myself into the windowsill with Humphrey on my lap. Two months ago Pet-dear and Hinny-luv had received a letter telling them that Kevin had been taken a prisoner. She cried a lot until he told her it meant Kevin was safe from the bombs, and had a better chance of surviving the war as a prisoner than as a soldier. She stopped crying for a while until she remembered that Stephen was not a prisoner of war, and he could still be killed. So I knew that wartime letters could contain upsetting news. I really was not prepared for what Trevor's July letter contained though.

My dear Ellen

*I hope you are well, and still helping Mrs Grainger,
like a good girl. We are both very proud of you,
suffering this terrible war without any complaints.
We are both well, and thinking of you. My business
continues to prosper fairly well as there is always a
need for cloth to make new uniforms for the soldiers,
and parachutes for the airmen. I am now working
mostly from our main warehouse in Lancashire, which
is why I could not come to see you in person as I
would have liked to do. Your mother is unwell at the
moment so she could also not visit you. I am sorry
about this.*

*I have some important news for you. Because of the air
raids that have begun in the northeast, your mother has
decided to go to America to live with her cousin Mildred
for a while. It will be safe there. So of course we ask if
you would like to join her? I will probably follow in a*

*few months, depending on finding someone to manage the
business for me.*

*Esther thought this was the moment to give you some
other news. It may come as a very big surprise to you,
and I hope it will not be too upsetting. We have always
loved you, done our best to be good parents. Though we
may not have done this perfectly well, we have always
had your best interest at heart. Now is the time to tell
you that, in fact, we are not your actual parents. Your
mother died when you were born and, out of the goodness
of her heart, Esther took you in and raised you as if you
were her own child. We adopted you, Ellen. But this does
not mean we love you any less.*

I read the last paragraph again, then I couldn't read anymore.
I tore up the letter, ran down stairs and fled out of the house,
a whirlwind of tattered thoughts flying after me, voices
clamouring inside my head. I heard myself crying out loud as
I ran up the lane and into the field, a roar like a wild animal
erupting out of me. I ran around the field in circles, clutching
my hair in my fists, shouting 'No, no, no!' at the top of my
voice, until Mrs Grainger came running after me, puffing and
panting with her plump bare arms and her face flushed red,
and begged me to stop. I let her catch hold of me and gather
me into her arms. I sobbed and blurted out what Trevor had
written.

'My mother's dead. My real mother's dead. They told me
lies. All these years they lied to me. I hate them! I hate them!'
I broke free of Mrs Grainger's embrace and began to stamp the
earth and fling my arms about, shouting 'I hate them' at the
very top of my voice, until Mrs Harris from next door arrived
to see what the commotion was.

'Come on, Ellen pet, let's go inside and talk about this.'
Pet-dear gathered me into her arms again and walked me

back to the kitchen. She sat me down and ordered me not to say another word until she had made tea. That gave me time to collect myself.

'I'm staying with you, forever,' I blurted out when the teapot finally arrived on the table. 'I won't go with her! I won't!'

'That's fine pet, ye can stay he-er as long as ye like. Ye'r part of wor family now. So don't worry yer little heed about all that.' She sat down beside me and poured us both a cup of tea. 'Now, for the life of God, please tell me what all the fuss is about.'

I told her.

So it was decided that I would stay with the Graingers and Esther went away, without even coming to say goodbye to me. I was relieved. I couldn't face meeting her, and I guessed she felt the same about me. I was so full of anger and hate that I didn't know what I might do if I saw her again, so it was better that she didn't come. For all those years she had tormented me, pretending she was my mother. When she wasn't.

Trevor did come to say goodbye – he would be moving to Lancaster for a while. He said Esther couldn't come because she was too ill, but I knew that was another lie. Our meeting was brief. We shook hands, very formal and awkward. He tried to hug me but I stepped back out of his reach. Never again would he trap me.

My life up to now had just been washed away like a riverbank in a flood, and I was someone new. But I had no idea who. I didn't know who my mother was, and I didn't know if I was a good person or a bad one. I wanted something terrible to happen to Esther and Trevor, so I guessed I was more of a bad person than a good one. And yet I also felt a terrible weight in my heart when I thought that I might never see them again.

It was hard to hold all of these different feelings inside, and I felt I might break apart if I moved at all. After Trevor left, I locked my bedroom door so that Daniel could not come in, and sat wedged into the windowsill. I hugged Humphrey tightly, close to my heart, and stared at the dirt streaks on the outside of the pane. I sat very still, the way Daniel sometimes did, like a river frozen to its banks. I sat like this for hours.

Act One

12

'Ellen, will you stop running about like that. You're going to break something.' She passes the door on her way up stairs, holding a bundle of ironed sheets laid out over her forearms like a small corpse, a cold baby offering.

I keep turning and leaping about the sitting room, twirling between the chairs and the settee, my arms sweeping up above my head, my hands clapping as they meet in the air. I'm not running. I am dancing. I spiral around, and my hand swings out and meets Esther's favourite vase where it poises graciously on a side table. The vase goes spinning to the floor. It breaks into a thousand shimmering flakes of white and blue and gold.

I stop then, and press my hands over my mouth. Now I feel really scared. Her dark, angry face comes down on me, harsh sounds pouring out. I don't hear the words, but I feel them. There's a sharp sting across the side of my head as her hand swipes by.

'Go to your room, and don't you dare come out till I tell you to! Your father will hear about this.' I understand this much. Then I hear a key in the lock of my bedroom door as it closes behind me. I'll be trapped here until Trevor comes home, I know it. Then he will try to sort things out in his clumsy old way.

'Trevor, she's impossible. She's like a wild animal, no self-control. I really can't handle her anymore,' Esther complains, when Trevor returns home from work that evening.

'Be patient dear – she'll grow out of it in time. I'm sure it's just a phase. You must try to understand her.'

'But how can I understand her when she won't even speak to me? There's something wrong with the girl.'

'I don't know, dear. She speaks to me when we're out, but I don't understand why she won't talk at home.' Trevor speaks in his most conciliatory tone of voice. It usually calms Esther down for a while.

'Don't you think she's not quite right in her mind? I mean, it's not normal, is it. To not talk, when she's perfectly capable of doing so. Why can't she be normal, like other children?' Esther is on the edge of despair – I can hear it in the high-pitched quaver of her voice. 'Do you think it's my fault?'

'No, I'm sure it's nobody's fault. She's just high spirited, impulsive.'

'Then she needs more discipline. You need to be firmer with her, Trevor, because I can't do anything with her. I give up.'

'Don't give up, Esther. She'll come round – I promise you.'

'I don't think so. I think she'll just get worse – and then what will we do with her?' The question hangs in the chill air, like a solitary icicle suspended from the gutter of a winter roof.

I'm lying on my bedroom floor with my right ear to a crack between the floorboards, where I can just hear their conversation. I feel cold. A draught is seeping up through the crack and my ear turns numb.

Act Two

13

A furious wind howled as the black of the night deepened. I watched dark clouds scud past my bedroom window, swept along in a frenzy of rain and trouble like nothing I had seen here before. Was this the war approaching? We hadn't seen much of it here in Bellingham – just a stray plane flying back in the night after dropping its bombs on some foreign city, or an explosion rumbling through the darkness from a far away place – though the voice on the wireless told us it was coming our way.

The night was wild. Nobody could sleep through all of that. The gentle tap-tap of a branch from the climbing rose – so pink and sweet-smelling in June, so dry and brittle now – had crescendoed to a frantic lashing, keeping me wide awake. Crack-crack against the windowpane. It stirred my heart up, beat it like a whip master. I remembered Miss Parker's ruler, the line of boys and girls standing at the front of the classroom with outstretched palms, waiting tremulously for the red lash to reach them, one by one. My palm began to smart at the very thought. I had stood in that wavering line several times now – just last week for turning up to class with a pencil as blunt as a tab end – as Ash would say. I was beginning to sound like her – 'A'm knackered as a bone', but still I couldn't sleep. Knick knack paddy whack, give the dog a bone.

It was a month since Trevor's letter had arrived and still I was full of a rage I didn't know what to do with. I felt strung out on my nerves, like a fly in a spider's web, spinning this way and that in the wind, but going nowhere. My head was thick and throbbing and my heart was rattling away like a steam train through the dark woods.

I heard a strange banging noise out in the night, distant, forlorn, swept up into the howling wind. Then I thought it must be inside my head, not outside.

Eventually I opened my eyes and gave up trying to sleep. The clock was striking four down on the mantelpiece in the kitchen, above the cosy fire, amid an assortment of candles, biscuit tins, photos of Kevin and Stephen. The all-important wireless sat on its own small lamp-stand next to the fireplace. I could see it all in my mind's eye, lit dimly by the glow of dying embers.

Then I thought the strange noise really had come from outside, and not from inside my weary head after all. I climbed out of bed and padded over to the window. It was not far – two wobbly steps and I was there. I peered out through the darkness and the wind seemed to be glad that I was looking at last, because it began to soften down a little. The clouds continued to brush by, but thinner now. I caught a glimpse of sky where a star seemed to skid between the curly edges of the clouds. At least the stars had not been blown away, I thought, then chided myself for such a childish thought. I was thirteen by now, not a child anymore.

As I peered out into the night something at the edge of the woods caught my eye – a lightness, a brightness, glowing against the dark shapes of wood and field and sky. Pale, shimmering, it seemed to slide down over the trees, slipping, curling, until the wind miraculously calmed and the slipping white thing came to rest. I saw it clearly now. The shape of a wing. An angel wing – it must be. Fallen out of the sky in the storm. There must be an angel out there in the woods.

I must find him. With no mother to love me, no father who might protect me, I needed an angel to save me from harm – from the dark and surging dangers that were welling inside me as well as outside in the world. I crept downstairs, gathered up my coat and shoes by the back door, and went out into the night.

The tree stood slightly apart, at the edge of the wood that bordered the west side of the village. In the grey light that signalled dawn approaching it looked spectral, the white luminous wing cascading down its branches insubstantial and shimmering. It was much bigger than I had thought, peering through the dark from my room. I kept walking, tripping over crusted cowpats and tufts of grass. My feet and ankles were wet. My heart was beating fast, my mouth dry. The tree itself seemed alive. It seemed to sway, although the wind had all but stopped now. The morning air hung heavy as a soggy blanket, like Daniel's sheets after one of his night turns.

As I approached, step by hesitant step, I heard a faint whispering amongst the leaves – "Who is it? What does she want?" the branches seemed to say. Fear gripped me.

Maybe I had been mistaken and the tree was the home of ghosts, wraiths who lingered, waiting to tell their stories, or to scare, or to punish the living for their bad deeds. But no, I had to believe, I *must* believe it was an angel's wing that draped graciously over the dark branches.

The early morning light hadn't yet reached the tree. I hesitated, afraid of what I might find. Would the angel be there? Or had his wing broken and fallen down to this spot, leaving him stranded somewhere else? Unable to fly?

I clenched my fists and my teeth, marched boldly across the last stretch of the field and right up to the tree. I stood beneath the canopy of damp branches, large droplets of rain splattering onto the ground below. The ghostly white drape glimmered in the eeriness of neither light nor dark that heralded the beginning of a new day, rippling softly. It had a sheen, soft and delicate, like silk. The feathers must have been so tiny I could not tell them apart, or so wet that they had glued together into a smooth sheet of uncanny beauty. I marvelled.

In a way that I never did in church, I felt the urge to kneel before it. An angel wing. I had found an angel. He had come to protect me. He would help me. I tried to pray to him, his broken wing fluttering all white and luminous up there in the branches above me.

'Angel, where are you? Please show me where you are.' No response, just the whispering of leaves and a glimmer of movement rippling through the softness of the wing.

I walked slowly round the tree. Nothing there. I looked all about me but there was no sign of an angel. He would turn up soon, I told myself. I waited. I walked around the tree again, first in one direction then in the other. My shoes were soaked through from the wet grass and I was cold from standing so long. Finally I had to give up waiting for him. I walked back to the cottage with a troubled heart, having swung from elation and awe to disappointment and despair, up and down like the swing in our garden back home.

A forlorn feeling swept over me as I remembered the familiarity of home, the garden with its hiding places, the swing, Trevor, sometimes kind to me. I could even miss Esther, ever so slightly – for a moment I missed the game of silence that I played with her. It had grown to be a part of me, and she had been right at the centre of my life, Act One, after all.

I arrived back at the cottage feeling very sorry for myself, but there was no time to wallow in it. Daniel, Pet and Hinny were already dressed and making breakfast in the warm lamplight of the kitchen. I had forgotten that this morning Daniel was to collect sphagnum moss from the fields with the younger children, and I had to go with him because this was his first time.

'Where've ye been, Ellen pet?' asked Pet-dear as I entered the kitchen, all wet and dejected feeling.

'Nowhere. Just for a walk,' I replied. She tutted, but said no more about it. She handed me a slice of bread and dripping and a mug of milk still warm and frothy from the cow, then I scurried upstairs to get properly dressed for the day.

'Now, Daniel pet, do what wor Ellen tells ye, won't ye, there's a good lad.'

Daniel wriggled into his coat and boots and stuffed the black felt hat into his pocket. 'Oh-kay,' he replied, frowning at me.

'Why don't ye leave the hat he-er, pet? It'll be fine with me while ye'r gone – ye don't want to be losing it in the fields, do ye.'

Daniel frowned at Mrs Grainger and pushed the battered relic more deeply into the spacious pocket of his overcoat. Now that I knew the hat had belonged to his mother, and that she was gone, and that this was all he had left of her (snatched from the cupboard when a neighbour found him hiding there and took him away from his home, forever) I understood his obsession. And now that I knew I had also lost my mother, I felt more sympathy for Daniel and his odd ways.

'Don't worry, Mrs Grainger. I'll make sure he doesn't lose it,' I reassured her.

'Ah, ye'r a good lass, Ellen me dear – when ye want to be.' She pecked us both on the cheek and steered us out of the door.

Daniel slipped his hand into mine and looked up at me with a deep longing in his eyes that unsettled me completely. I wanted to be alone this morning. I needed to return to the tree in daylight and look for the angel. I didn't want to share him with anyone, not yet. Maybe I would tell Ash later on, and perhaps Daniel if he didn't annoy me, but not today. I made a plan.

We walked hand in hand through the village until we

reached the field where the young children were gathering. I dropped Daniel's hand and swung my arms as I strode up to the gate, as I had seen the Landgirls do.

'Here, I've brought Daniel to help. He's really good at this sort of thing. He'll be no trouble.' Other little ones were running and skipping, falling into the clarty tire tracks that circled the field, and screeching at the tops of their little top of the range voices. Daniel stood patiently waiting for his orders.

'Good. Here Daniel, take this basket and follow me.' The tall lady in lace up boots, men's work trousers and braces, with her hair tied back in a red and white spotted headscarf, strode off into the grey morning. Daniel had no choice but to hurry after her. I waved as he looked anxiously back at me, then I turned up the track towards the woods.

A light mist lay over the fields and hills beyond, but I could feel the summer warmth begin to rise, setting the grass steaming as the dampness sizzled off. For a while the whole world shimmered in a silvery light, then a thin blue sky began to peek through and the day had begun.

I came to the tree, walked around it, sat down, stood up, stared into the branches. The angel's wing had gone.

It had to be somewhere. I began to search the woods, trailing this way and that, forging paths through the undergrowth where only rabbits and deer had been before. Brambles tore at my hands and my coat, my feet sank into damp mounds of sweet smelling humus. I peered around every tree, under stones, into the creek. It was nowhere to be found.

I emerged into the daylight again and sat down on a fallen log, the smell of wet grass and damp wood in my nostrils. I could have cried, but right then I noticed the small dark figure of Daniel standing in the middle of the field, shading his eyes from the sun as he slowly turned around in a full circle. Daniel was looking for me. I was looking for an angel.

I could have hidden before he noticed me, but I knew he would search all day until he found me. Daniel was the most tenacious, persistent, stubborn little boy I had ever met. I sat still, half buried behind brambles and a scrubby dogwood that was fighting for its life in this narrow and shaded spot. It didn't take him long to see me there. In his haste to reach me he stumbled over a clump of bracken and fell onto his knees in the wet sticky tangle. Green curly fiddleheads clung to his threadbare black coat as he found his feet again and picked his way more carefully across the field towards my log. He sat down beside me and joined me in staring out into the greening field, chin in hands and a frown on his brow that mirrored my own. I had to laugh, seeing him mimic me in this way. One thing Daniel could do quite well was empathy. It had surprised me to discover he had such a gift.

'Why have you left the others, Daniel? You're supposed to stay till you've finished picking, at least till morning break.'

'I have already finished. I am a quick picker and I am ready,' he replied in his solid German accent. He had placed the basket, half full of sphagnum moss, between his feet. The moss would be made into medicine to cure all kinds of wartime aliments, Miss Parker had told us, and we should be proud that we were helping the war effort in this way.

'You should have left that with the Landgirls. Now we'll have to go back to the field.' My irritation was rising again. I was trying to be patient with him since he had told me about his Mutti and Vati, how he had hidden in the big cupboard of their apartment, listening to her screams as the men in big boots dragged her down the stone stairway and far away from him, listening to the gunshots as they killed his father right there in the stairwell of the building. But it was hard to be patient with Daniel all the time.

I stood up and brushed the damp tree bark and moss off my backside. My coat was wet where I had been sitting, and my feet were cold.

'Come on, let's go back.' I sighed, feeling defeated and weighed down with too many burdens.

'Tell me what you were looking for first,' Daniel demanded, hunkering down onto the log, refusing to budge.

I feigned indignation. 'I wasn't looking for anything. I was just walking in the woods.'

'You were. I know you were.'

'How do you know that?'

'I know you went out in the night.' He was looking at me sideways to catch my reaction.

'I didn't!'

'Yes you did. I heard you leave the house. I heard the door. Then you were looking now in the woods.'

'I just went for a walk!' I felt angry with him. He was going to spoil it all. I turned away and started back towards the village. I knew he wouldn't have been able to see the angel's wing from his window, which was tiny and high up in the roof, and anyway on the wrong side of the cottage. At least I could be thankful for that.

Daniel quickly gathered himself and his basket up and tripped after me.

'Please tell me what you were looking for.' An expression of longing spread over his white face, seeping out of his big eyes; their darkness was intensified by a sand-coloured ring that circled the deep brown iris. I could not bear this expression and focussed steadfastly ahead.

We trudged back over the field in silence, the long grass now as dry as kindling since the sun had risen higher and burnt off last night's rain. I felt troubled. I needed to find the angel's wing, but now that Daniel knew I was searching for something he would not leave me alone for a moment, that I knew.

As if he could sense my wavering uncertainty, he began to prod again.

'Tell me, please. I can help you find it. I am good at finding.' That at least was true. Daniel had an uncanny knack of retrieving all kinds of lost objects – the sentimental, the useless and the absolutely necessary. I wondered if he went around the cottage hiding things just so that he could prove to us that he could find them again. Mrs Grainger believed in his talent, without a doubt, and praised him to high heavens whenever he dug out an old bobbin from between the cushions of the settee, or rescued a cooking pot from the garden shed. (Why on earth was it in there anyway?) I believed it gave Daniel a sense of usefulness, of importance in our lop-sided family, him being the smallest and the most recent to arrive as he was. It was a role he had created for himself so that he could feel he belonged with us. It seemed my role had become 'the one who looked after Daniel'.

I wavered some more. 'If I tell you, will you promise not to tell anyone. Nobody, especially not Mrs Grainger.' I stopped and faced him, held his gaze as he stared back at me with wide and earnest eyes, magnified and distorted by the now permanently smeared lenses. 'Can you keep a secret, Daniel?' I stared some more, to impress upon him the seriousness of the situation.

'Yes.' He stared back firmly, unblinking, his gaze continuing to hold mine with equal gravity.

I was still not sure. When he had his nightmares he sometimes shouted out in his sleep. He might give my secret away without even meaning to. Or he might just not be able to stop himself from blabbing to one of the other boys, just so that they would like him, or share their sweets with him. I didn't want him to tell. The angel was mine and I didn't want anyone to take him away from me. I could not bear to share him, at least not yet. But if I didn't tell Daniel he would pester me like mad and give me no peace. That's how he was. I had to ask Ash – she would know what to do.

'No, I need to think about it. I might tell you later, but I need to discuss it with Ash. She should know first.' I took his hand and started to march him over the rough field, the basket of early morning moss clutched tightly in his other clammy hand and his mouth pulled into a sullen pout. He could not argue with that. He knew, as Ash was the eldest, that she had the right to know things first. There were laws that even Daniel had to follow.

Act Three

14

The car lies mangled around the thick trunk of a tree. It has gouged a deep scar across the base, a bright opening into the heart of it. Drops of blood burst from the torn wood – glistening wet spheres that cling to the tree, showing where the wound is.

I am lying in a bed of leaves and damp soil some distance away. I feel nothing. My body is weightless, like a feather, transparent as glass. My mind is clear and lucid. As the drama of my life unfolds before my eyes I understand now that the freedom the war gave me also left me with terrible choices, responsibilities I was not prepared for. How quickly we all had to grow up, being without parents to guide us through those upending times.

My children have taught me about the deep dependency that vulnerability brings, but at that time I didn't know what was happening in Daniel's heart, or even in my own. We each became trapped by our own choices, like two babies who had crawled into places we could not get out of, and the freedom I thought I had was in fact an illusion. I could do nothing but follow the path of desires and needs distorted by the lies I had been told.

If I had grown up with Liza would I have acted differently during the war? And would I have been a better mother to Anita? She reflected back to me the emptiness inside my heart and I turned away from it. I couldn't bear it. I left her in her cot, crying in the dark, while I went out and walked the streets until my mind was as empty as my heart. I felt wretched, and I couldn't tell James. He slept right through it all.

My body lies motionless, yet I feel that I am curling in around myself, becoming very small. I begin to fall.

Why does nobody come? I feel so alone, down here in this dark place where I am falling, with nowhere to land, no one to catch me.

Now the words drift apart and my mind is dissolving, thoughts like grains of salt returning to the ocean.

Now the falling stops and I am being lifted upwards, riding on warm currents of air that spiral up out of the valley of trees and wreckage. I am carried on a white angel wing, up into a sky that is blue and wide. I am flying, at last I am flying. Soft white-feathered wings carry me.

It is so beautiful up here, James. Come with me. I reach out to you, my love, but I cannot find you. My heart reaches, but my hands lie inert and helpless by my sides, as if they no longer belong to me.

James, please come, help me. My babies – where are they? Martin, my brave boy. Anita, my little one – I am so sorry. You were crying and I could not comfort you. I pushed you away, too afraid of the pain your tears were opening up inside of me.

Panic is rising. My breath comes sharp, like thousands of tiny knives, carving me out.

Take care of my babies, James. If I die, please take good care of them. I have to go now.

★

I am flying, circling up and up. There is nothing to stop me now.

The angel's wing spreads and dips and flutters, delicate as silk in the warm current of air. It is taking me home, over the ocean, to my mother.

My mother – sweet words. I am on my way to you. I wonder if you will like me, still want to see me. What will you look like – brown eyes and auburn hair, like mine? I hope you are still waiting for me.

And what shall I call you? Mother sounds too formal, Mammy too personal for someone I have never met before. Can I call you Liza? I will be with you soon.

Please listen to my story so that you will know me. I want you to know that everything I did was because I needed you, and not Esther, to be my mother. And because a dark wish to punish them for their lies had surfaced and would not be pushed down again.

Amber leaves roll over me, like a carpet. There is a great light ahead, a stark white light, and a flashing blue and a red one. I can choose which one to follow. I think the red light will lead me to you, but I am not sure.

Red is Anita's colour. She is red like fire. From the moment she was born her face and her hair burnt red. They burnt right through me. I felt her pain, the pain of having a mother who could not love her. The pain of not knowing who her grandmother was.

Burning, burning a long narrow passage through my heart to yours. Are you still waiting for me, Liza? I hear voices. Are you there?

Something hard grips my face, pinches and forces into my mouth, swells out my lungs. I expand and float. Sweet bliss. Waves of light in my head, like veils lifting.

Words float in the air above me, disconnected words – '…

okay love … we'll get you … my hand … Jack, here … I've got it …' They waver and fade.

Then I am sucked out, hollowed, a cavern opening inside of me. The angel's wing has gone and I feel afraid. I am falling into the darkness that opens up inside me.

Until a light appears, and there is Ash, standing in a pool of watery sunlight that has fought its way down through the tangled tree branches.

Act Two

15

'Ye'r daft, man. There's nowt he-er. Ye must av imagined it, Ell.'

'No, I saw it! I know I did!' I was almost crying with frustration. And humiliation – I did not want Ash to think me daft.

She sat on the log that Daniel and I had occupied that morning, picking grubs of dirt from under her fingernails. She had come straight from her stint on the farm when I told her I had found something very special, and it was most urgent she meet me at once.

'A think that letter has sent yer heed a bit mad, Ellen, man. Why divint ye just drop it now?' In the distance an owl t'woo'ed, and the sweet scent of wood smoke drifted on the air. It would soon be evening and I could not bear to return home before I had found my angel.

I looked up at the tree, now bare of any shimmering wing, covered instead in a copper cloak of leaves as the sun set low in the sky and robed it in muted glory. We had looked all through the woods again. To no avail. Only trees, mud and brambles that had torn at our legs and made Ash curse the blinking woods a hundred times.

'If you don't believe me I'll have to ask Daniel to help me

find him, then.' I knew that would get the wind up Ash like nothing else.

'Now ye'r really talking daft.' A few drops of rain began to fall and she tugged at her jacket, now so tight that the buttons would no longer fasten across her chest. She relented. 'Aalreet then, A'll help ye, but what d'ye plan to do?'

'I don't know.' I looked forlornly about the field, back into the woods, up into the sky from which large wet drops were beginning to fall at a pace. 'How about we go to the hut to get out of the rain – we can have a think about it there?'

'Yeah. A conflab, like.' She grasped the idea enthusiastically and jumped up from the mouldering log. The hut had become our favourite place since the old tramp had been moved on – for molesting two village girls, Ash said. I didn't know exactly what molesting was, but it all sounded very serious – 'adult stuff', she told me in a whisper. Anyone acting strangely was suspected of being a Fifth Columnist, a spy or informer, so maybe that was why he was sent away.

We began to run as the rain fell heavier, with jackets held over our heads like spineless umbrellas. Through the hedge on hands and knees, streaks of mud and grass clinging to our skin and clothes, we arrived by the hut soaked and laughing. Ash always cheered me up with her jokes and her bad language. 'Bugger this for a lark. A need a pee', and she pulled up her skirt and squatted down at the edge of the field. I did the same, just for the hell of it. Wet grass tickled my bare bottom.

As I pushed open the creaking door and peered into the gloom, I froze. A man stood in the centre of the hut, staring back at me. He had pale blonde hair, sticking out in matted spikes. His shirt was torn to shreds and covered in mud stains and dried blood. So was his face. He leaned heavily on a stick, but still managed to stand up tall and face me square on.

'Are you the angel?' I blurted out, astonished, relieved, frightened all at once.

His eyes opened wider and he seemed speechless for a

moment. Then he recovered enough to reply in broken English, 'Ich bin Helmut. Please, no tell.' He brought his hands together as if in a gesture of prayer, taking a half step towards me. I returned the gesture.

'Please, Bin Helmut, have you come for me? Won't you stay? I need some help here,' I prayed back.

At that moment Ash pushed past me. 'Is this him, then?' She stepped up close and studied the man intently, up and down, back and front, like a museum exhibit. Then she stepped back to take in the whole of him. 'Not bad, mind.' She smiled and flicked a strand of wet hair behind her shoulder. 'What's his name then?'

'Bin Helmut, I think.' I hoped I had heard his name right.

'Helmut,' he corrected me.

'Helmet! What kind of a daft name is that, man? Blimey, ye two make a reet pair,' she mocked. 'But he's handsome, isn't he Ell. Shall we keep him?'

'Yes, of course. He's mine, anyway. He came for me.'

'Hmm,' grunted Ash, considering my claim carefully. 'We'll see about that.'

'Please. Very hungry – no water,' stuttered Helmut. Perhaps he had realised we were friendly and wanted to keep him, or maybe he was just desperate for food.

'Of course,' I cried. 'I'll bring you some food. Won't we, Ash?'

'Ye can do that bit. A'll make shuwer he cannit get away. He's wor prisoner now.'

'I don't think he'll run away. His leg's hurt.' We both stared at the wounded leg and Helmut sat down on the rickety chair to rest it. He dropped his head onto his chest and clutched at his side as he let out a sharp breath. There must be pain there too. In the corner of the hut, where there had been a pile of old blankets that the tramp slept on, there was now a heap of mud-splattered and torn, silvery coloured silk. It gleamed in the darkness. Helmut had torn off a strip and tied it around the hole in his leg. It was matted with blood.

'Shall A put a clean bandage on, angel man?' Ash put on a voice that both teased and mocked him. He looked confused, had no idea what we were saying or planning to do with him. He was completely at our mercy and, to be honest, both of us, in our different ways, enjoyed the feeling of it. Ash had never felt real power over a man before. I knew she was frightened of her father, despite the disdainful airs she put on, and she was going to milk this moment dry. I remembered the power I could hold over Esther when I refused to speak to her, and I could feel the sweet taste of revenge in my mouth. I did not yet understand it, but Helmut had just become entangled in my heart with the wish to hurt Esther.

'I'm Ellen, by the way. And this is Ash.'

He nodded to me. 'Miz Ellen. Miz Ash.' He gave Ash a quick sideways glance, then looked down at his damaged leg and winced.

Ash tore off a long strip of silk from the heap on the floor. He looked at her nervously as she began to pick at his make-do bandage, grimacing as peels of raw skin came away with the cloth. He didn't cry out, just held his breath and gritted his teeth. I could hardly bear to watch as blood began to flow from the open wound.

'A divint knaa if it's broke like. A'll bring some proper bandages and stuff from home, but this'll have to do ye for now.' She wrapped the strip of silk around the wound. 'Now lie down, man, and put ya leg up on the chair to stop the bleeding,' she commanded, once the dressing was in place. Then she stood over him, hands on her hips and a secret smile in her eyes. 'Ye'r me prisoner now. Ye'll do as A say, won't ye, man,' she said softly. Her voice was not unkind, but the way she stood over him looked threatening to me. Helmut looked so helpless and vulnerable lying there at Ash's feet with his leg all bound up and bleeding, and fear in his eyes, blue eyes that looked so innocent, like the eyes of a young boy.

'Ash, leave off. Let him rest now. Go get some bandages and

antiseptic – and he'll need clean water too. I'll see what food
I can find at home.'

Getting food to Helmut was harder than I had imagined.
Although country folk had more food than city folk during
the war, it was all rationed, every ounce and drop. Each egg
we collected from the big barn was counted. Every potato
plucked from the fields was earmarked for some house or other,
for some market town or city train. Mrs Grainger no longer
bought food in the shops with money, but with coupons, and
everyone had just the minimum amount to stop them starving.
I would have to give Helmut some of my own food.

That first evening I collected one slice of grey bread and
marmite, a soggy piece of Woolton pie wrapped in cabbage
leaves, and half an apple. Its sliced edge would be brown by the
time I got it to the hut. I filled a milk bottle with water and
hid the whole feast under my bed. It hadn't been easy though,
sneaking food out from under Pet-dear's nose.

'Come on pet, finish that up – there's a good girl.'

'I'm not very hungry – I'll finish it later.'

'What's wrong, Ellen pet?'

'Nothing.'

'Are ye not well?'

'No, I'm fine.'

'A'm shuwer ye cannit be overfed with the rations we have
these days. Ye'll be disappearing soon if ye divint eat up. Look
how thin ye've got.'

'I'll eat it later, I promise.' I began to nibble around the edges
of a triangle of bread, hoping she would turn her attention to
Daniel who was slurping his tea like a pig, but no.

'D'ye not like me Woolton pie then, pet? A thought ye did.
Look at wor Daniel – his 'as gone down a treat.'

'Can I take it up to my room – just so no one else eats it.
By mistake, I mean.'

'Why pet, ye divint think wor Daniel would take yer food

rations, d'ye? He's not that bad – are ye pet? Just always ravenous as a dog, A'd say.' She gave him an affectionate pat on the cheek. He tried to duck away from her hand, reddened with all the scraping and scrubbing, and knocked his fork onto the floor.

He scowled at me, but kept silent as he reached down to pick up the fork. I breathed a sigh of relief. I knew he could have blurted out about me searching for something in the woods, then who could tell what Pet-dear might have imagined.

'No – sorry – I didn't mean that.'

'So what's wrong with ye then? Have ye got yer – ye know – yer monthlies, pet? Ye can tell me if ye have.'

'My – what? – No. Please, can I leave the table now?' My face was burning with embarrassment. I wanted to hide.

'Just wait till we've all finished, pet. It's not polite.'

'Yes Mrs Grainger.' I hunched my head over and continued to nibble at the piece of bread.

'A'm not shuwer about taking food upstairs, mind. Could encourage the mice. I saw three in the attic last week! Frightened the living daylights out of me, they did.'

'I'll wrap it up in a cabbage leaf – that should keep it safe.'

'Ee, A divint knaa what's got into ye, Ellen pet. So awkward and moody these days. Are ye sure ye'r aalreet – not sick – missing home maybe?'

'No, I don't miss home. I'm alright, really I am. I just like to eat a bit now and the rest later. I sleep better that way.'

'Well, if ye must. Why not wrap it up in this clean cloth to keep it a bit warm then.'

Once I was sure everyone was sleeping, I crept down stairs and out of the cottage with the stealth of a burglar. Running across the fields with my precious bundle, I felt a rush of exhilaration, almost joy. Something wondrous had come into my life. I may not have a mother, but I had an angel, and that had to be just as good.

I stumbled through the dark, clouds hiding the moon and stars that night so that the blackness was almost total. After walking flat into the hedge and piercing my face on spikes of blackthorn, I went down onto my hands and knees to find the opening. The ground was damp and the chill crept up into my bones. It took some time to find the gap in the hedge, as I had to keep one hand free to hold the bottle of water upright. The bag of food soon became mashed as it jogged against my side.

When I arrived at the hut I could see pale slivers of dancing light through the cracks around the door. Helmut was awake, waiting for me. I tapped softly then pushed the door open. He sat huddled over a candle flame, his face eerily pale and long in the flickering shadows, cheeks hollowed out and brow creased like a sheet of unpressed linen. Worry was written on his face, loneliness buried in his eyes. I stepped back, unable for a moment to be with his pain, afraid that my own might leap up to be noticed too.

'Komm ein, Miz Ellen. Dank you to komm back.'

'Here, I brought some water to drink, and some food. It's not much, I'm sorry, but it's all I could get. Maybe tomorrow I can do better.'

'Is very gut, dank you.' He took the bottle and drank until it was empty, then watched as I unwrapped the food parcel.

'Oh!' Pie, marmite bread and cabbage leaves had disintegrated into an unidentifiable mush. 'I'm sorry. It's …' My utter dismay was out of proportion to the damage, but I couldn't help it. I felt devastated that my first gift looked so unappetising, inedible even. 'It was meant to be Woolton pie. It's very nice really.'

'I am sure, yes. No problem, I will eat.' He took the mush and ate the whole thing without so much as a glance at me till he had finished. Then he looked up, gave a crooked, one-sided smile, and thanked me again. 'Now I much better.' And indeed he did seem to be. A little colour was returning to his face and the furrowed brow had softened a tad. I sat looking at him over the candle flame, and saw that the loneliness behind his eyes had also softened into a sad but kindly smile.

'You can stay here till you're better. I'll bring you food, we'll look after you,' I told him. 'Don't worry about anything.'

'You very good, Miz Ellen.'

I could feel my heart beating against my ribcage, and in the quiet of the night the two solitary rhythms of our breathing began to find a common pace. I imagined that meant a common purpose. There was a purpose in our being together, and so my life had just found meaning. A sense of belonging, of an existence with meaning brought hope to my troubled heart.

Ash, Helmut and I were sitting on the floor of the hut discussing things. At least, Ash and I were discussing. Helmut was picking the last traces of spam fritter from the handkerchief I had wrapped them in. When he had finished he nodded politely to me and said 'Dank you, Miz Ellen,' before handing back the handkerchief. A tingle went up my spine. Helmut was so gracious, and I felt honoured to be helping him in his moment of need. I was growing thinner, but I didn't mind at all.

It was a few days since we had found him, and the wound in his leg had stopped bleeding. The pain in his side was still sharp though, and his breath came in short jagged gasps. He must have broken some ribs. Ash had embraced the role of nurse with charm and surprising dexterity. I had shown him the best way to the creek where he could wash, and had found, in the back of Kevin's cupboard, an old towel, a comb, a toothbrush and some spare clothes. There was no razor, so Helmut now had a fuzzy growth over his chin and upper lip, which gave him the grizzly look of a Border Terrier. It didn't suit him well, so Ash was considering how she might steal a razor.

'We want ye to stay handsome, angel man, divint we, Ell.' She ran a finger over his stubbly chin, looking at him coyly with her head tilted at her best angle. I was shocked at her boldness, but he didn't flinch. He took everything she gave him, from seductive caresses to harsh rejections when he dared respond to her gentle taunts with interest. In this instance, he tried to move away but Ash gently turned him towards her and drew her face closer to his. I thought she was going to kiss him. I could not let that happen. He was mine, after all.

'Ugh, looks like a pig's bum with all that hairiness.' She laughed and pushed him away. Helmut backed off, dragging the injured leg after him, and sat with his shoulder to the wall. He looked hurt.

'Ash, don't play with him like that. It's not fair.' I was feeling hurt myself, as if I was the one who had just been toyed with.

'Aw, he's not really minding it. He's just pretending, aren't ye, angel man.' She got up and made to leave. 'A've had enough anyhow. A'm going down to the village to see if owt's happening. Ye can stay he-er if ye like.' She opened the door and a whiff of cool air and a sneeze blew into the hut.

'Flippin heck! It's that bleeding Danny Boy! How long have ye been standing there listening to wor conversations?' She grabbed him by his jacket collar and hauled him into the hut, quickly surveyed the field to be sure nobody had followed him, and closed the door with a force that made the whole structure shudder.

'Daniel, how did you find us?' I felt dismayed. I thought I had hidden my tracks well.

'I am good at finding,' he replied, simply, stubbornly, truthfully.

I sighed and dropped my head into my hands. 'I suppose this will be the end of our secret then?'

'No, I won't tell. Promise.' He looked at me with that familiar unblinking stare, the one I didn't trust at all.

'Ye'd better not or A'll kill ye with me very own hands,' declared Ash, suddenly so protective of Helmut that I could have hugged her.

Daniel backed away from Ash, who was much taller than

he was and nearly twice as old. He looked at the man sitting hunched against the wall, who was trying to work out what was going on as he looked from Ash to Daniel and back to me.

'Who is that?' asked Daniel, pointing rudely at Helmut.

Helmut struggled onto his feet and held out a hand to Daniel. 'I am Helmut.' He must have guessed a small boy could not be too dangerous, but he might have been very wrong about that.

'Du bist Deutsch!' shouted Daniel.

'Shush Daniel. We don't want people hearing us,' I whispered, trying to calm the growing tension in myself and in the small wooden hut.

'He is German! This is how they look! I know it!' He was pointing at the badge on Helmut's leather jacket, which lay on the floor beside the chair. The silver eagle spreading its wings, a small swastika in its claws, was only partly hidden by the dry mud Helmut had not bothered to scrape off.

Helmut bristled and stood up as straight as his bad leg and broken ribs would allow.

'Ja, ich bin Deutsch. Bist *du*, auch?'

Now Daniel bristled and stood as tall as he could, chin up in a vain attempt to look taller, feet placed apart to look broader. I sensed an insult was passing between them but didn't yet understand the niceties of ranking that was woven into the German language.

'He is from Nazi army – flying man.' Daniel turned to me for support. 'Get him out of here. Get him out!' He was beginning to crack, his lip quivering and his clenched knuckles turning white. I took hold of his shoulders and felt his taut body tremble.

'Daniel, please calm down, it's alright. He's friendly. He's here to help us. And anyway, he's injured and can't walk.' I tried to calm my voice but it came out much too high and scratchy. I feared what Daniel might do.

'Du bist ein Hitler mann. Du bist schlimm,' Daniel spat out, stamping his foot and stepping forward to swing his boot at Helmut's bad leg.

Ash grabbed hold of him and didn't let go. 'Now what the heck are we gonna do?' she asked, looking at me as if I should know.

'Daniel, listen to me. It's very important that you don't tell anybody. I will never be your friend again if you do. Do you understand?' I was trying to sound like Miss Parker because I knew she had a way of frightening Daniel into submission. 'Please, Daniel, promise me this one thing. You'll see that he's really very nice, and he won't hurt you.'

Daniel tried to break free of Ash's grip but she held on for dear life until she was hugging him with a passion. Even Daniel could not sustain resistance to that. Ash's embrace and my words melted him down until he deflated like a balloon, sat on the floor and began to cry. Helmut sat down too, no doubt very confused by now.

It was up to Ash and me to sort this out.

'Are you really a German pilot?' Disappointment at this reality was overwhelming any possible embarrassment I might have felt. Of course I knew he was a pilot, but I was struggling to accept it. I didn't want to believe that he was not also an angel. In my world I could still believe in what I wanted to, like the fact that Esther was bad and I was right to want to hurt her.

'Course he's a German pilot, ye daft bugger. Did ye not realise that, ye divvie?' laughed Ash.

'Yes, Luftwaffe – airman Helmut Schmidt.' He drew his hand up in a defeated half-salute. 'First time to England flying. In woods come down.'

'In the storm – yes, of course.' I looked into eyes that were veiled and sad, and in that moment he looked so very young, not much more than a boy himself. He just wanted to be at home. Like a fledgling bird out of the nest for the first time, he had fallen and could not get back. We all four wanted to be at home, but none of us were. Ash's home was a warzone all of its own. Daniel's home was gone forever. Mine – I didn't have a place I could truly call home.

'Then we're all the same, the four of us. No home, no parents to look after us.' I looked at Daniel and he stopped crying to look at me for a moment. 'Daniel, we've got to stick together. We're all friends now, and when you share a secret, you have to be loyal to your friends.' I didn't reflect for too long on the rights and wrongs of befriending the enemy. That would come much later.

Daniel sniffed and wiped his nose on his sleeve.

'Come here you little rag.' I pulled him close and wrapped my arms around him. Despite it all, I had grown fond of the odd little Jewish boy. I would have to be his mother now, even though I didn't know what it was to have one for myself.

'Have ye heard the news, hinny?' Mr Grainger asked as he sat down for tea. It was Thursday, and September by now, about three weeks since we had found Helmut. He was still an angel to me, even if he was a German pilot too.

'And what news be that, pet?'

'Ower on the hillside, reet in the woods there, they've foond a plane that came doon. They divint knaa when. No pilot, nowt else there.'

I held my breath. I looked furtively at Daniel who glanced at me from beneath an errant curl of hair, then returned his attention to the plate of food that was being laid in front of him.

'Ee neva! He must be somewhere, running or hiding. Or maybe he's dead.' Mrs Grainger plumped down onto her chair and gestured for us all to begin. Sausage and mash, Daniel's favourite but not mine. They were nothing like the proper meat sausages we had before the war.

I had to think of a way to smuggle a sausage into my handkerchief, as Mrs Grainger had begun to object to me finishing my meals later, when everyone else had left the table and gone about their various jobs. Ash had given Helmut some matches and an old tin pot, so now I took vegetables from our garden and he made a fire and cooked them himself, but he would appreciate the sausage too. It gave me a thrill every time he said 'Dank you, Miz Ellen.' I felt proud and grown up and special. My angel was accepting my gifts, thanking me. So I did my best to take whatever I could to him every day, and dreamt at night of when the war would be over and Helmut, Ash and I, and maybe Daniel too, would be free to live together as we wanted to. Not that I wasn't happy to be with Pet-dear and Hinny-luv, but their sons would come back when the war was over and I wouldn't have a room anymore.

'Dangerous, if y'ask me, havin a German soldier wanderin aboot in the woods. Mind ye two luvs divint gan speakin to 'im if ye see 'im,' Mr Grainger said, pointing his fork at Daniel and me.

'Course we won't,' I replied quickly, jabbing Daniel with my foot under the table. He got the message.

'Of course we will not speak to him, Mr Grainger.' Daniel looked directly at Hinny-luv as he spoke – the way he always did when he was concealing something.

Pet-dear looked concerned. Whatever the old tramp had done to the two girls had worried her and she tried to keep me under her eye these days. I tried to get out from under it. I liked it better the way it was before.

'And now the war is up he-er in the northeast, we must all be gannin aboot wor business with more care,' Mr Grainger went on. 'Ye must take yer gas masks with yerselves at all teems.'

Daniel and I groaned. Pet-dear looked cross. Beneath it all I was worried that people might be out looking for Helmut now.

The four of us were huddled into the hut, Ash siting on the rickety chair, the rest of us on the floor. The air in the hut smelt of boiled cabbage, mixed with the raw, earthy scent of a man's body – sweat mingled with something else I didn't recognise. I sat between Daniel and Helmut, just in case Daniel tried to kick him again.

'The thing is, people are looking for you. They found the wreckage of your plane.' I spoke slowly in the hope that he could understand, but in the end I asked Daniel to translate and hoped that he would do it correctly. Daniel always turned out to be useful – no, necessary.

Lines creased Helmut's broad and handsome face. Worry seemed to narrow the pronounced bones of his forehead and eyebrows. He was now shaven and clean, his hair had grown longer and was swept back from his face in an elegant way. His nose was straight and his pale blue eyes had recovered some of their light. Exquisite shell ears softened the strong outline of his jaw. Today he had rolled up his sleeves, revealing a large purple scar on his left forearm. I wanted to touch it, to feel the raw and tender flesh that had been left naked when the skin was burnt away.

'I think we should find another place for you to stay, more hidden, less obvious.' Daniel translated my words for Helmut.

'Dank you, but I am too trouble for you. I think I must go now.'

'No, you can't go! We'll hide you and keep you safe. Don't worry, Helmut, it'll be fine.' It startled me to think he might leave.

'But must go home.' In that moment Helmut looked so vulnerable I wanted to weep for him. He was not much older than Ash and me, just eighteen. This was his first mission and I think he didn't like it very much. I was imagining his home, his mother and father waiting for him, just as Mr and Mrs Grainger were waiting for Kevin and Stephen to come home. I imagined a roaring fire and meat roasting in the oven. There were cakes and coffee on the table, and his mother standing at the door with open arms to welcome him back from the war. I began to cry.

'Please don't go, not yet,' I pleaded. 'You're my angel and I need you to stay.'

'Blimey Ell, divint be so daft. He's no angel, he's a pilot who's lost his plane.' Then turning to Helmut, she added, 'But she's right, ye cannit leave yet, man. We need ye he-er.'

Daniel translated, then asked Ash, 'What do we need him for?'

'Special service', she replied. 'Ye'll find out. We'll need him in the end.' She seemed very sure of this, so we said no more about it and began to make a plan to hide Helmut.

For the rest of the day the three of us worked hard to build a den in the deepest part of the woods, far from the village, where we hoped no children would dare to go if they thought there was a German pilot roaming about. We found a hollow in the ground and covered it with a mound of branches so that it looked almost like a natural part of the scenery.

That night, when I could hear that everyone was sleeping – Hinny-luv snoring, Pet-dear wheezing and Daniel snuffling – I left the murmuring house and crept across the fields and through the hedge to the hut. A half moon lit my way. The countryside had been strange to me at first, with its dark and still, silent nights, but by now my eyes had grown used to seeing by the light of the moon and stars. There was a whole rainbow of colours that was only visible by moonlight – a rainbow of subtle shades that had not even been given names. The colours of the unnamed world. I loved to be out alone in this world of mystery and silence – a silence broken only by the occasional hoot of an owl and the screeching of some small hunted animal. Tonight I didn't care if Helmut was a pilot. To me he would always be an angel and we were here to help each other through the war. Tonight I would take him to his new home, a safe place in the heart of the woods. I prayed he would like it and thank me for it.

I tapped softly and he opened the door. He was expecting me. His few possessions were packed into the old cloth peg-bag I had found in our shed. He bundled the mass of the silk parachute into his arms and followed me out into the night. Moths fluttered around us and a bat darted out of the trees. Our breaths misted in the air and mingled into a small cloud before dissolving behind us as we walked, Helmut limping slowly behind me.

It was harder to find the den at night, but after many wrong turns we finally stumbled upon it. I was tired by the time we arrived and would have slept right there, but I knew it was important not to arouse suspicion. After making sure that Helmut was pleased with his new hideaway, I trudged back to the cottage and was in bed and sleeping soundly before dawn broke.

The next thing I remembered was Mrs Grainger hollering up the stairs.

'Ellen, for heaven's sake pet, it's long past morning and ye have work to do. Get yersel out the bed now, there's a good girl.'

'I don't feel well, Mrs Grainger,' I called back. 'Can I sleep a bit longer?'

'Oh dear. A suppose so then. A'll be up later to see how ye'r doing. A must get down to the shops now before the rations all run out.' I heard her rustling around in the kitchen for a moment, then the front door banged shut. I fell asleep and dreamt of ice cream and angels in the sand dunes. I think Trevor was there. I was rolling down an enormous dune and he was tumbling after me. We just kept on rolling. It never came to an end.

Then I woke with a bump and I was lying on the floor beside my bed with a bruise coming up on my right elbow.

It was because I had stayed at home that morning, that I was there when the letter arrived for Mr and Mrs Grainger. He was out at work. She was still at the shops, or visiting Daisy on the way home. There was a knock on the door and I hurried downstairs, wrapping a blanket around me so that I was decent on the doorstep, not standing there in my nightie, which was far too short for me now. I had grown a great few inches in the last year.

'A letter for Mr and Mrs Grainger. Are they home?' A boy in a dark grey jacket and peaked cap, with a red badge on the front, stood there with his bicycle. He held out a brown envelope.

'No, they're out. Shall I take it?'

'Think I'd better wait.'

We stood for a while at the front door, waiting for Pet-dear to return. Finally I invited him into the kitchen and gave him a cup of tea. I thought that was what she would have done in my situation. He didn't speak except to thank me for the tea. We sat in stiff and awkward silence, our eyes shifting from the floor to the door to the window, so as to avoid contact and the possibility that conversation might be required. I felt embarrassed to be sitting there with a strange boy, dressed only in an old nightie and a worn woollen blanket, and he seemed to be embarrassed at some secret thing too.

After an age the door burst open. Pet-dear had returned and she poured a small mountain of groceries onto the kitchen table, the weekly rations for the four of us. The boy was sitting in the corner and she didn't see him at first.

'We have a visitor, Mrs Grainger. He has a letter for you.'

Time seemed to stop, to go into slow motion, even to start pedalling backwards. I'm not sure which is the most accurate way to describe this strange distortion of time that I felt as I watched Pet-dear take the letter, open it, sit down, begin to cry – in precisely that order. Then she began to holler and bang her fists on the table.

The post boy looked terrified and quickly took his leave, his job done.

'Shall I get Mr Grainger?' I asked, terrified too. I guessed what the trouble was.

'Oh yes, pet, get him to come home,' and she cried some more.

I ran up the stairs to pull on some clothes, then quickly down again. As I hurried along the main street I dodged a group of boys who were running in every direction, each one holding a piece of metal high above his head, sweeping his plane from side to side and roaring wildly. Debris from the crashed plane was prized highly by the city and the village boys alike, and the two sides had been in perpetual warfare since the plane had been found on the wooded hillside. Every now and then a boy would pick up a stone and throw it at one of the enemy planes, and the enemy would explode and fall to the ground in a dance of chaotic spirals, splutters and convulsions.

I found Mr Grainger in his workshop and told him there had been a letter and he should come home to Mrs Grainger at once.

16

After we learnt that Stephen had been killed fighting in France, everything changed in the Graingers' house. Pet-dear cried every day and nothing would console her. She no longer sat me down for a cup of tea and a chat in the afternoons, after school, or gathered us around her in the evenings to listen to the Home Service. Even her favourite comedians no longer made her laugh, and we didn't dare listen to Children's Hour because it made her cry some more. Pet-dear didn't care about the war anymore. Her heart was broken and she was completely lost to Daniel and me. Our home became a sad and solemn place.

I tried my best to cheer her up but nothing worked. I helped out more in the kitchen but she barely noticed I was there. When I brought her the biggest eggs the hens had laid, she cried some more as she remembered how Stephen had loved his soft-boiled eggs when he was small.

Daniel and I began to spend less time at home and more time in the woods, in the den with Helmut. Ash usually joined us, as there was often trouble in her house too. She never told me exactly what her father did, but I knew it was bad.

Daniel hated Helmut, but still he taught him to speak English. Being the teacher helped him to feel important and useful – and always right, of course.

'Wie alt bist DU?' he had asked one day.

Helmut bristled and sat up tall. 'Achtzehn,' he replied curtly. 'Und wie alt bist DU, Daniel?'

Daniel tried to bristle too, but he was faltering in the face of Helmut's great height and width and general sense of manliness. 'Neun,' he answered, a slight quaver in his voice. 'Und ich hier wohne, aber du sollte nach heim zuruck gehen.' I saw his leg spasm, the right leg that always wanted to kick Helmut, as if it had a life all of its own.

Helmut accepted the English lessons with as much dignity as he could muster. It was clear that his learnt hatred of Jewish boys ran deep, but he never lost his temper with Daniel. Daniel proved to be a thoroughly ruthless and authoritarian teacher. He followed Miss Parker's example and always held a wooden stick in his hand. He would flick it dangerously close to Helmut's face each time he asked a question or gave an order, and he gave orders often.

'Nein, dummkopf! Say it like I do!' or 'Learn these words,' and one minute later he would demand, 'Now say them.' 'No that is wrong, divvie.' This word he hard learnt from Ash.

One day I heard him tell Helmut, 'Now say after me – I am a murderer.'

Helmut's fists clenched tightly but he managed to stop himself from hitting Daniel. I saw the stiffness in his back intensify and angry red blotches came up on his neck. I didn't know if the rigidity in Helmut's body came from being alone in an enemy country where he had to be on guard at every moment, or whether it had been there all along – perhaps engrained from years under the military eye of his father General Schmidt, then the Hitler Youth Movement and military training. Or maybe it was just the pain from his broken ribs and leg that made him hold himself so rigidly. When Daniel was around, he had to use all his will to control himself and it made him even more tense.

'Daniel, stop that!' I grabbed him by the collar and dragged him out of the den. 'You can't say things like that,' I warned him, once I thought we were out of Helmut's hearing.

'I can say things if they are true,' he retorted stubbornly.

'Not here you can't. Not while I'm here, anyway.' And from

that moment I knew I would have to chaperone every lesson, every moment the two spent together. With me, Helmut was always polite and gracious, but with Daniel a side of him that was more like an angry, sullen schoolboy emerged. They each brought out the worst in the other and I feared that Daniel would come out very badly if they ever took to fighting for real.

Eventually they stopped competing over some imagined rank and accepted that here, deep in the heart of the Northumbrian hills, they were equal – equally German and equally troubled. But sometimes Helmut would be holding in so much bad feeling that the atmosphere in the den would be thick as a black fog. You could barely move or breathe. Even Ash noticed it.

'Blimey, that man's heed is full uv bleeding pig-swill,' she had said on one occasion. Helmut had sat for half an hour in a sour mood, refusing to speak to any of us, just snapping twigs and throwing them at a tree trunk. In the end I had asked if he would like me to help him collect firewood, and we had gone off into the woods together. After some heaving and chopping he finally relented and began to speak to us again.

We made the den as cosy as we could. You wouldn't believe what you could find around a village during wartime. We lined the roof with a sheet of old tarpaulin, propped up by branches, so it was like a tent inside. On the floor we laid some old rugs. They were dirty and damp, but Helmut said he was grateful and we shouldn't worry about it at all. He developed a bad cough though, so I knew it was not the best place to sleep. I began to wonder what we could do in the winter. Perhaps it would be safe for him to return to the hut, as people rarely wandered that far from the village during the coldest months. Besides, the excitement of the crashed plane had been forgotten. Nobody was still looking for a lost German pilot.

As the three of us reached the den Helmut was outside, boiling water over a small fire.

'We have tea, yes?' He waved a soot-blackened tin pot. Our breaths turned to mist in the chilly air. Autumn was well under way, wreaking its harvest on the land. The leaves had left the trees bare, lying now in slippery brown heaps on the ground. I felt bad about giving Helmut things that had once belonged to Stephen, but I knew he would not be needing his warm clothes now. My angel was wrapped up in layers of wool and gabardine. His cheeks were rosy red beneath his long fair hair, and the wounded leg had now almost completely healed, though he still limped badly. His good right leg would attempt to stride out with a fluid, confident swing, only to be brought up short by the left, then he would hitch up and drag the left leg along after him. It was not the walk of a proud military man.

Inside the den I put some cheese, dry crackers and onions on the upturned box that was Helmut's table, and took the tea caddy from a shelf made of three large flat stones. He made tea then we lined up on the log that was his seat, passing the enamel mug between us and blowing on our hands to warm them.

'How's yer leg, Helmet?' asked Ash. 'Is it better now, pet?'

'Yes, better. You very good nurse, Miz Ash.'

Ash blushed and smiled coyly. 'Maybe A'll join the army nursing corps when A'm finished with school.' She tossed her head back and laughed. 'Na, just joking. A plan to join the Lumber Jo's.'

Helmut didn't catch the joke, if there was a joke. I was not sure about that either but I laughed with Ash just in case, or maybe I laughed out of nervousness that Ash might be leaving us soon.

'Now I walk good.' He studied the ground for a moment, then continued. 'I think maybe it is time I go home.'

'Home? But how can you go home?' My heart jolted as if a hammer had struck it.

'I do not know. But must try. Maybe I find way.'

I looked at Ash. She looked at me.

'Flippin heck, Helmet, ye cannit get back yet, man, not till the blasted war is finished. Besides, we like having ye he-er, don't we, Ell.'

'Yes. We want you to stay.'

'But must try. My family – they not know where I am.'

'Of course – you want to see your family. You have a mother and father, so you should be with them.' I wanted to cry. I wasn't sure whom I was feeling most sad for – maybe Mrs Grainger, who had lost part of her family most recently. We had all definitely lost someone, even Ash who spoke about her parents as if they no longer existed. Except for Helmut. Most likely his family were still alive in Germany, or so I wanted to believe.

I liked to think of him at home in Muenster with his parents and his two brothers – the eldest one that he hardly knew, who was in the SS, and the middle brother who was like a best friend, somewhere on the way to Russia now. He was working as a doctor in a military hospital, Helmut had told me one rainy morning while we huddled in the den. I imagined them sitting around their dinner table with a feast of roast meat and vegetables and steaming gravy laid out in white porcelain bowls with curly gold edges, and silver cutlery shining in the light of a chandelier.

'He should go home,' said Daniel, standing up suddenly, as if to attention. 'I will send him home. On train.' I caught hold of his arm as he braced himself to kick Helmut, as if he were no more than a sack of potatoes lying on the ground. It was like a tic he couldn't control, and I knew how Daniel hated anything that made him feel out of control. He looked agitated now. He had sensed an opportunity to feel powerful for a moment, but it had gone – I had taken it away.

'Daniel, it's not so easy. He'll be caught if he goes on a train. Or a boat. Or any other way. I don't know how you could possibly get to Germany if you're a German pilot.' I looked helplessly at Helmut. He looked down at his feet. On the boot that belonged to his injured leg, the sole had come away from the leather and he had tied it together with string. 'You can't walk. You can't swim all that way.' I felt panic. I was going to lose him. 'Why don't you stay a bit longer? We'll think of something,' I suggested vaguely.

'Why don't you go home same way you came?' said Daniel. 'We will find you a new plane.'

'Now there's an idea, Danny Boy,' said Ash, suddenly alive with the possibility of an adventure. 'We can take ye to the airfield – there's one not too far from he-er, A think – and in the night ye can steal a plane and fly home!'

I looked at Ash, then at Helmut, aghast. 'That's a crazy idea. He'll be caught, for sure.'

'No, it is good idea,' piped in Daniel. 'My idea.'

Helmut frowned. He took some time to consider the preposterous plan. 'Will have to think. Not sure now.' He became silent and didn't say another word until we were all ready to leave.

'Maybe tomorrow I tell you what I do.'

I looked into his eyes and wondered if I could survive the war without him now that I didn't have a mother or a father, Pet-dear was lost in her own world of sorrow, and Ash talked more and more often about leaving Bellingham. His silver blue eyes looked into mine and I am sure I saw the beginnings of a tear there.

The next morning, while Ash was at school and Daniel was picking potatoes, I went on my own to see Helmut. I wanted to be alone with him. I needed to talk.

He was inside the den. I called his name then peeked under the curtain that served as a door. I had startled him. He was hurriedly stuffing something inside his coat.

'Sorry. Are you busy?'

'No, not busy.'

'What are you doing?' I asked, trying not to sound too nosey, but curious to know what he had hidden.

'Just writing letter, Miz Ellen.'

'Who are you writing to?'

'My mother. I write every day.' He didn't look embarrassed as he said this, not afraid to show this vulnerability to me.

'Oh, I see.' I felt sad that I had no mother to write to, but glad I no longer need feel guilty about not writing to Esther. Occasionally I replied, briefly, to Trevor's monthly letters, which he had continued to write even after the July news. Apart from that I had nobody to write to. I wished I did, and envied Helmut a little. For the first few months of the war Vera and I had exchanged letters, but at Christmas she had returned to Newcastle and stayed there. Then the letters stopped. I guessed she had found a new best friend, as I had.

'But you can't send letters, and I can't send them for you – not to Germany. People would be suspicious and they'd come looking for you. And for me – they might think I was a spy, then I'd be locked up with the Germans and the Irish, and the child molesters and suspicious neighbours, and…'

'No mind. I write anyway. One day I give to her and she me reads.'

I imagined him returning to his mother, one day, when the war was over, standing at her door like the postman with a large bundle of letters in his hands, offering them to her.

'What's she like, your mother?'

'She very beautiful. She play piano and sing, very nice.' He pauses, dropping his chin into his hands to stare at the floor. I notice the delicate curve of his fingers as they frame his cheeks. 'I wanted to play music too, but father said should become pilot. More useful when war comes. I not like very much.'

His face was full of sorrow. I wanted to take it in my hands and kiss the sadness away, but I didn't. Instead I pushed my hands deeper into my pockets to keep them out of trouble. I sat down beside him on the damp rug and took a deep breath.

'I'm sorry, Helmut – that you couldn't play music, that your mother is so far away, that you can't send your letters.' I felt helpless. I didn't know what to do. He looked into my eyes and it seemed to me that we shared a moment of understanding. The flicker of a sad smile crossed his face but he said no more about his mother, so I went on with my own news.

'I think it's safe for you to go back to the hut now. No one will go there in the winter, and it'll be warmer. Dry, at least. I've found a paraffin stove to heat it. You can't stay here much longer or you'll die of cold.' I didn't give him a chance to tell me what decision he had come to. 'Please say you will.'

'But I should… '

'Say you will stay, at least for the winter. Then in spring we can think about how you can get home.' This came out as a command, not a request, so I added, 'Please.'

'Ach, Miz Ellen, I think you are boss now! I must do as you say, yes?' He laughed. I could see relief as well as worry on his face. Human beings are such complicated creatures, always so many feelings going on at once. I feel love for Helmut and Ash, even for Daniel, I have to admit. At the same time I feel full of sorrow when I think of Mr and Mrs Grainger losing their son Stephen. I feel angry and hateful towards Esther and, these days, just indifferent towards Trevor. I no longer need him now that I have Helmut. The war makes me feel afraid, but it also brings lots of excitement – like the freedom to explore the countryside, to swim in the river with no clothes on when it's warm, just Ash and me, and to climb the heathery hills. We can grow vegetables and keep chickens in the back garden. And sometimes the village has fetes where there is lemonade to drink, and fairy cakes, and music – and boys wanting to dance with you.

One boy, a vacee from Wallsend, liked me a lot and wanted to walk out with me even though I was only thirteen, but I had to say no as I was afraid he would follow me around and discover Helmut. The village boy whose back I had jumped on was there too. He had his eye on me the whole time, but kept his distance.

'Yes, you must do as I say!' I declared triumphantly, laughing with relief. 'Look, I have brought you a present.' I pulled a pack of cards out of my coat pocket. I confess I had picked them up off the school playground and didn't return them to the boy who had dropped them. I reckoned Helmut needed the cards more than the boy did.

His face lit up with pleasure. 'Ah, wunderbar! I am so boring here.' He kissed the pack of cards, flipped them out of the colourful box and shuffled them deftly. 'You know how to play?'

'I can play Rummy. Trevor taught me how, and I must warn you that I'm very good! I nearly always win!' I was proud of this small achievement in a life that had been, otherwise, quite barren of successes.

'Ach, then I must try very hard to beat you,' he joked. He looked happy for a moment. Poor Helmut – how tedious life as a runaway pilot must be. I vowed to help him find a way home once spring came. Perhaps the war would be over by then and I could even go with him.

We must have played for hours because suddenly Ash's voice was right behind me and made me jump.

'Blimey, Ell, ye'll be in trouble if ye divint get back soon. Ye've missed lunch and yer class is about to start.' She wore scarlet lipstick, which made her washed out face look paler than ever, and her hair was waved up from her forehead and shining – the way that Esther's hair used to shine. A fleeting wave of disgust welled up in me at this likeness, but I pushed it down again.

'Crikey, is it really that late! Sorry, Helmut. We'll finish tomorrow. I must go now.' I jumped up, remembering the sting of Miss Parker's ruler.

'No worry.'

'And don't forget, I won two games and you won one!' I laughed, as I crawled out from under the curtain that served as a door. As I did, I noticed the black lines Ash had drawn up the backs of her legs, the way young women did those days, to make out they were wearing silk stockings when there were none to be had anywhere. They went dead straight, right from her ankles all the way up under her skirt. Ash was nearly sixteen by now, so I supposed she could do that if she wanted, but still I felt unsettled by her coming out into the woods all dressed up like that. A twinge of something sharp twisted in my stomach. Disturbed but not quite sure why, I paused outside the den for a moment, wondering if I should stay, but the threat of Miss Parker's ruler across the tender flesh of my palm sent me hurrying back to the village.

17

The day was chill, with leaden clouds hanging motionless over the village, threatening to drench us. Nothing much seemed to be moving that Saturday morning, no cats skulking in the lane, no boys out playing as they waited for the rain to fall or the clouds to pass over. Daniel was curled up in the parlour with his nose in a book. Once again I had taken to trying to sneak out without him noticing me. I wanted to find Ash.

I huddled behind a bush near the stream, out of sight. I knew she still went there sometimes, but after waiting half an hour with the cold nipping at my toes and the downpour still an imminent threat, I decided it was a waste of time. I scuffed back through the wilting grass and over the field towards the wasteland, where only a stray dog was sniffing and scavenging in a heap of thrown out junk. He would be out of luck, I was sure, as no one threw out food scraps these days, though maybe the treasure of a dead rat could be unearthed out of the discarded remnants of impoverished village lives.

I found myself making my way towards the woods. I had the feeling I was stalking Ash, though I couldn't see her. As if I had become attuned, like a fox, to the subtlest hint of a scent or sound, carried through the narrowing strip of air between earth below and rainclouds above, and was blindly tracing her steps.

Inevitably I arrived at the den – like a flake of iron drawn to a magnet – but something stopped me from entering. Instead I sat down on a tree stump a short distance away. From there I could see the entrance to the den but not easily be seen by anyone leaving or entering unawares. Unsure why I was behaving like this, I hunkered down to wait and see what would happen next. It was quiet, just a faint rustling among the leaves, an occasional twig scrunching or snapping as some small animal or bird hopped, scurried or burrowed above or below the ground. The earth seemed to breathe, lifting the branches of all the trees simultaneously in a soft, slow inhalation, then a long moment later allowing them to descend as if floating on some invisible tide. The whole forest breathed around me as I held my own breath.

I became convinced that they were in there. I can't say how I knew, except for a certain quality in the air, as if it magnified their presence and broadcast it throughout the whispering woods. I wasn't close enough to hear voices, but I imagined some of the woodland rustlings emanated from inside the den. Ash in the den, alone with Helmut.

A pain was searing through my chest and pushing up into my throat. A sharp pain, stabbing and twisting. Drawing with it a shocking realisation that once again all I held dear could be torn from me, those I loved could betray me, at any moment.

I couldn't bear it. I didn't want to see what would happen next. I stumbled off the tree stump and tripped over a rotten root, slid down a muddy bank, gained my footing again and began to run.

I ran. I ran, as the rain began to fall, and kept running as it fell in torrents between the bare canopies of trees. The trees thickened as I went deeper into the woods. The thorny undergrowth grew denser, slowing me down until I could run no further. I stopped and leant against a leaning trunk to catch my breath. As I had done so many times as a child, I was running away, but from what? A sight I didn't want to see, a truth I feared to know? I leaned in and held the tree trunk tight against my chest, feeling my heart beat thudding against it, flesh on wood, a drumbeat calling me to pay attention. I was being a fool. Was I not trying to run from something that was in fact inside me – a feeling, a fear, a refusal to acknowledge a truth? The feeling that lodged in my heart would come with me wherever I went. I couldn't run away from it.

As if the tree could hear my thoughts, it responded with a shower of raindrops and a pinecone, which hit my face and startled me back to the reality of wetness as the rain increased its force.

Turning to re-trace my steps, I slithered on the wet ground. As my hand reached out to stop my fall, plunging into shallow mud, I remembered that first time, seeing Ash in the dark muddy pool at the edge of the village, joining her there, both of us scooping handfuls of wet earth as if anointing ourselves in sacred ritual. A friendship sealed, secrets shared.

I brushed myself down and searched for the way back to the den.

It took some time, as the paths I thought I had followed, the turnings I had taken, had merged into non-descript tangles of tree and bramble and fern. Finally I saw the log that sat outside Helmut's makeshift home, and the curtain of branches that hid the entrance well enough.

This time I didn't have to wait. I darted behind a tree and crouched down as I heard someone approaching from the opposite side – it was Ash. She had a rain cape draped over her head, but I could see her hair swept up and shining, her lipstick glowing red against the dull browns and evergreens of the forest, and as she turned to step down to the den I saw the lines drawn up the backs of her legs, clear and precise like two parallel arrows hitting their target. Helmut was Ash's target. I was sure of this now.

I pressed my hands over my mouth to stop from crying out. Two parts of me fought for control of my body – one wanted to leap up and shout to Ash that she could not go in, not dressed like that, it wasn't right, it wasn't fair. But what right did I have to stop her? Another part of me wanted to crumple up on the forest floor and become invisible, disintegrate with the faded autumn leaves already crumbling to nothing on the wet earth. This impulse I followed.

I felt wretched, I felt sick.

But after some time I saw a rustling in the branches covering the doorway, then a sharp snapping sound as something broke, and Ash emerged, pushing her way through the curtain of twigs, knocking them into disorder. The cape trailed behind her, her lipstick was smudged, the black lines that shot up her legs were intact. She slipped on the bank where a meagre covering of grass had given way to bare soil, now turned to mud. Her hand and knee went down and she cursed out loud. Again I remembered her sitting in the muddy pool. It seemed to be her element, the one to which she would always be drawn back. For a moment my heart leapt towards her and I wanted to jump up from my hiding place and sit beside her in the mud again, the two of us, lost souls together in crime – but guilty of what? Of being never where we were meant to be? But I daren't let her know my own crime – how I had followed her and spied on her.

I watched as Ash stamped her wet foot in the mud, splashing the muck up over her legs and skirt, swearing as she stormed off through the sodden woods.

For a while I stayed hidden behind the tree, not sure what to do now. Eventually I decided I must see Helmut for myself. I was trembling as I carefully pressed the branches aside and found the entrance. I was cold and wet, but the tremors sprung from a place inside me where I felt afraid, confused and hurt, all at once.

'It's just me,' I called in a meek voice, hoping not to startle Helmut.

He pulled the curtain aside and nodded for me to come in, then he returned to sitting on the edge of the mattress and dropped his head into his hands with a sigh.

'I'm sorry, I'm disturbing you.' I was still hovering near the door. 'Shall I go?'

'No, come in. It is okay.'

'You look sad.'

'Yes, a little sad.' He looked up at me through narrowed eyes. 'What do you want from me, Ellen?'

Startled by the directness of his question, I opened my mouth to say 'nothing', but instead a rush of words tumbled out that I had not intended. Sometimes, when a person has something difficult to say, they take ages preparing for it – choosing the precise words, the tone of voice that will make them look strong and confident even when they don't feel it. (I had watched Trevor do this many times when he had to confront Esther.) But not me. The words just fall out and I must run to catch up with them if I can.

'Do you love Ash? Tell me honestly, because if you do I don't think I can keep on being your friend, and I want to know the truth. Please tell me the truth.'

I was shaking, but the blood had rushed to my face and I felt fierce and on fire now. I could have gone on, but I made myself wait to see if he would reply.

After a while he dropped his head again and spoke slowly, taking great care over each word. 'Ash has been good to me, she helped me get well. Naturlich, I have some feeling for her.' He looked up at me from beneath a tumbled wave of hair. The expression in his eyes held both a question and a plea – I don't know anything. Please don't ask me.

'And do you love me?' The words fell out before me and floated there in the space between us, unsure whether they required an answer or preferred not.

Helmut stood up painfully slowly, turning away from me as he did, so that I could only see his profile in the shadows of the den. I couldn't read the expression on his face, which left space for hope and fear to hover about me for a moment longer.

'Miz Ellen, you are very kind, and I am very grateful to you. You are the very best friend I have here, in England, and I always love my friend. I am more happy when I see you.'

He was standing in front of me now, looking down into my face, his eyes softer but his face lined and still sad. He lifted a hand and tenderly touched my right cheek. 'You very kind and very lovely girl.' A little shyly, he planted a quick kiss on my forehead. Then he stepped back and seemed to be smiling now, or so I imagined.

A hook had been dropped into my heart and as he stepped away the line pulled tight. My hooked heart was tied to his. I couldn't move. Helmut paced the three steps that took him around the den and was running his hands through his matted hair.

'Come, play Rummy with me, Ellen,' he said after a while, his voice tired but as soft as I had ever heard it. He pulled out the pack of cards and sat down by the upturned box table, inviting me to join him with a nod. The mood in the den lightened. I dropped my soaked coat onto the floor and accepted the invitation, grateful to be back on ground which felt familiar and secure.

Several days passed but there was no sign of Ash. She didn't come to the den and wasn't to be found down by the stream. I saw no sign of her leaving school at lunchtime and she didn't come knocking at our cottage door, as she sometimes did at weekends. I still had Helmut's friendship, and I was not quite sure but I thought he had said he loved me, and he definitely did kiss me, so that was good. But without Ash I felt bereft, despite this.

Finally I caught a glimpse of her talking to the boy she sometimes met on the wasteland. They were arguing, but then they often argued so this didn't concern me too much. I waited till he left, then ran up to her before she could slip away.

'Ash, wait. I've been looking for you. Where've you been?'

'Oh, just he-er and there.' She seemed dejected, her hair unwashed and out of place, faint traces of dried mud still on her skirt, but the lines drawn up the back of her legs were gone.

'I was worried. You haven't been to school or to the den. Are you alright?'

'Na, A'm fed up. What d'ye want anyhow?'

'Just to see you. Don't you want to come to the den anymore?'

'Na. Boring it is. A've got betta places to go now. But thanks Ell, ye've been a pal.'

'So is that it then?'

'Guess it might be. A divint knaa. Maybe see ye later, like.'

And with that she turned away and walked back in the direction of her home. There was no one at the kitchen window so I guessed it might be safe there for now.

<h1 style="text-align:center">18</h1>

Mr Grainger sat down and slapped both hands on the table, rattling the spoons and bowls. His jaw was set and his eyes aflame with a strange kind of glee.

'Well ye neva, who'd a' thought it.' He looked at each of us in turn as if about to announce some major personal triumph.

'What, dear? What's happened then?'

'They only foond the blasted Jerry, that's what!'

I froze. Must not give myself away now.

'And what Jerry be that pet?' her mind on other things.

'From the plane – the bugger what cam doon that neet.' Pet-dear glared at him for using language (don't use language in front of the young'uns, she would say), but he continued regardless. 'A poacher foond 'is remains in the woods, like. Not a pretty sight, A'd say – all pus and bones. Gan cold some time now.' He turned to look at Daniel and me. 'Now at least ye two'll be safe again when ye're oot there playin.'

I thought my face would explode. If I let out the breath I would scream and cry out so I clenched my mouth shut and felt my whole body stiffen with the force of it. My eyes stretched wide open as if I had indeed seen this horrible sight.

'Ah, look now, ye'r frightening the puwer lass. It's aalreet, Ellen pet, he's done with now. Ye divint need worry yer little head about him anymore.' Did she know I had been worrying about Helmut all along?

Daniel had begun rhythmically kicking the chair leg, as he

did when he was anxious. Pet-dear turned her attention to him and I was vaguely aware of her trying to comfort him, the soft tones of her voice filtering through a fog that was swirling inside my skull. I wanted to leave the room but couldn't work out how to do it, so I sat glued to my chair for an endless stretch of time, as she ladled out the soup and gave us each a thick slice of bread and dripping. When I tried to pick up my spoon and scoop up the watery gruel my hand was shaking, so I put it down again and sat looking at my bowl. Tears were brimming behind my eyelids, half-hidden by my uncut hair.

Pet-dear, bless her, could see I was in no fit state to eat, so excused me from the table. 'I'll keep the soup warm for ye pet. Come down when ye'r ready for it.'

I had the elaborate excuse of being thirteen, growing up during the war, far away from home, and the strange moods that came over me these days were generally passed over by Pet-dear.

Once in my room I locked the door, something I rarely did. That night I needed to cry, then I needed to think, both without disturbance from Daniel. I must go to the den to make sure, to see Helmut for myself if he was still there. I didn't care if he was all pus and cold bones, I would still love him.

The next morning, my eyes puffy from crying and my nose blocked from the tears that had not yet found their way out, I hurriedly ate the scrambled egg Pet-dear placed in front of me, keeping my head bowed so she might not see my face too clearly in the dim kitchen light. She had stopped pestering me with questions since Stephen died, and was anyway in a quiet mood herself. No doubt the death of a Nazi pilot was bitter justice for what they had done to her son. One of theirs for one of ours.

I was only half way down the lane when I heard our cottage door bang shut, and there was Daniel, running to catch up with me. We strode along side by side without speaking until we reached the wasteland.

'What do we do now?' He looked up at me as if I should know.

I studied his face for a moment. It was the first thing I had really looked at since last night's news had thrown my world on end, and in it I saw a strange light that I couldn't place. Something translucent shone through the thin and very pale skin, as if Daniel's soul had become naked and was exposed to the sharp light of the morning sun. Daniel was hurting almost as much as I was, and I couldn't understand this. I had thought he would be glad to be rid of Helmut, but he was clearly upset. Maybe in a perverse sort of way he had grown fond of him. Or, at least, he needed him. I supposed Daniel might be in need of a father as much as I needed a mother, and wondered if Helmut reminded him of his own father in some way, despite one being fair-haired and the other probably very dark. They both would have spoken German, anyway.

'I don't know. Maybe we should find Ash. She was involved too. Even if she's gone off Helmut now, she was his friend before.' I doubted the wisdom of this, but felt the need for Ash by my side. She always gave me courage.

We went to Ash's house, round the back where I knew her bedroom was, the window on the left, above the kitchen. The kitchen window was empty.

'Find some small stones, Daniel – no, small – we don't want to break the window.' We hid ourselves at the bottom of the narrow strip of garden, behind a bush, and I took careful aim. One small stone landed just below the windowpane, but the second one hit the target, and the third. After a moment Ash's bedraggled head appeared above the sill. She peered out, yawning, and stretched an arm up behind her. I must have woken her. She wouldn't be pleased. As she was turning back into the room I threw another stone. This time she opened the window wide.

'What the flippin heck was that? Hey Romeo, wither off man!' And the window was pulled shut again.

I threw once more, hoping to God that her father wasn't at home. This time, the moment she opened the window I shouted in a hoarse kind of whisper – wanting to be both heard and not heard – 'Ash, it's me. Come down. I must speak to you. Please, it's very urgent.'

'Aw Jesus, bugger and blast. Ye woke us up man.' But a few minutes later she appeared at the back door, hastily dressed in her old skirt and jacket, and came down the garden path to join us behind the bush.

'What the heck d'ye want, Ell. Ye must be mad, throwing things at me flippin window. If me dad had been home he'd av flayed the both of ye.' Daniel winced.

'It's Helmut. We think they've found him and he's dead. You've got to come with us.'

'Are ye right out yer heads. He'll be fine, man.'

'No, honest, they found a dead German pilot. It must be him. Come with us, please Ash. We must find out.'

In the end curiosity overcame whatever reluctance Ash felt about seeing Helmut again, or spending time with me, and I hoped there might still be a touch of concern for him in her heart too.

I approached the den with dread. Daniel was dragging behind, scuffing his feet through the damp remains of leaves along the path that we had worn over the autumn months. Ash strode out ahead. I held the tension in the centre, fearing a lifeline was about to break.

Was it a ghost? Stranger things have happened. A cracking of branches, the swish of an arm, sleeved in thick wool and carrying a stick. Something fell to the ground and there was scuffling, a dull thud, silence. My head was pounding with the thickness of blood stopped up behind a dam. I tried to peer through the branches but my eyes were stinging, still swollen from last night's tears. My mind began counting – one, two, three, four – a habit, something to occupy it when I was scared. Footsteps fell into rhythm with the count – five, six, seven. As if we were marching together. I remembered the small army that was Trevor and me. For a moment I was back in Newcastle, marching the city streets.

A foot appeared in view, from behind a tree, and another. The steps continued. I was afraid to look up to see the face. Helmut's face.

Yes, it was. There he stood, startled to see the three of us – each just as startled to see him. Even Ash, whose heart had believed my words even though her mind had not, looked shocked to see him standing there in the woods and very much alive, the corpse of a squirrel hanging from one hand, the weapon of slaughter in the other.

'Jens – Jens Werner. Good friend of me, best friend. Like brother.' Helmut spoke quietly, sadly of his co-pilot. 'I look for him but no find. So thought he must be dead. Now I know he dead.' He wiped a tear from his cheek and looked at us pleadingly. 'What will they do with him? Will they send him home, or bury him here, far from the Vaterland?'

'I don't know Helmut. We can try to find out. Someone will know.' When Helmut was sad I always felt like crying too, and that's what I did then, though my tears were also of relief.

Ash had been standing quietly by the door of the den, ready to leave if she felt it necessary. Daniel was huddled on the ground in a corner, plucking at the fur of the squirrel, as he had done with the feathers in his mother's hat before the hat had become completely plucked of all its feathers.

'Why did ye not tell us about yer friend, like?' Ash finally chipped in.

'Was afraid you might tell and he get shot. I look for him every day, when I can walk again – but not find. No parachute. Maybe he die in plane. Not jump.'

'Did you not trust us to help your friend, Helmut?' I asked.

'Not sure. Sorry, Miz Ellen. Me know you friend for me, but not sure for Jens.'

We all fell silent, taking in the complexity of it all, the vulnerability of Helmut's situation and how under our power he must have felt.

'A'm sorry we couldna help yer friend, Helmet. A'll take it on mysel to find out what they've done with him, if ye like.'

'Dank you, Miz Ash. You very kind.' They nodded politely to each other. Maybe they could be friends again, after all.

'I think we should take you back to the hut. It'll be safer. There could be poachers in the woods and they'll find you here.' I had to be the practical one right now, as things still seemed delicate between Ash and Helmut and she had offered as much as she could.

'What are poachers?' Helmut asked, startled.

'They shoot animals in the woods, steal other people's animals and eat them.' Daniel had suddenly come back to life as if he had found his rightful place again. 'Like you do.'

Helmut laughed. He could have been offended, but he saw the irony of it all.

We helped Helmut return to the hut that evening, once it was dark, all four of us trampling through the woods, skirting the village, across fields, under the hedge and back to the comfort of the four rotten walls that now felt like our home. Things seemed to return to normal, though Ash kept a little more distant from Helmut and I was not so sure of Ash as I had been before. But we seemed to be friends again, as far as anyone would notice. The knowledge that any one of us could die at any moment had drawn us back into the web of friendship, and the bound and complex patterns of power and dependency that we had created seemed to draw even tighter.

19

*Why don't you come home for Christmas, Ellen dear?
You know I would love to see you – it's been such a long
time –* Trevor wrote in his December letter.

*No thank you. I have to help Mrs Grainger now that her
son has died. I will be fine here –* I wrote back.

My life in the city was behind me now, and I had no
intention of returning to it, ever. Esther had settled in America
and wanted him to follow her very soon, he said. I wrote back
to say that I was happy in Bellingham. He should join Esther if
he wished, and not worry about me. I had a new life now. He
wrote back to say that he could not leave me here alone – he
would stay in England until the war was over, then we could
live together again, in the countryside if I wished. I thought
that he should not wait for that to happen, but I didn't write
again. I knew he would go to America eventually, without me.
Esther would insist on it.

Christmas came, and it passed. It was a sad time, with
Stephen gone and Daniel missing his parents and his real
home in Berlin. There was no tree that year, no ring of holly
on the front door, but Pet-dear and I cooked a nice dinner
for the four of us, and Daisy came for tea in the afternoon
while we listened to the King's Christmas message on the
wireless. He told us, in a slow and crackly voice: '*War brings,*

among other sorrows, the sadness of separation. There are many in the Forces away from their homes today because they must stand ready and alert to resist the invader should he dare to come, or because they are guarding the dark seas or pursuing the beaten foe in the Libyan Desert.' Pet-dear burst into tears and buried her face in her handkerchief.

When he went on to talk about us, the children, he said: *'To all of them, at home and abroad, who are separated from their fathers and mothers, to their kind friends and hosts, and to all who love them, and to parents who will be lonely without them, from all in our dear island I wish every happiness that Christmas can bring.'*[1] And there the tears sprang into my eyes too, for I was thinking of my own mother and that she might have been lonely without me, if she hadn't died. By the end of the king's speech we were all crying. Hinny-luv was so moved by the words of hope and pride in the British spirit that big tears rolled down his crumpled cheeks, and Daisy joined in because she had lost her sweetheart in the first Great War and never found another to replace him.

It was a cold winter with lots of snow that kept people indoors when they didn't need to be out. In the mornings a thin film of ice coated the inside of my window, rippling the clean white lines of the fields and the brown trees beyond the glass. Mrs Grainger didn't wonder at all why I went out every morning, no matter what the weather brought, and there was nobody else around to see where I went. Except for Daniel of course. Sometimes he came with me, but mostly he stayed at home and helped Pet-dear to feed the chickens, or pull frozen sheets through the mangle, or mop the muddy floors one more time. And of course Daniel always did the homework that we had been set. Sometimes he did mine too.

---

1 [https://en.wikisource.org/wiki/Christmas_Message,_1940 Accessed 30-1-2016]

Helmut was surviving, but only just. In the autumn he had hunted for rabbits and pigeons, but now everything with any sense was sleeping in some impossible cranny of shelter, or had escaped to a warmer place. Even Hitler's planes seemed to be hibernating now, or else he had forgotten about us in the northeast for the time being. Now Helmut depended totally on the food I brought, so Ash began to help too. She didn't care if her parents realised she was stealing rations because she would be leaving home very soon.

Ash had turned sixteen and immediately stopped going to school. No one missed her there. No one at home seemed to mind at all. In fact no one had ever questioned that she kept going to school for so long. She could have left when she was fourteen, got a job somewhere, but there were no jobs for a girl like Ash in Bellingham. And no one at school or at home seemed to be paying much attention to what Ash was doing. So she kept on going to school when she felt like it, though she had learnt very little there.

March came. The snow melted. Rain and cold winds blew about the hut, and sometimes beautiful bright crisp days arrived, setting all four of us itching for something to happen. Ash was first.

She arrived one Saturday morning and burst through the creaking door, nearly flinging it off its rusty hinges.

'A've had enough! A've really had enough this time!' She plonked down on her knees and burst into tears. I had rarely seen Ash cry. I knew it must be very bad.

'What's happened, Ash? Is it your dad again?' I knelt down beside her.

'Bastard, bleedin bastard he is! A hate him! A'm neva going back, eva. A mean it.' She cried some more and we tried to comfort her. In the end Daniel trumped. He brought out a square of chocolate and offered it to Ash. I knew what a sacrifice this was for him. So did Ash. She was touched, took the chocolate gratefully, broke it in two and gave half back to

Daniel. They both sucked on the delicious brown sweetness, smiling at each other. A truce had been made, which was just as well considering what was about to happen next.

'Thanks, Daniel, ye'r a real mate,' she said, and Daniel beamed.

'What will you do then?' I asked.

'A'm off to Scotland to join the Lumber Jo's. A said A would do it and no one eva believed me, but now A'm going.'

'You have to be eighteen though,' I pointed out, unhelpfully.

'A can look eighteen if A want to.' She plumped her hair, now cut in a stylish bob up around her chin, and glanced at Helmut.

'How will you get to Scotland?' asked Daniel. 'On a train?'

'Divint knaa yet. A'll work it out.'

'Then I'm coming too,' I stated, suddenly very clear about my future. 'I can look eighteen too. I can be a Lumber Jo as well. I helped Helmut chop branches for his fire, didn't I, Helmut?'

'Yes, but very hard work for girl. Not good idea, Miz Ellen.'

'You can come too, Helmut!' I cried. 'We can help you get home on our way to Scotland! What a great plan. It will work out for all of us.'

'Yes, I think now it is time for me to leave,' he said slowly, deliberating on each word – evidence of Daniel's strident lessons.

'And me too. I come too,' chipped in Daniel.

In my moment of excitement I had forgotten about Daniel.

'No Daniel, you are much too young. You still need to be at home, to go to school. You must stay here with Mrs Grainger.'

'No. Go with you, Ellen. I go where you go. I will look after you. I am nearly ten year old now.'

I looked at Daniel. He was not much taller than when he first came to live with us, as if the shock of it all had stunted his growth. Skinny legs protruded like sticks beneath knee-length grey trousers that were much too big for him –

Stephen's pass-me-downs, of course. But the navy blue cap he insisted on wearing all the time made him look much older than his ten years. My heart was suddenly so full I reached my arms out and gave him a hug, knocking the cap to the floor. He dived to rescue it and pulled it firmly back over his ragged head.

'Well – maybe. Let's talk about it later, Daniel,' I said.

'Jesus, he cannit come with us, Ell. Are ye barking mad? He's just a baby,' whispered Ash, but Daniel, sharp as a toothpick, heard her.

'I am not a baby!' he shouted, jumping to his feet and stamping a foot on the rotten floorboards. The over-sized boot clacked feebly against the wood, sounding more like the rap of a tap-dancer than a strong willed ten year old. 'You wicked. Give back my chocolate.'

'Oh, heck, A can't be dealing with aal this right now, Daniel. A've things to work out for mesel. Look, man, A didn't mean it. Ye'r a good lad, really, but ye'r too young to be travelling to Scotland with us. And there's nowt else to say about it.'

'Daniel pet, maybe you should go home now, and I'll talk with you later, when we've made a plan. Go on, there's my boy. And here, have this.' I took my last square of chocolate out of my pocket and pressed it into his sticky palm. He accepted begrudgingly and sulked out of the hut. I felt so bad about what had just happened, but we had important grown-up things to discuss.

'Can A stay he-er till A'm ready to go away,' Ash was asking Helmut when I turned my attention back to them. He looked about the tiny space awkwardly, then glanced at me. This arrangement didn't feel right to me, and I couldn't be feeding both of them.

'You can stay with me. Mrs Grainger won't mind. We can sleep head-to-tail, and talk all through the night if we want to – it'll be fun,' I offered.

'That's good. Not many room here, Miz Ash.' He was always

so polite to us, so charming. If he was not an angel, then he certainly was a nice young man. I would like to marry someone like Helmut one day. No – I would like to marry Helmut. When the war was over of course, and I was a bit older.

'Well, it'll only be for a few days anyhow, till A get me plans sorted.' I had the feeling Ash was disappointed to be staying with me, but she said no more about it.

We sat in silence, each of us trying to think of a plan. Helmut shifted on the precarious chair, challenging it to stay upright and in one piece. His leg still ached and might give him some trouble on a long walk.

We sat for a long time, shuffling our feet, scratching our heads, rubbing our chins, hugging our knees, then we decided to sleep on it and meet again the next day. As we stepped out of the hut into the bright daylight, Daniel was squatting by the gap in the hedge. I sighed. I felt so many responsibilities sitting on my shoulders. You had to grow up quickly in the war. I guessed we would all survive it together – Daniel, Ash and me. But what about Helmut? I couldn't bear to think that I might lose him.

Daniel trailed ahead of us as we walked home, and my feet trailed behind me as I studied the brown earth and the green springing grass along the edge of the field.

Mrs Grainger seemed neither happy nor cross when I asked if Ash could stay for a few nights, we wouldn't be any trouble, she could help out, she had her own coupons with her. This last point wasn't true, but Ash knew how to get extra rations. She knew the right people, she told me.

'Please yerselves, if that's what ye want to do,' Pet-dear said, eyeing Ash briefly with an expressionless face. The life had gone right out of her. Here was the other reason I should leave – I had become a burden for Mrs Grainger and I should get out of the way so that Kevin could come home and have his room back. So it was decided in my mind. I would go with Ash and Helmut. We would try to sneak away without Daniel, but I knew that would be difficult, and probably impossible.

The three of us tried to be good as we sat down to tea. When the war broadcast came on the wireless we sat still and listened attentively. And I am very glad we did.

'Two members of the IRA group were arrested near Belfast yesterday, after British intelligence services learnt of a German plot to invade Northern Ireland. They planned to drop thousands of paratroopers into the country, enabling Luftwaffe fighter squadrons to land on captured airfields. The IRA has been known for a long time to be aiding the German forces with information and communications, in the hope that Germany would in turn support their campaign for Home Rule by supplying weapons. The plan has been thwarted and the subversive activities of the IRA undermined.' The posh voice on the wireless continued to crackle and splutter through the airwaves.

Ash looked at me, wide-eyed, and began to fidget in her seat.

'A need a pee,' she whispered urgently. 'Come out with us to the nettie.'

We excused ourselves and went round the back and leant against the middin, out of sight of the kitchen window. It smelt bad because they were due to empty it the next day. There were beautiful pink and red and purple streaks of clouds arcing right across the sky, and down the lane a cat was mewling loudly. The smell of boiled cabbage and smoke from the coal fires seeped through the evening air.

'Are ye thinking what A'm thinking?' Ash asked.

'Well, sort of. The IRA are friends with the Germans – but how can that help us?'

'Divint knaa yet, but A bet they can. If we can get wor Helmet to them, they'll be right glad to see him, A reckon.'

We looked at each other, our eyes bright with excitement. A plan was forming in our minds.

Act Three

20

Perhaps I was searching for you, Liza, that first time I tried to reach Ireland, not even knowing you were alive – having no idea that you might be in Belfast.

With my three friends, I set out on a journey.

Yes, we had to take Daniel with us. He did not let me out of his sight for a moment so in the end I told Mrs Grainger that I was visiting Trevor, and Daniel was invited too. A holiday for us both.

I have been searching for you all along, without realising it, even when I believed you were dead. Are you still there? Can you hear me now? I am on my way. Maybe this time I will reach Belfast, and all will be well.

I hope you will understand why I wanted to take care of Helmut, and not blame me, the way I know Esther and Trevor would have done. Befriending the enemy would have been a betrayal of all their values, their hopes for me, their great and good efforts. It would have shocked and hurt them to know what I was doing. And it gave me some satisfaction to know it. Do you think I am a bad person for this?

Everything I did was because I wanted you, and not Esther, to be my mother – because I was so angry with them for lying to me. I wanted to punish them. Does that shock you? I did not really understand that there was something else driving me to this act of betrayal too – something deeper, visceral, in my blood – a force that pulled me towards Helmut in a way that I was unable to resist.

Now, none of this really matters. The only thing left to do is tell you my story, to let you know what I did, how I have used this short life you gave me. I want you to know who I am.

I will be with you soon. Then you will see what I have made of myself.

Now I am floating. Silver light shimmers all around me. The angel's wing has gone.

Liza, can you hear me?

'I'll be back by six, Ellen,' James shouted up the stairs.

'Eleanor,' I shouted back.

'Sorry – Eleanor.'

He never got used to calling me Eleanor. I never stopped asking him to. It was the beginning of lots of conflict between us.

James was so angry with Esther and Trevor, angrier than I was in the end. Once I had given up all my desire and longing, and the grey mist had taken me in, I felt nothing, but James kept the flame of anger burning for me.

He was angry with you, too. Because of your letter – because everything changed after that. We had been happy together, but when I discovered the truth my whole life fell apart. It crumbled like a lie in the face of insurmountable reason. It changed me. The love I had felt for James and my babies was buried somewhere deep inside, away from the light, under the grey blanket of mist that had smothered me. I could not reach it anymore. Poor James. Poor Martin, Anita.

I used to be called Ellen Rushton.

Then for a while I was Ellen Rose.

Now I am Eleanor Rose. I like that name.

But who was I before all this? What was my mother's name, my father's?

There is pain piercing right through me. I don't know where it begins and where it ends. It simply exists inside me, and all around me. I want to scream but there is no strength for that, no pathway for my voice. The pathways through my body have been scoured clean with knives. Oh, help me, somebody.

I am being tipped and pulled, pummelled and rocked. The air has become hard and angular, pressing on me from every side. I am being slowly tipped upside down until I am falling again, down through layers of darkness.

I hear a voice, shouting. It seems to come from above, then beside me, then far behind. Now I am being spun like a top and streamers of coloured ribbon are flying out from me. Like a Maypole, like springtime, like Anita in her yellow dress dancing around the Maypole, bright with laughter.

'Hold on there – this way – careful, mind the – still breathing – got you.' The words circle around me like a bat flitting through the darkest of nights.

James, are you there? Are you coming for me? I will wait here for you.

Don't forget Martin's swimming lesson. Anita likes orange juice, not apple, and remember to give her a Farley's rusk at bedtime, dipped in warm milk. I'll be home soon my love, once I have told Liza all about my life.

James – my rock, my shelter. With your anger you wanted to protect me, but you did not know about my angel. You did not know that I had been saved, despite it all, from the sorrow and the lies. I will tell you about him when I come home. I want you to know that I loved him because he came into my life just as the empty space my mother should have filled became so vast that I could not bear it. And because his helplessness touched my own. Perhaps I thought I could save myself by saving him.

The bright lights have stopped flashing and turning. It is dark. I am struggling to breathe, it hurts to breathe. I am cold, in my bones I am cold. I think my body is shivering but I cannot feel it. I can barely feel my body at all – a jumble of dry sticks and sallow cheesecloth wrapped loosely around the tangled mess. There must be blood somewhere, a lot of blood.

I am not ready to die yet. Please don't let me die.

Act Two

21

'Tickets please,' called the inspector as he edged towards us. A large peaked cap almost covered frameless spectacles that perched halfway down a long hooked nose. He was tall and thin, and quite old, which is why he was not a soldier I suppose.

'Just don't say a word, Helmut, or you, Daniel. Let Ash and me do the talking,' I mouthed behind a cupped hand. I didn't dare shout above the uproar of the train – the screech and rumble of the engine cantering over the buzz of human voices laughing, shouting, jeering. Soldiers in their uniforms filled many of the seats. Some hung out of windows smoking, others jostled for space in the aisle. Every other kind of person was there too – people in strange foreign clothes, old men in threadbare coats that looked as if they hadn't been taken off since the war began, women with young children who ran up and down the aisle between the lounging soldiers, shrieking each time the train rolled and they were tipped into a stranger's lap.

Here on the train I felt I had finally arrived in the war that we had listened to on the wireless every night, but that never really came our way – except for Helmut, of course. Everyone seemed to be on the move, fleeing the war, or going into war, or just feeling restless because when the bombs fell they had no idea where it was safest to be. It was best to keep moving on, dodging the air raids, like jumping back from a big wave as it crashed onto the beach or over the seawall.

Ash had found half the money to pay for our tickets to Newcastle. She said that in the war everyone had to share, so there was nothing wrong with taking her share. Daniel and I had saved up just enough from our pocket money – the ha'pennies that Pet-dear and Daisy gave us each week for helping out. I was glad I hadn't spent all mine on sweets like some of the children did. Pet-dear had also given us a little money and coupons for food, our rations for two weeks, so we wouldn't starve.

'Tickets please.' The inspector towered over us so that I had to crick my neck to look up into his dour face. I handed him the four tickets and four ID cards, bundled in one pile, Helmut sandwiched between Ash and me. She had borrowed her brother's card – said he wouldn't be needing it, and if he did, she didn't care – it served him right. The inspector punched a hole in each ticket and handed them back without even a glance at Helmut.

'See, nowt to it,' said Ash. She was enjoying the ride enormously, smiling at the soldiers who looked her way, crossing and uncrossing her legs, checking her hair was still in place. Today she wore bright red lipstick and the miraculously straight black lines drawn up the backs of her legs.

The four of us had to make do with the old and scruffy clothes that were all we had. We didn't have a choice in that, but, 'No harm in making the best of what A've got,' Ash had said, when I had told her it wasn't a picnic we were going on. We were all nervous and it made us irritable with each other.

A middle-aged woman sitting opposite Helmut tried to draw him into conversation.

'Are ye going to the town, pet?'

Helmut looked at me, alarm in his eyes. After living in near isolation for months, the noise and commotion of the train was making him jumpy. I came to the rescue.

'He can't speak, our cousin. War damage, y'know.' I knew all about not speaking when you didn't want to. Daniel had taught Helmut to speak English. Now I was teaching him to not speak when there were strangers nearby.

'Oh, my dear!' she said, in a tone meant to convey sympathy but sounding more like the voice you might speak to your cat with. 'Here pet, have these.' She pulled out a packet of boiled sweets and passed them to Helmut. He looked at me again, fear in his eyes. I nodded. He accepted the sweets and gave one to each of us, including the woman, who took this as an invitation to continue the conversation.

'A'm off to Gateshead, meself. Me sister lives there and A haven't seen her in ages. Told her to come out and live with us for the war, A did, but she's so stubborn, like. Prefers the air raid shelters to the comforts of me own home, would ye believe it. But now of course she's sick, what with the stress of it all, so A'll have to look after her A suppose.'

Helmut retreated back into his corner by the window to watch the countryside flash by. Ash had cut his hair short and blackened it with boot polish so that he wouldn't look too German, she thought. He was wearing Daniel's peak cap to shade his ice blue eyes from view. Daniel had on one of Stephen's woolly hats to keep his mass of dark curls at bay. Across the left lens of his spectacles ran a grubby strip of sticky tape, tentatively holding the pieces of broken glass together. For most of the journey he clutched a bag of marbles, every now and then taking one out and tossing it from hand to hand while swinging his legs and kicking his feet annoyingly against the seat. Occasionally he would pull the black felt hat from his pocket and pick at a stubby quill, the last remains of the feathers that had once graced it.

I wore my best cotton dress and a brown wool jacket that was much too big. 'Room to grow,' Pet-dear had said, as we shaped her old coat down to a grow-into size for me. Ash, of course, looked lovely in her flowery cotton blouse, the one

she had worn all last summer, and a tight grey skirt that she
had made out of her unflattering school tunic as soon as she
stopped going to school. It came down just below her knees,
with a slit up the back so she could walk.

I began to relax and enjoy myself, just a little, now and then
nodding or saying, 'Yes, how nice, oh dear, no thank you,' to
the very friendly woman sitting next to me as she told me
all about her sister, her sister's family, her neighbours, their
family, and all manner of people whom I had not met and
never would, but my mind was busy thinking about what we
would do when we reached the city. Our plan was to take
Helmut to Ireland, but first we must find a way to get more
money for the train fares, and food coupons too, in case it
took longer than two weeks to get there. Ash said she could
easily get a job in the city.

'And where y'aal going?' the woman asked me at last.

'We're taking our cousin home. He's been to visit us in
the country.' This was not the total truth but not a complete
lie either, so I thought it would do well enough. I glanced at
Helmut and noticed a faint line of grey trickling from under his
cap down the side of his neck. The heat of the sweaty carriage
was melting the boot polish. I pulled up my own collar, staring
at his neck. He got the message and did the same, only partly
hiding the tell tale sign of a slowly dissolving disguise.

Eventually the woman finished her story, closed her eyes,
and nodded off into a contented sleep, snoring very softly and
leaning heavily against my shoulder. My attention now released
from the effort of listening and not listening at the same time, I
looked around the carriage. One of the soldiers across the aisle
from us was staring at Ash, winking whenever she glanced his
way, which she did often. I sighed and sank back into my seat.

I must have dozed too, for the next thing I remembered
was the long curve of the railway line that was sweeping us
towards the city centre. The familiar arc of the Tyne Bridge
came into view. Below, I could see the grey ribbon of water

threading between houses and factories. We swung around and were coming into the city from behind.

The war had been here. Hitler had bombed Newcastle and left behind great holes and mounds where factories and warehouses had once stood. People's homes, too, had been bombed to the ground. The train toiled through the industrial heart of the city, past piles of brick and stone, tangles of metal and wood, great mountains of junk and fallen roofs. Chimney pots and bathtubs lay where people had once lived and worked. Broken cars and prams and bicycles were piled up in heaps on scraps of wasteland.

After the green of the countryside, the city was full of grey – grey clouds above, grey walls still standing, grey rubble lying over the tired earth, the grey thread of the river winding through it all. The train added to this by leaving its own thick trail of steam along the valley.

I had been here with Trevor once, but what I saw now was a very different world. His warehouse had been in this part of the city, off the Scotswood Road. I strained to see if I could recognise it, if it was still standing. It was hard to tell one ruined wall from another. Bleak stretches of empty land lay between them.

Trevor had not mentioned the bombings much, but I know this was to protect me from the war. In his letters he never complained. He tried to sound optimistic and cheery, though I could often read something else behind his words: *"Dear Ellen, Next week I will be travelling to Lancashire where my company's main factory and warehouses are now. I will be staying there for a while, as work has slowed down considerably in Newcastle, and the business is now centred in Lancaster. I will send you my new address as soon as I know it."*

I imagined Trevor on a journey, like me, not knowing where he was going. For a moment a pang of sadness distracted me, thinking of him as homeless and alone in a strange city, his business struggling and Esther and me both far away. I was brought back to the present by Daniel dropping a marble on the floor and diving under the seat to retrieve it. He bumped my legs and I toppled sideways. The woman leaning against me woke with a startle. Then everyone was reaching up for bags squeezed into the racks above their heads, and putting on coats and hats. The train jolted and shuddered to a stop, belching out a last huff of steam. The soldiers were pushing towards the door and swinging down onto the platform before the train came to a stop.

I was back in Newcastle. In the excitement of planning how to get Helmut to Ireland then Ash and me to Scotland, I had forgotten to consider how returning to my old home might feel.

Act One

22

Trevor holds my hand tightly as we walk back from the football ground. Each Saturday afternoon, after the match, he buys me a bag of sweets. Today it's sugared almonds, last week, cinder toffee. Dolly mixture, wine gums, pear drops, chocolate eclairs – there's no end of lovely things to buy. I suck on the sugary coating while Trevor hums the tune all the men had been singing at the match. I was more interested in how they jumped up and down and waved their arms and scarves in the air, than in how the game was proceeding. They seemed just like me, hardly able to keep still for a moment. I feel at home there.

'I need to drop by the office, Ellen. It won't take long. Maybe you'd like to see where I work?'

I nod, my cheeks stuffed with almond sweetness.

'Good. Let's take the bus then.'

We climb up to the top deck so that we can look down on the city crawling by. It's a relief to sit down for a while. After all the standing and jumping and walking, my legs are tired. The bus jogs along slowly, dropping off the boys and men in their flat caps and black and white scarves, until there are just Trevor and me and two old men left. Finally we clamber down too.

We arrive in front of a high red-brick building with six rows of dark, steel-framed windows running from end to end. They are grimy with soot and fumes from the traffic that trundles past during the week. Today the road is quiet. Up five steps, then we enter the warehouse through a big wooden door with wrinkled glass panels. Trevor switches on a light and we're standing in a lobby with dark wooden panelling on the walls, and several doors leading off it, all in the same shiny wood. He opens the door to our left and beckons me to follow him. I don't know why I feel afraid to enter, but I do. I peer through the semi-darkness into a large square room lined with glass-fronted book cabinets. A big table with a leather top sits in the centre of the room, an upright chair in front of it and a big leather armchair behind. Along one wall stands a row of six more upright chairs, in case Trevor has more than one visitor, I suppose. On the desk are four neat piles of paper arranged symmetrically around a large sheet of blotting paper. At one side, an inkpot and a black pen, its top ringed with gold. A brass lamp with a white glass shade sits to one corner of the desk.

Trevor sits down in the comfortable chair and indicates that I can sit in the other. I twine myself around the doorframe like a mountaineer around a craggy outcrop. I'm not going to let go, to fall into this gloomy cavern. The air smells of stale cigarette smoke and I begin to feel sick. Trevor looks at me, shrugs, and turns his attention to one of the piles of paper. Once I see that he's engrossed in his work, I slide away and sit on the floor of the lobby in the one thin trickle of sunlight that has found its way through a small cob-webbed window high up above the entrance. I close my eyes and turn my face into the light, imagining I am on the beach at Bamburgh.

I can hear Trevor chuntering to himself as he scratches some figures onto a sheet of paper. I begin to hum a tune – one I make up as I go along, not a real tune like on Esther's wireless.

Suddenly the telephone in his office rings out, loud and shrill in the empty building. His voice is low, mumbling – 'Yes … No … Not yet … Sorry … Alright then … No, we'll be home soon.' He slams the phone down hard, which means he's angry. And that was Esther, I'm sure. How does she know we're here? I guess there'll be another row when we get home. I take my bag of sugared almonds out of my coat pocket and pick a green one and a pink one. I put them both in my mouth at the same time and begin to crunch into their nutty centres. Before I've finished Trevor comes out, slams the office door shut, takes my hand and pulls me to my feet without a word, and out we march.

That was my only visit to Trevor's office. I still had no idea what he did.

Act Two

23

We lost our way three times and it was dusk, almost night, by the time we reached the house. I thought I knew the way but the city had changed. Streets had disappeared, shops were no longer where I expected them to be, my school was hidden behind a wall of corrugated iron so I didn't even know if it was still there.

Helmut was obeying orders well. He hadn't spoken a word since we left Bellingham but now, as we walked down another street that looked just like the one before, he checked there was nobody behind us then stooped to whisper in my ear.

'We stop soon, Miz Ellen?'

'Yes, soon. Is your leg bad?' I whispered back.

'Yes, bad. Big pain now.'

He was limping heavily. The wound had not healed as well as we had thought. Probably the bones had broken and not set well.

'I am sorry, Helmut. I am sorry we could not take better care of you.' My words limped out, mimicking the rhythm of his broken English. Recently I had taken to speaking to him like this in the hope he would understand me more easily. Pigeon English — I was talking like a pigeon.

'No, not your fault. It is not so bad. Just need to rest soon.'

He tried to reassure me, but the lines on his face showed that he was struggling to control the pain.

'We nearly there. I think it is the next street.'

Yes, this was the very crescent I had gone down that first time I tried to run away. One more block and I would be home again. I knew Esther was in America and wouldn't come back whilst the war was going on, and Trevor was living in Lancaster now. But what if he had decided to come home, just a short visit, to check on things, collect mail, make sure the house had not been bombed?

It had seemed a good idea to come here when we were making our plans from the safety of the hut – a place to hide out until Ash earned enough money to get us to Belfast. But now that we were here, looking down the street where Act One of my life had taken place, a shiver of fear ran through my heart. My knees buckled as if they could no longer hold me up. If Trevor returned he would never allow me to go to Scotland, or even return to Bellingham. Helmut would be caught and sent to a prison camp – or worse, he might be shot. I dreaded to think what Trevor would make of Ash, and what he might do with her. He would surely be shocked to meet my new friends, and would take me to live with him in Lancaster. With these fears jumping in my mind, my heart beat faster and my words seized up again. It was as if the ghost of Esther was still here, and I became mute.

I grabbed hold of Ash's arm and pulled her into the shadow of a tree as I heard footsteps following us. Helmut and Daniel darted in behind me.

'Hell, Ell, what's up with ye?' cried Ash as she stumbled over a tree root and fell against the roughened bark of its trunk.

I waved my arms in the dusk air, unable to utter a sound, gesturing towards the footsteps, but they had stopped. No one was following us.

'Flippin heck, Ell, get a grip on yersel, man.' She shook her arm free of my grasp. She was annoyed that the soldier had not made an arrangement to meet her, but had jumped off the train with the others and disappeared down the platform without even asking her name. Ash had been in a foul mood ever since.

'There are plenty more soldiers,' Daniel had said, trying to be helpful. All three of us had glanced at Helmut, without really meaning to. It was just that he was a soldier – well, sort of – and we sometimes forgot this but we all knew it deep inside, and we knew what it would mean if someone found out that we were harbouring – that was the word they used, like a ship sheltering from the storm – the enemy. We would be made prisoners too, sent to a camp, or shot for treason. My unruly mind was running wild with these dark thoughts.

We finally arrived at the house. The low brick wall and narrow strip of front garden looked much the same, except that weeds had taken over where summer roses used to grow. Night was falling. Every window on the street was blacked out and nobody was about. I led them into the narrow gap between our house and the neighbours'. There was no way of knowing whether Mr and Mrs Dempsey were at home. An eerie silence hung over us as we huddled along the hedge that ran between the high brick walls of our house and theirs. Though none of us would admit it, we were all afraid. I had to think quickly, take charge. It was my home, after all.

'Wait here. I'll check round the back.' Because of the blackout I couldn't tell whether anyone was in the house – Trevor, or someone he had rented it to perhaps. I stood by the back wall and looked down the garden. The swing was still standing, but Esther's flowerbeds had been dug over and I could just make out the abandoned remains of a vegetable patch. Behind it, the Andersen shelter. I crept along in the shadow of the hedge, holding my breath, praying that nobody was peeping from behind their blackened windows, disobeying orders, to gaze out into the night. Through a thin layer of cloud, the half moon cast a faint shine that was just enough for someone to see me by.

As I passed between the hedge and the swing I ran a hand over its sturdy wooden frame, touched the rope that hung motionless, just as I had left it nearly two years ago. An impulse surged in me to feel the sweeping arc of movement once again, to feel the freedom of flying. To push through the night, my heels thrusting forwards, my mind forgetting all the worries and responsibilities I had gathered about me since I was last here. I snatched my hand away from the rope. I must control this childish urge.

Reaching the shelter, I tested the door. It was open.

I retraced my steps until I was in the shadow of the house again, and gestured for the others to follow me. I didn't dare look at Helmut. What was he thinking right now? What on earth had I got him into? A wave of homesickness swept through me – for Bellingham, for Pet-dear and the cottage, and our hideaway in a broken down hut in the corner of a forgotten field. I wondered why we had left, why we could not have stayed there until the war was over. There we were all friends, and each of us needed Helmut to be there with us to help us through the war. To help us suffer our own private loss. Here in the city I felt danger all around me and I knew that everything had changed forever. Helmut was a German pilot and we would be seen as Fifth Columnists if we were discovered helping him. We were like spies.

For a moment a ripple of excitement overran the fear. For one crazy moment, as I crept along the hedge, stooping low so that I would be out of sight of the Dempseys' window, I imagined the life of a spy, the adventure, the risk, the glamour of it. Now that would truly annoy Esther and Trevor.

Then we were stumbling into the dark of the shelter, down two narrow steps into a hole in the damp earth.

Daniel, always the most organised, as well as the most fearful, was first to pull out his torch the moment the door was closed. He flashed it around the shelter – about six by eight feet of dark enclosed space – then sat himself down heavily on one of the wide benches that ran along each side. Ash found the other bench and lay down full-length so that I had no choice but to sit next to Daniel. Helmut sat on my left and groaned as he stretched out his leg. We were exhausted, too tired even to eat, so we sat in silence as we waited to see if anyone would come and find us there.

Soon I could hear the soft purring of Ash's breath. A dark curl of hair fell over a pale cheek, giving her a look of innocence that had long since abandoned her waking self. Daniel curled up beside me and laid his head on my lap. I felt the weight of his skull press into my bones, hard and angular. My fingers ran absent-mindedly through his hair, smoothed the contours of his forehead as I traced the line where wiry hair met smooth, cold skin. In sleep he too could look angelic.

To my left I could feel the big, warm contours of Helmut's arm and his thigh. I dared to lean a little closer, to take in the strong reassuring feeling of his body so close to mine. My angel. I wanted to drink him in, to melt into the fullness of him. Amidst all my fear and worry, and the sense of responsibility for all of us, for one moment I felt small and young and safe as I rested against his side – as if he could make our troubles go away and everything be well again. As I took in a deep breath my hand brushed the back of his, just a light touch. I didn't draw away. I let my fingers slide beneath his broad palm, where they wanted to go, and bury inside his hand. He gently squeezed my hand and we stayed like this until sleep found us.

A shrill noise tore me from my dreams. Daniel, screaming, clawing at my neck. Instinctively I reached for his mouth and tried to silence him. He bit me hard and I felt a warm trickle of blood run down my wrist. I yelped. He kept screaming. The sound echoed through my tired brain and stretched into the darkness of the night.

'What the hell!' gasped Ash.

Helmut leapt up, banging his head on the corrugated roof of the shelter, and cursed in German – 'Scheisse!' As my support gave way, Daniel and I came tumbling to the ground.

I was clinging tight to Daniel, trying to stop him from wriggling out of my grasp and running, hiding somewhere. We were already in a dark cupboard so there was nowhere left for him to go. He thrashed about in my arms. A torch was switched on.

'Helmut, grab his legs, stop him kicking,' I gasped. Helmut understood what was needed and took hold of Daniel so firmly that he began to whimper as the breath was squeezed out of him, and then finally to cry. Ash sat upright on the bench, her face white with shock. Helmut and I sat on the damp soil holding Daniel as he sobbed.

I knew there was no point telling Daniel not to do this, and I also knew that he could give us all away if a neighbour heard him screaming out in the night. I listened for footsteps, but no one came. Still, none of us felt like sleeping after that, and we waited for dawn.

The hut was so well sealed that morning was hard to recognise. Every now and then Helmut cracked open the door, until finally a trickle of grey light entered and told us that a new day had arrived and our torturous night was over. I shivered with cold and fear, wondering what we should do next. My head was thick with tiredness, my body aching and stiff.

We dug into our bags for our morning rations – two slices of grey bread and dripping each, stuck together like a sandwich, and two apples between us. One by one we crept round to the back of the shelter where an overgrown patch of garden behind some shrubs would be our make-do toilet, until we worked out something better.

'Flippin heck, Danny Boy, divint eva do that again,' Ash demanded, as we sat around to discuss our next move. She sounded authoritative, like Miss Parker, as if it were as simple as telling him not to fidget when she was talking.

'He can't help it, Ash. He's scared. Just try being nice to him and he's less likely to do it.'

'A knew he should neva 'av come with us.' She began picking dirt out from under her fingernails with a nail file, concentrating hard.

'But I can help,' said Daniel, afraid he might be sent back on his own. It was odd how Daniel was so frightened and yet so curious and brave at the same time.

'How, like?' asked Ash

'I will find food. Nobody will notice me.'

'That might be true – you look like all the boys look now – like ragged street urchins,' I said. 'Why don't you come with me to find a shop, Daniel. First thing is to get something to eat.'

'And A'll go look for work in the city.' Ash was combing her hair, trying to get it back into shape after her rough night on the bench.

'What will you do?' I was curious about this big world Ash was about to step into.

'A can work in a shop or a bar – or in a factory. There's lots of things to do now that the lads are off fighting.'

'Hmm, I suppose so. Helmut, you must stay here and hide till Daniel and me get back. And listen out for any signs of people in the house. I doubt anyone'll come, but if they do, just keep pretending you can't speak.' Helmut was silent. He looked down at his boots and frowned, but didn't say what was on his mind.

'We won't be long.' I peeped out of the shelter and saw that the blackouts were still drawn over the windows of our house. That was hopeful. Probably it was empty.

I went out first, creeping behind the hedge so that Mr and Mrs Dempsey wouldn't see me if they happened to be looking out of their kitchen window as they made breakfast. Daniel and Ash followed me, hats pulled down over their eyes like real spies. I had changed a lot since I left home two years ago, but people might still recognise me, so I kept my head down as we walked through the streets. We walked a long way, to shops that were in another district where I wasn't known. Ash caught the number five bus into the city.

Daniel and I returned with a bag of groceries, to find the shelter empty. My heart skipped a beat then thumped hard against my breastbone. Helmut must have been discovered and taken away. But Daniel soon found him lying in the long grass at the bottom of the garden. Maybe I did need Daniel after all.

It was impossible to stay in the darkness of the shelter all day, so we joined him and watched clouds roll by over our heads as we waited for Ash to return. Every now and then I peered between the bushes to watch the house. The blackouts remained down, the house empty and silent. We would wait till night, then find a way in when we were sure there was nobody inside.

It was dark when Ash returned. Her cheeks were flushed and her eyes bright with excitement. I felt a little envious, wondering if I was old enough to get a job too.

'So?' I asked, as she squeezed into the shelter and secured the door behind her. 'Did you find a job?'

'Wey aye.'

'Doing what?'

'Selling things.'

'What kind of things?' asked Daniel, wriggling down from the bench that we all understood to belong to Ash so that she could stretch out her tired legs.

'Just ordinary things – stockings, hats, that sort uv stuff. And cigarettes. Maybe perfume if we can get it.' She pulled a small bundle from her pocket and unfurled a pair of real silk stockings. A smug smile spread across her face. She kicked off her shoes and reclined, as if on a comfortable settee, dangling the stockings above her head to admire them. I imagined her behind the counter of a glamorous department store, helping beautiful women choose hats and silk stockings. I had no idea how scarce these things had become. To me, the city was still a place of plenty and only in the countryside did we have to make do and mend. In my fantasy of Ash's new world I forgot for a moment that the war had robbed the whole country of luxuries.

'I wish I could work. D'you think I'm old enough to get a job too?' I asked.

'Not right for you, Miz Ellen,' said Helmut. He was looking at Ash with a strange expression on his face — a dark hunger buried beneath a mask of suspicion that narrowed his eyes and drew his lips tight. I didn't like this cold look — Helmut's face was usually kind and thoughtful, intelligent, though sad at times. I could see he was trying to protect me from something, but I didn't understand what. He sighed and leant back against the wall of the shelter. 'I should get job.'

'Not possible!' I exclaimed. 'You'd be caught straight away.'

But his thoughts had slipped far away from us, perhaps back to the home where his mother and brother, who was like a best friend, were waiting for him. He was imagining a job back at home in Muenster, not here in Newcastle with us.

'Maybe I find my way home now. Ships on river sail to many countries. I am too much trouble for you, too much danger I think.' Helmut had been quiet since we arrived in Newcastle, though he was thinking hard, I could tell.

'Helmut, don't go yet,' I whispered, as if the others might not hear me in the cramped space of the shelter. 'Please stay till we can make it safe for you. We'll get you to Ireland, I promise.' I looked into his eyes and there again was the sadness. His face was drawn with lines that had not been there when we first met, almost a year ago now. The skin looked grey. He was as good as a prisoner, trapped in a damp shelter with us, in a city full of enemies and threat, people who would kill him if they could. It occurred to me that he might be better off being captured and imprisoned in a proper camp. But I banished the thought as quickly as it had come. I needed Helmut to stay with me as much as he needed to return home.

'Did they pay you?' Daniel was asking Ash.

'Not yet. Just the stockings, but they're expensive, like.'

'When?'

'Soon. Now stop interrogating me. Is there any food? A'm famished.'

I took out the bread, spam and carrots we had bought earlier, and two more apples we had brought from Mrs Grainger's tree, stored through the winter in the shed and looking soft and wrinkled now. We each stared at our meagre rations but no one complained.

'Sorry, it's the best I can do right now.' I felt the need to apologise even though it wasn't my fault. 'If we can get into the house we'll be able to cook. I'm sure it's empty. Shall we try tonight?'

There was silence. They looked at me, three pairs of eyes sunken within dark hollows cast by the watery torchlight. Three vacant expressions. I turned to Helmut. 'What d'you think, Helmut?'

'I think yes, we try house tonight. I come with you.'

'Thank you.' I sighed with relief. I didn't want to do this alone. 'We'll wait till after midnight, to be sure all the neighbours are asleep, then you can help me get in through the bathroom window. It was always a bit loose and I know how to wriggle it free. We'll need something metal and thin.'

Ash had resumed her manicure.

'That's perfect, your nail file will do it.'

She hesitated, reluctant to give up this small relic of civilised life. 'Divint break it, man, will ye.'

'No, it'll be fine. Thanks Ash. We'll come and get you and Daniel once we've got the back door open. Let's try to get a bit of sleep first.'

Helmut took hold of my hand and smiled at me. His eyes crinkled up and shone in the torchlight. 'You brave girl, Miz

Ellen.' I felt a warm glow spread from my heart, rippling all through my body. What could go wrong with my angel by my side?

This time it was not Daniel but the wailing of the air raid siren that woke us. The sound reverberated through the city and set the corrugated roof of our shelter vibrating each time it soared to an eerie caterwauling. The four of us were immediately sitting bolt upright on the edge of our bench, ready to run. But there was nowhere to run to. We were already where we were meant to be. In Bellingham, the air raid drills had been a wartime game. Here, it was for real. It meant that German planes were coming and might choose us to drop their bombs on tonight.

The faint sound of engines grew louder and rumbled through the night towards us. Daniel suddenly leapt up. As if he had just remembered what the war was about, he grabbed hold of the nearest weapon he could find and lunged towards Helmut. The torch hammered down onto Helmut's skull before he had a chance to defend himself. Daniel began kicking his shins.

'Du Hitler-Mann. Du bist ein Moerder. Scheisse! Arschloch!' he screamed.

'Oh my God! Daniel, stop it!' I tried in vain to hold onto him and drag him off.

Helmut planted his feet on the ground and straightened his back, crossed his arms over his face, and let Daniel beat hell out of him. Daniel pounded his small fists against Helmut's sturdy arms, bone thudding into bone. Ash and I watched aghast, paralysed for a moment.

'Bleedin heck, Daniel, man!' Ash grabbed one of his arms, I grabbed the other, and we wrestled him to the ground. The three of us lay tangled on the damp earth, Daniel pinned down by my knee in his back and the weight of Ash pressing down into his shoulders.

'You alright Helmut?' I gasped.

'It is alright, yes. He had to do this.' He knelt down awkwardly beside Daniel, wincing with pain, and looked into the tear-stained face. He met Daniel's eyes, full of fury and hurt. 'I am sorry for what we did to you – to your family. It was unspeakable bad and wrong.'

Helmut hauled himself back onto the bench and dropped his head into his hands. Daniel huddled against the wall of the shelter and whimpered.

The sirens were still wailing. The engines of the planes rattled and coughed as they ratcheted across the sky. Explosions every few minutes now, booming across the city from some distance away. With each one, my ear-drums throbbed and my heart hollowed out, like a drain sucked dry.

Then a sharp crack, and the door flung open. Two blinding beams of white light flooded into the shelter.

'Who's in there?' a man's voice demanded from behind the light, as it darted about in the darkness. All I could see were streaks of brightness bobbing across my eyeballs, the after-glow of the torch beams striking them. I froze, unable to breathe, my hands caught mid-air as they reached up to rub my throbbing ears. As if I might scream, but I had become mute again. I knew these were my neighbours and they would surely recognise me. The silence sat heavily in the fractured space between us, until finally Ash spoke.

'A'm Marjorie. Is this yer place, like?'

Mr and Mrs Dempsey stepped down into the dampness and closed the door. Ash shuffled along to make room for them on her bench. Daniel slunk up from the ground and perched on the very edge of his, ready to flee if the situation required.

We sat in silence while the sirens continued to whine and the angry planes battled in the night sky above us. I kept my head down, letting my hair fall over my face, afraid they would recognise me. I could feel their gazes scrutinising us. Helmut's body was as taut as steel next to me.

Mr Dempsey shuffled on the bench and his wife moved along to make more room for him. As he shifted to the side, he flashed the torch briefly at Helmut, then me, then Daniel, and back to Helmut. We all ducked our heads down. My hands, still hovering in the air in front of me, came in to shade my eyes from the light. I was burrowing my face deeper into the shadows, hoping not to be seen. The mass of Helmut's body was shrinking beside me, clawing inwards.

I glimpsed Mrs Dempsey nudging her husband's arm and whispering in his ear. He lowered the torch until it was shining on Helmut's foot, stretched out at the end of his wounded leg. The boot with its sole tied on with string was visible. Helmut shifted uncomfortably and drew his leg in as far as the pain would allow, trying to get out of the spotlight.

Eventually Mr Dempsey turned to Ash and answered her question.

'This is Mr Rushton's shelter. We share it with him.'

'It's lucky for you he and his family are away – or there'd be no room for you. It's so cramped,' added Mrs Dempsey, relieved the silence had been broken, wanting to chatter on to hide her nervousness. I had always liked her. She was kind in the way that Mrs Grainger was kind. 'But you must stay now. Oh my goodness, I wonder what they will hit tonight.'

'Bloody Germans. They should come down here and look at the damage they've caused to people's lives. I'd shoot the lot of them if I had the chance.' Out of the corner of my eye I could see him shaking a fist at the roof of the shelter. I remembered Mr Dempsey's tirades, and how Esther would complain about him getting on his high-horse again. Trevor would tell her he was harmless, all bark and no bite, and she should not be upsetting herself about him. The atmosphere in the shelter was sharp as knives. My skin was prickling with the tension. I held tight to Daniel's hand, hoping to stop him from jumping up or screaming or hitting Helmut again, afraid that Mr Dempsey would set him off too, and then all would be lost.

Squeezed between Daniel and Helmut, I could barely breathe. It was as if a fight was still going on between them but it was happening invisibly, inside my body. I began to feel nauseous. To steady my nerves I tried to think of something nice. I remembered rolling down the sand dunes at Bamburgh, but that made the nausea worse. Then I thought about the swing in the garden, but when I realised it was not a distant memory but stood just a few feet outside the shelter, motionless now, this thought brought me right back to where I was. So I tried to remember the day that Helmut and I had played cards all morning in the den, laughing and teasing each other, having fun like a brother and sister might do. This memory worked for a while, and my stomach began to calm.

I slipped my hand into my pocket to see if the pack of cards was there. Maybe I had brought them with me. No, I hadn't. But there was a stone I had picked up from the stream, rubbed smooth and translucent green when washed by the running water, silvery grey when dry. I wanted to take it out to see if my sweaty palms had turned it green but didn't dare draw attention to myself. I kept as still as I could, my hand clasped rigid around the stone.

Mr Dempsey coughed and fidgeted with the woollen blanket he had laid over his knees – in case he was to be stuck in here all night, I supposed. Mrs Dempsey finally broke the uncomfortable silence.

'So, d'you know Mr Rushton?' She directed her question to Helmut who was clearly the eldest of us four, and sitting directly opposite Mr Dempsey. In a normal situation they would have had a manly chat about the war. This wasn't normal though. I could feel Helmut hold in his breath. I felt it in my body – a tightening ring around my throat, and pressure growing from inside my chest, pushing at the ribs, pushing them out. It hurt – they might break. I feared he might explode. I wriggled, nudging Helmut's side. I must get him to breathe. He shifted and half turned his head towards me. He couldn't speak. I couldn't speak.

'Me aunt does,' Ash finally said. She had realised it was up to her to save us now. 'We're on wor way to her place, taking me cousin back.'

'I see. And where is your place. Are you from the city?' she turned to Helmut again. His shoulders twitched with the tension they were holding. Daniel began kicking his feet against the leg of the bench. I hooked my right foot around his left leg and pinned it back, but his right foot kept kicking. I wanted to yell at him to stop, he was driving me crazy.

'He was injured in the war, like. He cannit speak now.'

'Oh dear, poor man,' Mrs Dempsey said, staring at Helmut. I know she would have been genuinely curious about us, but her husband was a nosey parker. I could feel him glowering at Helmut, even though I was looking down at the floor.

Helmut buried his face deeper into his coat collar. I reached out to hold his hand but he pulled it away. I could hear his breath now, sharp and quick. I feared one of us might snap, but Ash kept calmly chatting to Mrs Dempsey about her aunt and their big house in the country.

'She's got six other children, three girls and three boys. Luvly kids, they are. Clever, all at school except wor Edward he-er.' She nodded her head towards Helmut. 'They grow all their own vegetables now, and the girls knit socks for the soldiers. They do what they can, ye know, to help A mean. Me uncle is a train driver.' As Ash prattled on, I thought she was describing her dream of the happy family home she had never known.

The planes finally retreated into the distance, eastwards over the sea, without dropping their bombs on us.

'Must have hit some other buggers south of the river,' grunted Mr Dempsey. He seemed disappointed, as if he had really wanted a battle with the Germans that night. 'Might as well go back to me bed then.' For a moment he didn't move. He looked expectantly at us, waiting for us to leave first. When we didn't, he humphed as he gathered up the blanket he had wrapped around his legs, and stamped heavily up the steps of the shelter. 'C'mon love.' He took one last furtive glance at Helmut before he disappeared into the night. The air tangibly lightened and a certain stale smell that had sifted in with him could now escape.

She followed obediently.

'Take care of yourselves, won't you. Are you off to your aunt's tomorrow, then?' she asked Ash, as she stepped outside. A rush of cool air swept in, a balm to our jangled nerves.

'Expect so, or the next day.'

They left the door ajar, expecting that we would follow them and return to the house. We waited until they were back inside their home then closed the door.

'Jesus, man. A was right scared. What the blazes will we do now?' Ash dropped her head back and looked up, as if answers might be found in the corrugations of the roof.

'You did real well, Ash.' It could've been much worse if they'd recognised me.

'A divina. Now we cannit stay he-er, can we.'

'I guess not. Maybe a day or two, but not long.'

Daniel stood up and faced me. 'I want to go home,' he declared.

'Where? Bellingham?' I asked.

'Home. Berlin. I go with Helmut.' He kicked the dirt and slapped his arms down at his sides. 'Home is better than here.'

'I don't think you can do that, Daniel. Berlin's not safe for you any more. D'you want to go back to Mrs Grainger's?' I meant it kindly, but it came out stark and bare.

He plopped down onto the bench and scowled at me. 'Only if you go too.'

'Once we get Helmut away, I can take you back. Or we can put you on the train tomorrow. Maybe that's best …'

'Only if you come back too.'

Because I knew Daniel in his stubborn moods, I decided to say no more. I was getting a headache. I felt trapped and all I longed for was slipping away. I didn't even know what

I longed for any more, except that it would have to include Helmut. He had gone outside while we were talking. I went out to find him.

Against the orange glow of a sky lit up by fires, I could make out his tall shape between the dark walls of our house and the Dempseys', just before he disappeared into the street. I ran after him. I was always afraid he might leave, without a word, without warning. His injured leg, clearly more painful after Daniel's beating, slowed him down and I easily caught up with him.

'Are you leaving us Helmut – without saying goodbye?'

'No, I just need to walk. Need to think.' We walked for some minutes in silence. I hooked my hand into the crease of his elbow and he squeezed it tight. I knew he liked me, but maybe not as much as I liked him. And I was not sure if he needed me any longer.

'What d'you think we should do?'

'I cannot put you all in danger like this. I will find way by myself now. You and Daniel go back home on train, then I leave.' He glanced at me then took a deep breath and looked straight ahead, his jaw set and his arm pressing my hand firmly against his side. 'I will be o-kay, Miz Ellen, do not worry.'

'I want to come with you.' When I felt Helmut beside me, I felt a man with a family, a history, a home, a mother and father. I wanted him, and I wanted all that was part of him, but it was impossible to tell him this. 'I'm going to stay with you, Helmut. Please don't stop me.'

'You very kind. After war is over, I write to you and we meet again. You good friend to me, Miz Ellen.'

That sounded so final. Tears pricked my eyes as we walked through the night streets, arm in arm. Helmut my angel, my brother, my friend. I didn't know quite what he was to me. In that moment, I thought he was everything, and once again in my life everything was about to be taken away from me.

<h1 style="text-align:center">24</h1>

It seemed best to enter the house, in the dark, as we had planned. The Dempseys would be suspicious if we stayed all night and all day in the shelter, like uninvited guests, which, of course, we were.

Helmut helped me onto the roof of the small porch that sheltered the kitchen door and handed me the nail file and a torch, just in case the electricity had been switched off. I thought I could find my way in the dark and didn't need a torch – I knew my way around this house blindfold – but I didn't know what Esther might have left to trip me up. It was easy to wriggle the nail file under the latch of the bathroom window and prise it open, but harder to unstick the tape that kept the blackout in place, then slide myself through the narrow opening. I landed in the washbasin. A pool of cold water had gathered from a dripping tap. I thought it was odd that Trevor had left the plug in, but I suppose he was closing the house up against all possible invasions and spiders used to enter this way.

A damp musty smell filled the house and the air felt cold and thin, despite it being nearly summer. The electricity hadn't been turned off, but still I used the torch as I crept down stairs to the kitchen, like a burglar, and opened the back door.

'All okay. Get the others,' I whispered, and Helmut slipped back through the shadows to bring Ash and Daniel to our new hiding place. We were all tired. Tomorrow I would show them around the house, but now all we wanted was to find somewhere to sleep.

That night I lay on my own bed again. It had been stripped of sheets so I wrapped myself in a scratchy woollen blanket and tried to sleep. The dip in the middle of the mattress, the lumpy edges, the two pillows, one too thick and one too thin to be really comfortable – all so familiar that my body yielded into the shape I had made for it in my younger years. But I had grown and it was no longer a cosy fit. The springs of the old iron bedstead creaked as I turned and wriggled, trying to find the hollows that would hold my new shape.

The blacked out darkness of the room unnerved me, so I switched on a side lamp but that was too bright and still I couldn't sleep. I looked around my room, my childhood room. My toys had been stored away somewhere, or perhaps thrown out, and only a few small china animals that I had bought in seaside gift shops, one each year on our annual holiday, sat in a row along the top of the dressing table. The room was so tidy I barely recognised it as my own. The flowery wallpaper was the same but the paintings of trees and birds that had hung there were gone. Only rectangles of brighter colour remained where the wallpaper had been protected from the dust and sunlight. It was as if my spirit had been erased when I was sent to Bellingham.

Ash slept on Esther and Trevor's bed, with instructions not to go inside the clean crisp sheets. I would never have dared to sleep there. I could smell Esther's perfume in the tired air. Her ghost hovered, as if she were already dead and seeking to wreak her revenge on me for loving a German pilot more, much more, than I loved her.

Daniel fell asleep on the floor of the spare room, amidst boxes and old clothes, a sewing machine, brooms and other odds and ends that, like Daniel, had no home of their own. Helmut had the settee downstairs. He would keep watch for anyone trying to enter the house. This was his first soldierly duty since his plane had crashed and he seemed relieved to take on the responsibility of protecting us, though his presence there was the biggest risk of all for us. We each knew this.

After the dank earth of the shelter and sleeping upright on a wooden bench, the comfort of a lumpy mattress and pillow seemed a luxury. We had an indoor toilet and running water to wash in, though we couldn't work out how to heat it. In the morning Ash and I scrambled our egg substitute ration on the gas stove and made toast, then she left for her job in the city. We felt almost like an ordinary family preparing for the day. I found a copy of *Robinson Crusoe* for Daniel and he retreated into the front room, grateful for this escape into another world. Daniel needed books like most of us need food, water and friendship – this I had learnt about him very early on. Probably he wouldn't make the connection between the castaway's situation and his own – better not to compare realities too closely.

Helmut and I sat in the kitchen with Esther's green teapot and two matching green cups full of the hot and bitter liquid on the table between us. I treasured these moments when there were just the two of us. For a while we sat without words, before a loud rap on the kitchen door startled me out of my private thoughts. I jumped up to open it and there was Mr Dempsey standing in the doorway, dressed up for work in a brown tweed suit and matching waistcoat that was so tight it almost burst its buttons off. He had put on weight despite the rationing. His shiny bald head glistened in the grey morning light.

'Ah, good morning. Just thought I'd check you were all okay, have everything you need?' He was looking over my head and surveying the kitchen, examining Helmut, so had not really taken me in. I turned away to hide my face.

'Yes, fine thank you Mr Dempsey.' As soon as I said it I realised it was a mistake. They hadn't introduced themselves last night. He turned to look at me and stared for a moment,

then his eyes and mouth opened wide, as if his brain had lit
up with the realisation that had landed there.

'Aha, young Ellen isn't it? I didn't recognise you in the
dark last night. My, you've grown.' He kept staring, boring
with his eyes right through mine like a miner digging for coal
in the dark. I tried to hide myself from his gaze, putting up a
barrier behind my own eyes, but he kept on coming after me.
'You didn't introduce yourself to us. Now why could that be,
I wonder?' I was silent, my words had dried up again, so Mr
Dempsey turned his attention to Helmut. His blonde hair and
blue eyes were like a ray of sunshine in the dingy light of the
kitchen. All signs of black boot polish had gone.

'And you're the cousin who can't speak.' He spat this out
as if the words offended him. 'I wonder why Mr Rushton
never mentioned you – a brave soldier in the family – I'd have
thought he would be proud to tell us all about you?' Helmut
simply nodded and looked down at the table. Neither of us
could answer, but Mr Dempsey kept talking anyway.

'Odd that Mr Rushton didn't mention you were coming
home.' He was addressing me now. I was shrinking into myself,
becoming smaller, bone by bone. Becoming the young girl who
couldn't speak again. He must have sensed this and barrelled
on even more forcefully. 'He wrote to us just last week, had
some post he wanted us to collect for him – before he comes
for his monthly visit. Always visits at the end of the month,
just to check up on things. But I expect you know that. No
doubt that's why you've come now, so you'll see him.' His
eyes burrowed further into me – a question, a judgement? 'A
bit odd, we always thought, that you never came back to visit
your parents, but it's not really our business, is it.' There was an
unpleasant smirk on his face, just a hint, an odd way that his
lips widened towards a smile then turned down at the corners
at the very last moment. His eyes narrowed as he spoke to me
and I felt accused. I had been a bad daughter and now I was
up to something no good, though he didn't know quite what.

Keeping up a one-sided conversation clearly proved a strain, even for the loquacious Mr Dempsey, so eventually he left, assuring us that he or his wife would drop by later to make sure we were alright.

'Ellen, I will go today. I know you do not want, but I must go. I am too danger for you all. You could stay here if you like, live in your house. Why not?' Helmut's face was drawn with tension, his eyes deep with anxious fear.

I felt miserable. This house was like death to me, and I would rather risk everything than stay here without him, but I knew he was right. Now that we had been discovered we couldn't hide Helmut here much longer.

'I'm coming with you. I will help you find – something – a ship to Europe, a train to Ireland – I don't know.' I flailed my arms about as I spoke. Words were deserting me again. I battled to pull them back. 'Where will you go? Let me come with you, Helmut.'

I would not hear no. In the end we agreed that I would take him as far as the city, then he insisted I must abandon him to his fate. So we left the house, with Daniel immersed in Robinson Crusoe's world and a convenient mist outside to shroud us as we walked towards the city centre, hats pulled down over our eyes and collars turned up. We marched, swinging our arms, attempting to look bold and purposeful.

If I had looked back I might have noticed a flicker of the net curtains next door, glimpsed Mr Dempsey watching us from his sitting room window. But I didn't look back. I didn't understand how much suspicion was on every street corner, in every neighbour's heart.

Act Three

25

I am looking down on my young self, fourteen-year-old Ellen, as if from a great height. Her face is pale and gaunt, framed by auburn hair that's un-brushed and uncut, hanging limp over her shoulders. Her limbs are thin and too long for her clothes, her shoes scuffed and worn. I am filled with sadness and concern. I see her in danger, naïve, brave, reckless. Take care Ellen, I cry out, but my voice is lost in the distance between us. I look into eyes that are no more than dark hollows and I feel afraid. It is myself I am looking into.

There's a face hovering over me. She has kind eyes. Her hair is grey and crinkled. Is it you Liza? Have I arrived?

'Liza – my mother?' I reach out to take your hand but it slips through my grasp like smoke. Now I hear you.

'I think she's conscious. She's trying to speak,' I hear you say. 'Now you just relax love. Try to stay calm … 'Your voice wavers and vibrates in the shimmering air, then falls away like a waterfall cascading over the edge. Everything trembles. The world is rushing up to meet me and my heart is pounded into my throat. I am choking with the force of it, the force of my heart pushing up. I cannot breathe, I cannot swallow.

I feel your hand come into mine, squeeze it gently. There is the scratching sensation over my face again, and then a rush of air fills my body so that I blow up like wings. I am swept up in my angel's wing once more.

'Let me tell you what happened next. Please listen.' But I can't speak now. The breath is rushing out of me. I feel you holding my hand but I am soaring upwards and must let go. Now I am drifting in the sky. It is white. You would not believe how white the sky is here.

'Helmut!' I gasp. Now I see his face, up in the sky above me.

Act Two

26

We stood on the Tyne Bridge, Helmut by my side beneath the grand steel arches, looking out along the river, east and west. It glistened through the mist like a snaking ribbon of silvered glass. Downriver, every ship was painted the same flat grey and flying the British flag, bristled with guns and radar. Of course, if Germany had defeated the countries to the east, across the sea from us, no merchant ships would come from there. I had imagined he might stowaway on a ship to Europe, but not on these killing machines.

'No chance. You could never hide on one of those – not even get on board.' We peered down on the massive grey hulks that billowed up towards us through the mist. I felt an uncomfortable fascination, mingled with a shiver of fear that ran up my spine and made me clutch my jacket tight across my chest.

'I'm sorry – I thought it would be easier. There used to be fishing boats and big ferries – all along there.' I waved my arm vaguely downstream, where the riverbanks were now clad in grey instead of the colourful flags and clanking ropes of hundreds of small vessels.

'No. Train is better chance.' Helmut looked nervously

about, knowing that his broken English could give him away. Every word he spoke was like a beacon to his enemies, my countrymen, people like Esther and Trevor.

'Let's go to the station then. See what we can find out there.' His jumpiness was contagious and I startled as a truck flashed by, honking its horn at a boy who had leapt off the path and sped across the road in front of it.

Helmut glanced to his right, along the path of the bridge, and I felt a jolt go through him. His shoulders tensed as he took a sharp breath. I followed his gaze to where two men were standing, some distance from us, also looking down on the ships below. He was gripping his hands into fists and breathing fast. I felt the blood freeze in my veins.

'No, I go alone. It is time I leave now. You stay here, Ellen. Please, not follow me.' He took hold of my shoulders and looked straight into my eyes. 'Thank you for everything. We will see us when the war is over. I promise.' And with that he turned and limped briskly along the bridge, away from me, out of my life.

For a moment I felt paralysed as I watched him stride out. Then the two men in dark brown coats and trilby hats were running past me, coats flapping and pigeons skittering out of their path. I glimpsed a flash of polished metal poking out from beneath a coat sleeve – each had a pistol in his hand, held ready. Now Helmut was running too. I began to run after the men in the hats who were running after Helmut. How did they know?

A group of people crossing the bridge jumped quickly out of our path. No one tried to stop me and I kept up with the men. I was a good runner. It was in my blood, Trevor used to say.

Once over the bridge Helmut ran faster than I thought possible with his bad leg – along busy roads, weaving between market stalls, and finally disappearing into a narrow alleyway. We followed, but I couldn't keep my eye on him as he darted through a crowd, up a short flight of stone steps, and out of sight. I ran after the two men, but they had lost sight of him too. They stopped and turned to see me some distance behind them, flushed and breathless. One of them began to walk back towards me, his eyes intent on me, burning through me. I turned and fled the other way.

I knew I was in serious trouble now, but still I wanted to find Helmut, still sure I could help him. I darted and dodged between the people and the cars and buses on the street, past a rubble heap that had once been a building, past the drab shop-fronts and broken windows. I slipped through the big glass door of Binns and mingled with the women shopping for cloth and shoes and underwear, until I was sure the man was no longer following me.

To give myself time, I picked a skirt from a rail and asked the shop assistant if I could try it on. In the changing room I sat down on the floor and waited for my breath to ease and my heart to stop pounding against my ribs. It felt bruised, but more from the wrench of losing Helmut than from the effort of the chase. I could not let myself believe that this was the end of him – that we would never meet again.

'Are you all right in there? Would you like to try another size?' came a woman's voice from outside the cubicle. I startled to, confused and for a moment uncertain of where I was.

'I'm fine. No, I don't need another size, thank you.' I scrambled to my feet and took the skirt from the hook, still on its hanger, all clean and pressed and modestly navy blue. For a second I longed to be able to buy the new skirt, but what use would it be to me, really? I handed it back to the sales assistant.

I would make my way back to the alley where I had last seen him. Foolish perhaps, but I could not just let him slip out of my life like this, not knowing. A force I had no control over was drawing me back to him – a deep physical need to feel him by my side. This was a new feeling – the sense of comfort and safety and warmth that I had when Helmut was near. I wondered if this was what it felt like to have a real mother, and a father, but there was no time to dwell on such a question now.

As I emerged onto the street three soldiers ran past, faces red and sweating from the sultry warmth of the afternoon, guns slung over shoulders that knuckled down to the chase. Low clouds were gathering above the city, threatening rain. I followed the soldiers, sure that they must have been called in to capture Helmut – or worse, to shoot him dead.

I had to keep them in my sight without making it obvious that I was pursuing them, but I was small enough to hide in the crowd and I knew I could out-run them if I had to, burdened as they were by heavy boots and thick army clothing. As they drew to a halt at a street corner, I turned to look in a shop window, keeping them just in sight, in the corner of my eye. My heart was racing, my palms sticky and my mouth sandpaper dry.

With his injured leg, I knew Helmut couldn't have gone very far. He would have to depend on something other than speed if he was to escape them. I had to think like him, work out what he might do, but I had no idea how he really thought, what kind of tactic or skill he might use. With some dismay I realised that I barely knew him at all, how he felt, who he loved, what he remembered from the past, how he imagined his life in the future would be. I only saw the man I wanted him to be. All I knew was that he longed to return home. And I longed for him to stay here, with me. With some shame, I realised that my intentions were purely selfish. I didn't really want him to find a way back to Germany. If we could help him reach Ireland, I would stay with him there. But I had no vision of a life beyond that.

The three soldiers stood at the corner, unsure which road to take. There was a heated discussion. After a while they split up, one continuing along Market Street, another turning up a road to the left, and the third coming back the way we had come. Under the awning of the shop, I turned my back to him as he marched past, staring at the scant display of pipes, tobacco and cigars.

Remembering our journey into the city earlier in the day,

calculating how quickly Helmut had been able to walk, I began to work out how far he might have gone since I lost sight of him. In my mind I created a map of the area he could have covered, then I went back to the bridge and began to follow the route he had taken. As I hurried back through the streets I was trying to get a sense of how he might have been thinking – did he have a plan, any idea at all how to escape the soldiers? What would he have done once he threw them off his trail? I arrived back in the lane where I had last seen him.

Soot-blackened walls pressed in on the claustrophobic alleyway, their grimy windows criss-crossed with iron bars. Here and there a few worn stone slabs led up to a closed door, giving no clue as to what lay behind the walls. As I reached the top of the flight of steps at the end of the alley a light rain began to fall. I pulled up my jacket collar as I stopped to get my bearings. Ahead was a small cobbled square with five narrow roads radiating from it. There were five ways I could go.

A numbness settled into my heart, but it helped me to focus on the task, allowed a stubborn determination to take over. I stopped thinking about whether I was right or wrong to want Helmut to stay with me, whether he might be shot or imprisoned if he were caught, and set my mind to simply finding him. I began to run, up one lane then down another, bumping into women who stood on street corners in tight gossiping groups, peering into open doorways, down alleys, this way and that, until I was exhausted.

A persistent drizzle had set in and my jacket was damp right through. I could not find Helmut.

I arrived home late that evening to find Daniel wandering about the dark house from room to room, clutching his mother's hat. Ash was not back yet and Daniel was alone and frightened. He glowered at me then stomped off into the front room, slamming the door behind him. I waited a few minutes before following him, opening the door slowly and tiptoeing in so as not to startle him.

'Sorry I'm late, Daniel. I lost Helmut. I don't know where he is.' I dropped into an armchair and burst into tears. 'He's gone. Soldiers are after him – if they catch him – they'll shoot him,' I blurted out between sobs.

Daniel came over to me, shuffling through the dark room from the corner where he had been slumped, and put an arm awkwardly around my shoulder. 'Don't worry. I help you find him. I know how.' The tense, bony embrace gave me little comfort, but I was grateful for the intention behind it.

'I know you do, Daniel. But this is serious, and dangerous. I can't let you get involved.'

'He is my prisoner too. I will find him and keep him.'

I smiled grimly to myself. Poor Daniel. Believing that Helmut was his prisoner let him feel there was a possibility of avenging his parents' deaths. It was the only way he had to feel strong – a sense of moral superiority his only way to feel he possessed anything at all in the world. Hatred sustained him to the point where he was almost as dependent on Helmut as I was.

We were still crouched in the dark like this, me curled up in the chair, Daniel sitting on the arm beside me, when the back door opened and closed with a bang.

'Crikey, are ye's all dead in he-er?' Where's everyone?' The light went on in the hallway and after a few moments of clattering about with shoes and bag Ash found us there, huddled in the darkness of the front room. 'What's up with ye both? Has owt happened?'

'Helmut's gone. Soldiers were after him.' I didn't have the energy to say more. I uncurled myself out of the chair and left Daniel to tell her whatever he wanted to as I went up to the sparse sanctuary of my room.

True to his word Mr Dempsey knocked on the kitchen door

the next morning, at exactly the same time. I realised this could become a habit.

'Good morning Ellen, Marjorie – ah, the young lad's here too. And what's your name, sonny?'

Daniel looked at me. I nodded. There was not much point in hiding anything from Mr Dempsey. He would find out what he wanted to know one way or another.

'I am Daniel,' he answered in his dense German accent, then returned to his book and didn't say another word. The bald, overweight Mr Dempsey raised his eyebrows, but didn't comment. He turned to Ash and me.

'So – when do you plan to take your cousin home – to your aunt's house, you said, did you not? Or has he already gone?' Mr Dempsey was looking towards the open door and listening for signs of Helmut in the house.

'He'll be going very soon, Mr Dempsey. Now divint ye worry yersel about him like. It's all in hand,' Ash said in a firm tone that shut him up for the moment. 'Now, if ye divint mind, A must be going to town now.' She opened the door and gestured for him to leave. He looked ruffled by this, by Ash's manner, but he left, tipping an imaginary hat towards the two of us and muttering something about Mrs Dempsey coming round with some bread tomorrow.

'Bleedin nosey-parker!' Ash exclaimed the moment the door was shut. 'A divint like people nosing in me business. He'd better watch out, that man, or A'll have his guts for garters.' I wished I could feel as brave as Ash, but Mr Dempsey was making trouble and I was getting scared that Trevor would come home soon. Perhaps Mr Dempsey had already told him I was here, and that he should come quickly. He would do something like that, I was sure. Interfering pompous old fool – that was one thing even Esther had been right about.

Daniel and I went with Ash to the city, travelling on the

morning bus. I wanted to see where she worked but she said no, I couldn't go there, and anyway, Daniel and I had important work to do ourselves. So we got off at the Haymarket while she stayed on to the end of the route. We were armed with a big potato sack that I had found in the pantry, and a plan that Daniel had drawn of the steps leading to the cobbled square, and the five roads leading off it.

We stood at the top of the steps, Daniel holding the map as he instructed me.

'We begin with first street on the left. We go up left side to end, then down right side, back here.'

'But how far? When will we know it's the end?'

'Like you measured. How far he can go.'

'But by today he could have gone further.'

'Never mind. We go far, and see when we get there.' Daniel was enjoying his own sense of organisation and would not be swayed by my doubts. He was like Esther in this and it irritated me intensely, but I had failed on my own to find Helmut so today I would put myself in Daniel's obsessive hands and do as he told me.

We turned down the first road where there were several shops before an endless row of terraced houses began, their front doors opening right onto the street. Daniel went into the first shop and I followed, the sack tucked under my arm. He had a good look round the shop while I talked to the assistant.

'Good morning, Madame. We're collecting old clothes and shoes for the homeless, for the soldiers, cloth for bandages, anything useful for the war effort. I wonder if you have anything at all you could give?' I asked in the politest way I knew.

She looked at me with suspicion. 'Does your mam know you're out doing this?'

'Oh yes, she's collecting too – Women's Institute, you know.'

'I see. Well, let me have a think.' She opened a door behind the counter and disappeared into the dark. Daniel was there right behind her, peering in, taking in every detail of the gloomy room – its one chair, a small table, a sink, an empty fireplace and no window. Stacks of cardboard boxes sat along the walls. The woman ignored these, went over to the sink and pulled out some cloth from a bucket that sat beneath it. We darted away from the doorway as she turned back to the shop.

'That's all I have at the moment – but maybe it'll do for bandages or the like. They're clean.' She handed me the bundle of tea cloths and I put them into the sack.

'That's very kind of you. Thank you.' We quickly took our leave.

'Anything there?' I asked Daniel once we were out of view of the shop window.

'No, nothing there, no way out, no place to hide.' He made some notes on his map, in German, then we went to the next shop.

The smell of baking bread set our taste buds tingling and for a moment we both all but forgot why we were there. I stood in the queue of women while Daniel mooched around unnoticed amidst the lively conversation and the bustle of the baker's assistant and the shop girls. The baker's was always busy – everyone wanted bread in the war, to fill up their empty stomachs.

It was odd how Daniel could become invisible if he wanted to, when usually his insatiable need for attention pressed his presence into my awareness at every moment. He slipped into the back room, the bakery, behind the assistant who carried an empty tray ready to be refilled with the grey loaves we all had to eat during the war. Five minutes later he came out carrying a brown paper bag, the ends of two stale loaves sticking out. It was my turn at the counter so I got out my coupons and a few pennies and bought a fresh loaf, before joining Daniel on the road.

'We must look behind.' Daniel marched off down the street to find the wooden door that led down a passageway to the back lane. We found the back gate of the bakery unlocked and slipped inside. There was nobody around so Daniel poked and peered while I stood on guard. A shed was full of junk that left no room for a human intruder to hide, and there was nothing else of interest there.

We returned to the street. In the barber's I asked if they could spare any old cloth for the war effort.

'Nothing like that he-er luv, though the missus might have some old clothes back home.' The barber eyed Daniel. 'The lad could do with a cut though. How about it son? No charge for ye this time, since ye'r helping the war effort, like.'

I opened my eyes wide at Daniel and nodded, to indicate 'Go on.' With a pout of resistance he nevertheless climbed into the chair and submitted his tangled mass of dark hair to the barber's scissors.

'Could I possibly use your toilet while I wait?' I asked, again in my politest voice.

'Course luv. Out back, in the yard.'

I searched carefully. No sign of a German pilot hiding, not in the back room or the yard.

The barber tried to give Daniel the pudding bowl cut that all small boys wore in those days, but it didn't quite work out on his wiry curls. He ended up with something that looked like a small black umbrella perched on the crown of his head. Daniel scowled at the barber, then at me, but to his credit he didn't complain.

'Don't worry,' I whispered as we reached the street again. 'Ash can tidy it up for you when we get back.' He scrunched up his face in disgust, but didn't say a word. It was, after all, a small sacrifice in the greater scheme of what we had set out to do.

The day passed. We went up the first road and back down, knocking on every door, asking for donations for the war effort, getting into the houses when we could. Some people were kind and even gave us tea to drink. Others shooed us away and slammed doors in our faces. Those people we suspected, and found ways to creep round to their back yards.

After we had scoured the first three roads, night was setting in and we had to go back, exhausted and dejected – me because I had not found Helmut – Daniel because he had failed at the task he had set himself.

The next day we continued searching the area – the shops, the lanes and back yards, knocking on each house door, peering into every coal shed and outside toilet we could find. By the time we had covered the five roads that led off the cobbled square our potato sack was full of scraps and Daniel's map was covered in spidery scribbles as he noted every detail of our search. But we had failed to find Helmut.

I was careful to leave the sack of rags for the poor and the homeless outside the Women's Institute hall on our way back that second evening. It would have been dishonest not to.

Daniel and I were in a dark mood when Ash arrived home. She was wearing a new red dress that hugged her body tight, and thick make-up around her eyes. She laced herself around a kitchen chair and crossed her legs.

'Well? D'ye like it?'

'Ash, you were meant to be earning money to get us to Ireland, not buy dresses.' I was angry and could have ripped the dress off her back.

'A hav'na bought it. Me boss gave it to us. A present for me good work.'

'Ash, what did you do?' I felt suddenly afraid of this grown up world that she had inhabited, so easily, so naturally, as if she had been born for it. A world that I knew nothing about.

'A've acquired some special goods. Perfume – it's rare these days, ye know. He's right pleased with us.' She grinned and slid her hand into her bag. 'An look, me first wages as well.' She took some food coupons and two pounds in silver coins out of a small brown envelope and placed them on the table.

I wanted to be pleased at this, but the fear was growing into a fist in my stomach. I was not sure what I feared exactly, but I knew that something had changed and the ground beneath me was giving way. Helmut had gone. Ash was behaving strangely. Still I had a plan to go to Ireland, but without him, why would I do that?

'We've lost Helmut, you know.'

'Ah, flippin heck, man. Ye should let him get away. He'll be aalreet, like as found his way back home by now.'

'Can't you help us look for him, Ash? He's your friend too – I thought you liked him.'

'Wey aye, A like him, but he's not wor problem, really.' Ash took out her nail file and began the ritual that indicated the conversation was over as far as she was concerned.

'Ash, we have to leave here. Mr Dempsey – he's nosing around too much. And I'm afraid Trevor might come back any day now. It's nearly the end of the month and Mr Dempsey said …'

'Aw, ye divint wanna be listening to that ol' divvie. A bet he's lying about that.'

'He might not be, and I don't want to be here when Trevor comes back. Let's find Helmut and go to Ireland.' I must have sounded as desperate as I felt because Ash became exasperated with me.

'Hell Ell, ye cannit find Helmet. The two of ye should go back to Bellingham if ye divint wanna stay he-er.' She put the nail file down on the table between us and looked at me for the first time since she had come in. 'An anyway, me boss says A can stay at his place if A like, so A think that's what A'll do.'

Now the ground inside me was crumbling. I felt sick and the strength was draining from my legs. I stared at Ash but she began to blur around the edges, like a reflection in restless water.

'Don't leave us, Ash,' I tried to say, but no sound came out.

At that moment there was a knock on the door and there stood Mrs Dempsey, holding a loaf of fresh-baked bread in her hands.

'I thought you might need some more, the four of you,' she said, offering the loaf to the room in general. None of us moved. I was in shock at what Ash had just said. She was uninterested in Mrs Dempsey's loaf. Daniel was in a foul mood and wouldn't take his nose out of his book.

'Shall I just put it here then?' She stepped into the kitchen and took a step towards the table.

'Oh yes, thank you, very kind of you,' I muttered, recovering a little bit of myself.

'So your father will be back home in a couple of days. That's nice for you. I expect you'll be staying till he comes then? You must be looking forward to seeing him, Ellen pet, after so long away from home.' Her voice was soft and rather wistful. She was a thin and fragile woman, timid beside her husband's bombast and bluster.

I couldn't think what to say, so I just looked at her. She understood. She had known me as a child with a habit of not speaking, and would assume I still had this affliction.

'Never mind, pet,' she said, as if to confirm this thought. She backed awkwardly towards the door when still none of us responded. 'I'll be going then.'

'Yes.' How rude I sounded, but I just could not muster the energy to say anything else, after two whole days of speaking politely to strangers. Mrs Dempsey left and closed the kitchen door behind her.

'Well, that's it then.' I got up from the table. I had no idea what *it* was, but I knew I had to prepare for something else to happen very soon.

<h1 style="text-align:center">27</h1>

That night I couldn't sleep. I tossed in my bed until the blankets were twisted around me so tight I couldn't move at all. Then I gave up struggling to fall asleep and surrendered to the tears that my frayed nerves had pushed to the surface. I felt lost and utterly alone. Even Daniel couldn't help me now, as he had sunk into a morass of sullenness. The feeling of failure was unbearable to him and I did not have the will or the energy to coax him back to life this time.

I wondered if I should continue to search for Helmut around the back lanes and yards of Newcastle, but I had no idea where to look next, and the city was big and sprawling. I needed Ash's help more than ever. She always had a bright new idea. With her on my side I would feel bold and brave again, but without her I feared my own despair might take me down with Daniel into a private hell that neither of us could crawl out of. One thing was certain. I must leave before Trevor returned – that gave me less than two days.

By the time the house began to stir I had finally fallen into a restless sleep, and it was hard to pull myself back up again. I could hear Ash and Daniel arguing about who was to use the bathroom first – Ash won the argument, of course – a door slamming, footsteps on the stairs. I missed the sound of Helmut moving around in the room below.

A head thick with tiredness, my eyes red and itchy, I untangled myself from the blankets and stumbled out of bed. I peeled open the blackout and a watery light trickled into the room. It hurt the backs of my eyes. My nerves were jangled with exhaustion and a wave of nausea held me in its grip. I could have fallen right back into bed and slept all day, but I knew I didn't have a day to lose. Trevor would be on his way home soon and I must act now if I was to avoid being imprisoned in his and Esther's world again. I pulled on my clothes and splashed cold water on my face, then stepped dizzily down the stairs.

Predictably, Mr Dempsey arrived while we were eating our bread and dripping. We had finished all of Mrs Grainger's apples, so there was nothing to sweeten the bland taste but a cup of tea – with one spoonful of sugar each, half our daily ration.

'Good morning, Ellen – Marjorie – Daniel.' He looked pointedly at the kitchen door and raised his eyebrows into a question mark, expecting an explanation as to where Helmut was, but he got none from us.

'Morning, Mister. On yer way to work then?' Ash looked at him defiantly. He looked down. He could not face Ash eye to eye – she had a power over him, and this was not a situation he was familiar or comfortable with at all. He was used to intimidating people, if he so chose, not the other way round.

'Yes, on my way. Life must go on, despite the war,' he muttered. His vain attempt at sounding wise and philosophical came across as painfully banal. Daniel noticed this, and for the first time that morning he looked up from his book and glared at Mr Dempsey.

'No, not all life goes on. Some life does not go on.' He was staring darkly at the startled Dempsey, as if he were the one responsible for shooting his father on the Berlin stairs. The man's eyes seemed to sink into his podgy pink cheeks and shrivel back inside his head, like the lashless eyes of a pig.

'No, of course not,' he declared, too loudly, and coughed, trying to salvage something of his dignity from this unsettling conversation. 'Well, I'll be on my way then.'

'Aye,' said Ash.

I observed all of this in silence, wondering what he would tell Trevor about me and my new friends when he saw him.

'Blimmin heck, what a divvie!' Ash glowered at the door as it closed behind him. She finished her breakfast and put her plate and cup in the sink for me to wash up later. I was looking at Daniel who continued to stare at the space Mr Dempsey had just vacated.

'Daniel, wake up.' I gently tugged at his sleeve. We could do without one of his turns just at that moment. 'Look, why don't you stay in today and read your book. I'll go to the shops on my own – and see if I can find out about trains while I'm there.' I was not sure which trains I wanted to find out about, but at least I would feel I was doing something. Daniel scuffed off to the front room, carrying his book in one hand and a piece of dry bread in the other. He was miserable. I regretted that we had brought him with us and had no idea what to do with him now. Perhaps we should go back to Bellingham, as Ash suggested, but once Mr Dempsey had told his tales to Trevor I was sure he would come looking for me there. I felt the world was closing in on me like a vice. Once again I was trapped in our house in Newcastle, with nowhere to escape to.

Ash was picking up her handbag and coat. She had on her red dress and lipstick to match. I felt a hint of envy creep into my heart. She seemed free. Whilst the three of us had become imprisoned in our suffering, she had broken out of hers and had stepped into an exciting new life. War had liberated Ash. I thought it had brought me freedom too, but now everything was going wrong.

All I had to hold onto now was the idea of Ash's bright future, as if maybe this could save all four of us. After she left the house I put on my jacket and shoes and followed her, keeping far enough behind so that, I hoped, she would not see me if she turned around. When she caught the bus and disappeared from view, I waited until the next number five came along. I knew she took the bus to its final stop.

It was near the station, the goods station. I was surprised to find that I was where I needed to be.

Later I would look for Ash, but first I snooped around the station, checked departure boards, inspected wagons all hooked up and ready to be loaded or waiting to leave the station with their cargoes of coal and food, wood and steel, petrol for the cars and bomber planes. The whole story of the war could be read here in this railway depot, the scarcity and the preciousness of goods exchanging hands, being moved across the country, keeping the whole great war machine going. A long trundling train arrived while I was there. I watched the men who set to unloading the wagons. Great cranes took hold of heavy containers like a child's fist picking up an empty matchbox. There was much commotion as vehicles came and went, containers were emptied, filled, moved, replaced with others. I could sit invisibly in the shadows of a brick arch, one in a long row of arches that overlooked the platforms. It wasn't yet clear to me how I might make use of all this information, but I was sure it would help once I found Helmut. We could surely find a way onto a goods train bound for Ireland.

I must have sat for hours because eventually I realised I was hungry and thirsty. I left my hiding place and slipped unnoticed out of the station. The unfamiliar road ran through an area of factories and warehouses, interspersed with patches of derelict land. There was not a tree or blade of grass in sight. The grey road and blackened walls of factory buildings merged with the leaden sky to create a grim impression, a kind of purgatory of the senses. All I could smell was coal smoke and rotting sewage that had leaked out somewhere. I walked until I found a road with a few shops, a terrace of small houses, and a pub on the corner.

As I walked past the pub I peeped in. I was hungry, thirsty and desperately needed to use the toilet. I didn't know if I dared go into such a place as this. The room was dark and smoky, full of men's voices and coarse laughter. The occasional chime of a female voice rose above the grumbling din. I stood in the doorway, between the daylight and the murky world inside.

'Come on luv, get a move on,' a voice behind me chided. An arm scooped around my shoulder and propelled me into the bar as the man and his mate squeezed through the narrow doorway with me. I was inside. Stronger than anything else was the urge to pee, so, without further thought, I searched for the Ladies sign and boldly crossed the room. Relief.

I didn't dare ask for food or drink here though. I was heading for the exit again when a flash of red from the corner of the bar caught my eye. It was Ash. Sitting at a table, with two men. Drinking an amber coloured liquid from a tall glass and laughing at their jokes. She appeared happy and confident, sitting as she was with her long legs crossed and her hair shining in a streak of sunlight that fell through the frosted window across her shoulders. Like a queen with her courtiers around her, I thought, she seemed perfectly at home here. Suddenly I understood the new life she had found, and why she didn't want to leave it.

I felt small, dull, insecure and defeated. Beside Ash I was insignificant. I couldn't possibly let her see me – my hair limp with grease and coal dust, my clothes plain and old. She would guess that I had followed her and I couldn't bear the humiliation of being found out, this heaped upon an already dwindling sense of myself as a person with any worth at all. Dazed, my mind reeling with the revelation of Ash's new world, I slipped invisibly out of the pub and leant against the wall outside to recover my balance. My breath was short and jagged and a lump had lodged in my throat, a thick ball of lead that I could neither swallow nor spit out. I knew that I had lost Ash forever.

28

I forgot my hunger and thirst. I barely noticed the air turning cold as steel clouds gathered overhead, blotting out the last thin trails of sunlight. With no idea what to do now, I trudged back to the station, the only familiar landmark in this part of the city. Still dazed from the sight of Ash, beautiful in her red dress, shining amongst the dark-coated men in the smoky shadows of the bar, I watched for a while as the endless business of loading and unloading went on, each man knowing his place, his job, the parts fitting together like a clockwork toy as the long noisy trains shunted in and out of the station. My mind sank into a pool of dullness as I watched the monotonous coming and going.

Eventually, stirring myself from this aimless reverie, I began to walk. Along the wall of arches and into the goods yard where enormous stacks of crates and containers towered above the men below – row after row of them, like a city suburb with its criss-crossing roads. Nobody noticed me, in my drab grey skirt and faded brown jacket – Pet-dear's hand-me-down. I found a path that led towards the river, over some wasteland and past the thick legs of the stone arches that stretched down to the bridge – I trudged on, not knowing, not even hoping any more. I felt empty, my future bleak and shapeless as the weight of cloud that had descended over the city.

Just before I reached the riverbank I came to the last of the massive towers that levered the bridge up into the air, high over the water. A wooden door in the side of the tower was open. Without thinking at all – of why, or whether I should be there – I entered the dark space and found a flight of stone steps. They led me up to the bridge, to a precarious walkway under the black metal beams, beneath the railway track. I was suspended high up over the sulking river, standing on a metal lattice path with nothing between me and the dirty water but air and a few iron beams. I took a few steps, trying not to look beyond the pathway, but my gaze was drawn down to the swirls and eddies of the tidal flow.

Then the whole structure began to vibrate. A train was approaching, rattling the bolts of the bridge and shimmying the skin of the river far below as the air was set in motion. It thundered towards me and over my head. I was lost in noise and billowing clouds of grey steam as the massive wheels turned, just feet above me, and hammered against the rails. The bridge trembled and I held my breath, afraid the whole edifice might collapse under the weight of the groaning train. It took forever to snake past and into the open mouth of the station.

I held onto a rail to steady myself and felt the damp sweat of my palms sticking there. Down below me, through the metal struts, I could see the river swirling seawards, grey-brown and sluggish. I felt faint and sat down on the cold metal lattice. The slushing of the water tugged at my belly, my brain, drawing me towards it. A magnet, pulling me down to meet it. I felt I could slip, so easily, through the gaps between the metal beams and into the grey-brown sludge below.

'Don't give up.' A voice inside my head seemed to be calling me, urgently. 'Don't give up, Ellen, not yet.' It brought me back to the bridge, to the dangerous ledge I was clinging to. I looked behind me but there was no one there. 'Don't let go – hold on, hold on,' the voice kept calling.

Struggling to my feet, I shook my head to get rid of the dragging feeling and the voice that swirled around me. My body was trembling and I felt as cold as ice. With one hand holding the rail to keep my balance, I walked slowly, stepping carefully over the empty space below, back to the firm ground of the riverbank.

I retraced my steps – along the path and into the goods yard, through the arches and back to the station platform. To the shadow of the arch where I had sat earlier – before Ash in the red dress, laughing and talking with her boss in a pub – before the bridge and the mass of water that churned beneath it. Before I had lost hope.

The men in their flat caps and coal stained trousers were still loading and unloading trains. Now I took some comfort in watching their repetitive movements, back and forth, up and down the platform, even paced and sure. A group of them were sitting on crates and smoking, taking a break.

I watched as two men emerged from an arch at the far end of the platform and walked towards the station entrance with some purpose in their stride. Then I noticed the odd limp of one of these men, the way he hitched up his left leg. Just as Helmut had done. My heart rose then sank, all in one beat, as a flicker of hope was followed quickly by the memory that I had lost him and might never see him again.

But as I studied the man I became convinced that, yes, it was Helmut. The feel of his body was so familiar to me now – his height and breadth, the square angle of his shoulders, his spine held upright and a little stiffly, the bold swing of his good leg followed by the painful hitch of the other. Now I was quite sure it was him. A miracle had brought my angel back.

I scrambled to my feet, aware again of how hungry I felt, but once more another need was more urgent. For the second time that day I began to follow, invisibly, some distance behind, keeping just out of sight. I wanted to be sure. I needed to know where he was going.

They followed the route I had taken earlier, talking intently as they walked, heads bowed towards each other as if they spoke in whispers. Before they reached the pub where I had seen Ash they turned left and kept walking down a long and straight road that had been pummelled by the bombing raids. They walked down the middle of the road to avoid the wreckage of brick and plaster that lay in mounds where the pavement used to be. I kept a good distance behind, closer to the wall where I could disappear into shadows if they turned around. After a while they stopped outside what was left of a tenement building. The second man, short beside Helmut, and dark-haired, exchanged a few words then looked furtively over his shoulder. I ducked into a doorway and studied the ground, glancing sideways to see him hand a haversack that he had been carrying on his back to Helmut, then hurry on his way up the road. Helmut disappeared inside.

Once the short man was out of sight I ran to the building. Most of its windows were broken. On the right side of the entrance, part of the wall had collapsed to rubble, revealing the rooms inside, several floors high. Each one had been covered with a different patterned wallpaper, now peeling and scorched in places. Some rooms were empty, some still held odd pieces of furniture, broken, tipped over, a settee resting vertically against a wall, chairs without legs. A picture of a woodland scene clung tenaciously to a wall, hanging at an angle but still in its place.

I clambered over the rubble that lay in grey and powdery heaps around a large crater in the road. The bomb had just missed falling full and square onto the building. The main door was open. Inside, the hallway was unlit and smelt strongly of urine. Metal-railed stairs circled upwards, winding around the vertical shaft of the stairwell. I could hear Helmut's uneven steps, tap, tap against the bare stone steps. I held my breath and tried to gage how far up he had gone. As my eyes became accustomed to the dimness of the building I saw his dark shape moving towards the top floor. I pressed myself into the shadows of the wall so he wouldn't see me if he looked down. He shifted to the left, the faint click of a door reached me, then there was silence. I released my breath. I had found him.

Tiptoeing, clutching my chest where my heart was thumping so loud I thought it would give me away, I went up, all the way to the top. The building was uncannily still and quiet. It seemed deserted – probably everyone had left after the bombs fell. Everyone except Helmut, alone now in this fragile shell of a hideout. Outside his door I sat down, leaning my back against the wall, to recover my breath and wonder what he would think of me turning up at his new hiding place like this. I wondered if he liked it better than the hut or the den, or Esther and Trevor's house. I wondered if he had a plan to leave England – on his own, without me.

I could hear the faintest of sounds from inside the room, but when I finally mustered the courage to knock, the sounds stopped abruptly and I felt the stillness inside the room seep out and surround me, like a landslide of mud pouring over a green valley. It was suffocating. In my mind's eye I could see him on the other side, wracked with tension, standing there facing me through the closed door. I tapped again, very gently and whispered through the crack at the side of the door, 'Helmut, it's me, Ellen.'

The uneven tap of his steps on the wooden floor, then a click and the door cracked open. I saw one startled blue eye looking out at me. He opened the door wide enough for me to enter, pulled me inside and glanced down the stairwell before quickly closing it again.

'Mein Gott, Ellen, what are you doing here? How did you find me?' He sat down on one of two wooden chairs that faced each other, one on each side of a small table, and gestured for me to sit on the other.

'I'm sorry – you're not pleased to see me.'

'It's not that. Just that it is dangerous. How did you find me? Did anyone follow you?'

'No – I don't think so.' My stomach turned over. I hadn't thought of this – that while I was following Helmut someone else might have been following me. I looked at the door, half expecting it to burst open. It didn't.

'It is not safe for you here.' His tone was as stern as I had ever heard him.

'Nor for you either,' I retorted. In my longing to help, I had made things worse for him, and to keep my shame at bay I felt irritated with him, with myself, with the whole damn situation. We sat in silence for a while, until I could bear it no longer.

'Please, Helmut, tell me what you plan to do. I'm sorry if I shouldn't have come, but at least let me help you now I'm here.' The words came out impatiently. The tone of my voice reminded me of Miss Parker, and for a moment I almost wished I was back in the classroom with her rapping my knuckles for some petty crime – for spelling 'occurred' wrong, yet again, or not sharpening my pencil.

He stayed deep in thought – staring at the table, looking at the door every time there was a faint rumble of a sound from the street below, clenching and unclenching his fingers – working out what to tell me, what needed to stay hidden.

'Surely you trust me, after all we have been through.' I hadn't meant to say those words out loud – it was a private thought – but the membrane between private and public was wearing thin and words began to tumble out. 'Please talk to me. What are you going to do? Tell me what happened after the bridge, Helmut,' I demanded. I stood up as I said this, but quickly sat down again. I felt nervous and afraid.

Desperate for something to help me, I looked around the room. It was tiny. Apart from the table and the two flimsy wooden chairs, there was a narrow mattress on the floor along one wall, tucked in beneath the eaves, a sink with a shelf above it, a paraffin stove, and a small skylight window. A small box with some stale bread and a few wrinkled potatoes sat on the floor by the sink. It really was no better than the hut, and once again I wondered why we had left Bellingham. I had been happy there, and Helmut seemed to be mine. Now he, like Ash, was slipping away from me, swallowed into a world of shadows, furtive conversations, secret dealings. And danger.

'Okay, I will tell you. You have been kind, so I owe you this much,' he said at last. 'Yes, I trust you Ellen, but this really is secret. You must tell nobody – not Ash, or Daniel, and especially not that stupid man next door.' He stuck out his belly to be sure I knew whom he meant. I wanted to laugh but knew the situation was really too serious for that.

'Of course not.' My heart warmed as he took me into his confidence. I felt safe again. For a moment I was back in the den, one of those special mornings when it was just the two of us, playing cards, going into the woods to snare a rabbit or catapult a pigeon, or to collect firewood. Once he had shown me how to carve a rabbit out of wood, watch it emerge from the shapeless stick, pale and smooth, like magic.

'I won't tell anyone, I promise.'

He sighed, seemed to be searching for a way to start.

'Tell me where you went after the bridge, after the steps in the alley, when the two men were chasing you. Daniel and I looked for you everywhere, you know.'

Helmut raised his eyebrows. 'Daniel?'

'Yes, he helped me. He wanted to find you too – so he could beat you up again, I suppose.' Helmut smiled for the first time since I had entered his secret hideaway – just the faintest reflection of his old smile, but I saw the light was still in his eyes. His face was pale and drawn, but for a moment it seemed to soften.

'I cannot run far, I must hide. I go through a door between the shops, through to the back lane, and run along there. Then the man is ahead, so I go through a door on the other side of the lane. I am in a kitchen, someone's home.' His brow wrinkles up in a gesture of surprise, his eyes opening wide. 'A baby is there, sleeping, but no one else. I creep through the house and out of the front door.'

'Gosh, you were lucky no one saw you. Were you scared?'

'Ach ja, scared, but I must keep going. I am in the hallway of a big building, like this one. A stairway goes up, and doors come off at each floor. I go up to the top and find the roof. I walk along the roof, one building to next. I am up high, many floors, so I cannot be seen from the road.' He pauses, glances towards the door, listens for a moment then continues, speaking in a hushed voice as if there were neighbours to hear. 'When I reach the end, I go down into the last building. I am in a big room — above a shop. Men carry boxes back and forwards, up and down stairs, so I pick one up too — it hides my face and I go through the building like this, until I reach a shop floor.'

'What kind of shop is it?'

'They sell clothes. A big shop, many rooms.'

'You must have been in the same shop where I was hiding! I bet it was. And I didn't see you.'

'I try not to be seen.'

'Me too. But if I had seen you then …' I stopped. There was no point in going over what might have been. 'What happened next?'

'I find way out, onto the street, a busy street. I walk away, in other direction, away from the bridge and the place where the men chased me.'

'Of course. You were too clever for them — you really fooled them. Daniel and me too.'

'I walk until I come to the station, near this place.' He stops, frowns.

'What happened then?' I encourage him to go on.

'I am tired, my leg hurts too much, so I find a place to rest — under the bridge where the trains go over the river.'

Late that evening another man had joined him under the bridge. It didn't bother him that Helmut had a foreign accent — there were many strangers in the city during the war, including Jews who had fled from Europe. Perhaps he didn't recognise him as a German — or perhaps it was simply that they were both homeless and that was a bond stronger than any other. They slept the night beneath the bridge and the next day scavenged for food together in the lanes and back yards.

On the second night some others joined them.

'Three Irish men, just passing through they say, here for a meeting. When they hear I speak German they very friendly to me. Say I can help them. I tell them I want to leave England and they say they will help me too. One brings me here the next day. Tells me I can stay here while they work things out.'

'Was that the man I saw you with?'

He becomes agitated again. 'Where did you see me?'

'At the station, then walking back here with another man. I followed you.'

Helmut dropped his head into his hands. 'If you can find me, I am sure they can too.'

'How d'you know they're still looking for you?'

'I am sure they will be.' He glanced at the haversack he had been given, sitting on the floor by his feet.

I followed his gaze. 'What is it? I saw him give it to you.'

'Miz Ellen, this is very secret. I think you should leave now. If you know too much you could be in big trouble.'

'No, I will help you. Whatever you are doing I will help. You will need me.' The possibility of assisting Helmut's war effort took hold of my imagination, gave me a momentary sense of importance. I guessed we would be doing something that would help the Irish and the Germans, but I didn't care. I would become a spy if that was the only way to stay with him. This thought ran riot in my mind, throwing up images of adventure and danger — a life of espionage. My life too could become glamorous, just as Ash's had.

I looked at the haversack, its angular edges and odd shape. I looked at Helmut. I sat stubbornly rooted to my chair.

He always found my pleas hard to resist, and finally gave in. 'Okay, I show you, but then you must leave. Please.' He squatted down on the floor and peeled back the canvas bag. Inside was a black metal box, which he lifted onto the table. It was heavy. On the front of the box was an array of dials and knobs and gages, an elaborate toy that Daniel would have loved. Given a chance, he would have taken it apart just to find out if he could put it back together again.

So I was right. Helmut was a spy and he was helping the Irish men. He had been given a radio so he could communicate with the Germans for them.

In that moment I saw him in a completely new way – not as someone wounded and lost who I could rescue and nurture back to health, but as the man he was – a German pilot on a mission to destroy my country. I felt fear and I felt utter fascination at the same time. Once again I felt the impossibility of these conflicting feelings living inside me at the same moment, pulling me two ways, threatening to tear me apart. I stood on a hair's breadth of certainty that being with Helmut was where I needed to be. On either side was a deep chasm that I might fall into and never return from. The dragging sensation of vertigo that I had felt on the bridge swept through my brain again, and churned my stomach over into a tumult of fears and forebodings. If I lost Helmut, my angel, forever, I knew no way to go on living my life. If I followed him into his life of espionage and danger, I risked everything that was right and good and sane in my world. I risked my life.

I had a choice between love and life. I could not have both. Perhaps I could have neither.

He was studying my face hard as these thoughts ricocheted back and forth. His hand slid towards mine, around the clumsy presence of the radio that sat, cold and lifeless, on the table between us, and gently took my hand in his.

'I have trusted you with my secret, Ellen. Now you know what I do. So now you must leave. There is no other way.'

I couldn't bear it. Tears welled in my eyes. I squeezed his hand tight as they spilled out and rushed down my cheeks.

At that moment there was a loud crash and the insubstantial door was flung from its hinges, falling onto the floor with the snap of splintering wood. A storm flooded in from the silent hallway. One large figure dressed in khaki but wrapped in darkness barged in. Another followed. I saw the shapes of others outside. I had been followed after all.

There was a gunshot and Helmut slumped to the floor, without a sound – just a thud as his knees hit the wooden boards of the attic room. I screamed.

Someone grabbed my arms from behind and twisted them into a knot so that I was almost tipped over. My head was jerked forwards and I saw blood pooling on the floor. Helmut was looking at me, still breathing, clutching his left shoulder where the dark red blood was seeping between his fingers. One of the soldiers kicked over a chair as he lunged for the radio, snatched it up and hurried out of the room. Other men, two or perhaps three, gathered Helmut up and dragged him towards the door. He was trying to say something to me as he vanished from view behind a tall and thick-set officer. I sank to my knees, but the one who was holding my arms pulled me back onto my feet.

I wanted to say so many things, but no sound came out. Once again words had forsaken me.

I reached the street just in time to see Helmut's face, white and cold as marble, eyes glazed and mouth set tightly, looking out from the back of an army truck as it jolted into life. His gaze met mine for a moment as the truck began to move away. I could read nothing in the blank stare. I wasn't sure he even saw me. Just before he disappeared out of sight, he dropped his head and looked down. In that movement I read despair. In my heart I felt the cold stab of fear – for him, and for myself.

The soldier that had brought me out of the building tugged at my arm and yanked me towards a black car that waited in the middle of the derelict road. A small crowd of people had gathered on the opposite side to watch the drama that was unfolding. Even the children stood still and quiet, wide eyes and jutting chins turning towards me as Helmut's truck disappeared round a corner. One little boy with a grubby face and matted hair stuck his tongue out at me.

'Traitor,' hissed an old woman, as I was led around the car and passed near to her. I was pushed roughly into the back seat.

As the door slammed shut another woman shouted out, loud and shrill. 'Traitor!'

Once I was safely behind the glass screen of the car window, a chorus of voices rose up.

'Traitor, traitor, shame on you, traitor!'

It became a chant, a tuneless angry chant. These people were loyal, they had suffered beneath the rattling grey machines of the Luftwaffe, and they had no sympathy for the likes of me. I was their enemy. I had betrayed them.

As I had betrayed Helmut. I had not meant to, but I had unwittingly led his enemies right to his door.

Shame flooded through me and I hung my head.

The soldier climbed into the back seat beside me. My wrist was handcuffed to his, but I had no intention of trying to run away this time. I knew there was no point. The other soldier got into the driver's seat and started up the engine. We drove away.

It was a short distance to the police station. I was led into a grey-walled room, empty but for a table with a chair on each side, facing each other full on, ready for combat. I was pushed into one of the chairs then left alone for some time – to reflect on my sins I suppose. I did. Again the confusing mixture of feelings that battled and contradicted each other – and now, on top of it all, shame seeped through the layers into the very core of me, into my heart and my soul, until I was swallowed up in it, like quick sand, sucking at me, dragging me down. The pain of losing Helmut stabbed into the heart of it all. A raw, sharp wound, it wrenched out my tears eventually. This had to be the most miserable moment of my life.

When, maybe an hour later, two men returned to the cell and one sat down opposite me while the other stood behind my chair, ready to catch me if I tried to escape, I had nothing left inside of me. Shame and tears had flushed it all away – the hope, the strength. I sat very still while the man sitting across the table fired questions at me, but his words made no sense. I heard only a loud buzzing noise, rumbling and roaring into my ears. I couldn't speak. I was silent as the blackest night.

I was back at home, sitting on the cold linoleum floor in the middle of the kitchen. Esther rushed in.

Act One

29

My back is turned to the door so I don't see her but I hear her footsteps approaching, quickly, click-clack behind me. I am quiet. I have been watching the play of sunlight through the leaves of the apple tree in the garden, streaming into the kitchen and falling in quivering threads over the patterned floor. The light tickles my bare feet and I curl up my toes in delight. A giggle is rising into my throat just at the moment Esther comes in, a big bag of groceries in her arms so that she doesn't see me sitting there. She trips over me. There is a string of banging sounds as the groceries are flung across the table and bounce onto the floor, each neat parcel of food bursting open into showers of powder and rolling potatoes and slabs of meat. Esther comes crashing down beside me, landing on hands and knees and banging her head against the sharp edge of the table.

I see blood burst out of the spot on her forehead where the table caught her fall. It's so bright, so red, bubbling up into a bead before it trickles down her face. I am marvelling at the bright redness of it. How it shines in the flickers of sunlight that find their way into every crevice of Esther's angry face, lighting up the whiteness of her skin, emphasising the glint of her eye.

She curses. I scream. My back hurts where her foot kicked me on its way to tripping her body right over me and onto the hard floor.

Then she turns to me – standing on her hands and knees she is at my level where I sit. I stop my crying as I see her turn her anger towards me.

'You stupid girl! I've told you not to sit there. Now look what you've done!' Then she wipes her fingers through the thin line of blood that has trickled past her eyebrow, looks at the red smear on her fingers, and begins to cry.

She lifts her other hand, the one without the bloody fingers, and I think she will hit me, but instead she moans and pulls her arm into her side as the pain in her wrist stabs. Her thundering eyes come down on me, black as coal now, searing into me like fire. I feel the anger. I feel the sharpness of her hand against me even though she cannot hit me, with one hand all bloody and the other perhaps broken. Tears roll down her cheeks and all I can do is stare at her. I am frozen – I cannot move even a finger or toe.

The world becomes dark. The flickers of light go out and I feel the air pressing in on me, squeezing the breath out of my lungs. The room swirls about me and Esther is now standing up and walking away. She seems to wobble and sway. Her edges waver and begin to dissolve.

Then I remember no more until Trevor comes home in the evening, comes up to my room, tells me I have been bad and must stay there until I tell Esther I am sorry. But I cannot speak. I am too young to speak. So I stay there for a long time, in the darkening room, hugging Humphrey to my chest and keeping very quiet.

Act Two

30

I spent a sleepless night on a hard bench, curled against the cold, only a thin pillow and one grey blanket to protect against the darkness that had crept inside of me. I was in a cell with bars from floor to ceiling, not even a door to hide behind. There was no window to show me when morning had begun.

I dropped into a fitful dream, but was startled awake by the image of Helmut's pale face staring at me from the back of the truck as it shuddered into motion. Staring right through me, as if he didn't see me.

The next morning, early, with just a cup of lukewarm tea and a slice of stale bread to fill my grumbling stomach, I was pushed into the back of an army truck, perhaps the same one that had taken him away. For a moment I dared to hope that I would be taken to him.

There were three other prisoners, handcuffed, like me, to metal loops on the sides of the truck. One was Italian and muttered now and then under his breath, as if carrying on a conversation with himself. Another had a thick accent, from somewhere in the heart of Eastern Europe perhaps. He spoke politely but scowled so furiously I thought his face must be in pain from the tension of it. The third was a local man. He grunted and complained constantly.

'What ye done t'end up he-er, lass? Young'un like yersel should'na be caught up in aal this.' He gestured vaguely to the city street we were bumping along, the people shambling about, minding their own business

I kept silent, stared at the floor.

'Please yersel then,' he mumbled, and turned his attention to the Italian. 'Bleedin war. Cannit even leave a man to make his own livin in peace these days, they cannit.'

The Italian didn't understand, but nodded and replied with what sounded like friendly agreement – none of us spoke Italian, so he was going to be on his own for the journey. We all were. Each of them looked at me now and then, furtively, glancing sideways from under hats or bushy eyebrows. I kept to myself and soon they seemed to forget about me, each sinking back into his own troubled world, his fears of what was to come next.

I was frightened. Just yesterday with Helmut, in the attic hideaway, I had felt grown up as he shared his dangerous new world with me, took me into his confidence. I glimpsed a life of adventure that could be mine. Now, with all that snatched away in one brief flash of splintering wood and gunshot, I felt like a small child again. I had nothing with me but the clothes I was wearing when I left the house just the day before, and my belly had begun to cramp. My bleeding would begin soon. What would I do then? I couldn't ask these men for help.

From the open back of the truck I could see countryside flying by. Roads, towns, green woods and a black mountain of coal as we passed a colliery. Now and then we crossed a river and the landscape flattened and opened out. The air was lighter here, with thin, translucent clouds drifting through the wide skies. Then we were going up, into the hills. At first I wondered if they were taking me back to Bellingham, but I didn't recognise these hills. The direction of the sun showed me that we were travelling south, to another part of the country. Far away from all I had ever known. Away from Helmut and Ash – and Daniel. What on earth would happen to Daniel? I hoped he would be sent back to the Graingers', but he would be angry with me for leaving him behind.

The long journey gave me lots of time to think. After the landslide of events that had swept through the last few days I felt the need to catch up with myself, as if part of me was still back in the air raid shelter, waiting for the right moment to enter Esther and Trevor's house when a blinding flash of light pierced the darkness and Mr Dempsey had barrelled into our world. That was the point where it all began to go wrong, where our plan started to unravel. The interfering old man must have set the army onto our trail the very next morning. I should have known he would give us away. Which would lead to me betraying Helmut in the end. I could hardly bear to think of this, but I must. My actions had led to his arrest and I couldn't run away from this fact.

I wondered if this was punishment for wanting to betray Esther and Trevor – for helping a German pilot so I could hurt them, get revenge for what they had done to me. Things come around. Even though I was still only fourteen, there was enough of a life behind me that I had to be accountable for what I did. I was old enough for this. I was guilty and I had been caught. Maybe I would be shot. I was sure Helmut would be, and I didn't really care what happened to me after that.

The truck bounced along, over the high hills and past wondering sheep that stared for a moment then returned to chewing grass that was already as short as the haircut Ash had given Helmut. Before we left Bellingham. Those seemed happy days now. How quickly time had eaten up all the happiness and freedom I thought I had.

As I looked out over the round green backs of the moors, I longed to run free. I knew I could outrun the lumbering soldiers who were accompanying us. They were not real soldiers – Home Guard, old men really. But I was shackled to the truck. Even when we stopped for a pee one of them kept me handcuffed to him – just turned away so he would not see me squatting with my bare bum to the earth. I felt humiliated. If I ran, he would be dragged along with me and I would get nowhere. Besides, they all had guns – the one driving and the two in the back with us. They chatted and joked and spat and now and then smoked a cigarette. The horrid smell made me cough but they kept on smoking anyway. I didn't count anymore. What I needed was not important to anyone but me. I would have to take care of myself as best I could, so I turned my face to the fresh air and the open view retreating behind us, counting each tree and sheep and farmhouse we passed to keep my mind from sinking further into the dark places that lurked inside to trap me.

I must have dozed, because I came to with a start as the Italian, sitting next to me, let out an enormous sneeze. I had slumped against his shoulder and was almost toppled to the floor when the sneeze jerked out of him.

'Maledetto tempo inglese,' he muttered, as he wiped his nose on a dirty coat sleeve. How shocked Esther would have been to see that, I thought, smiling to myself – then I remembered all that had happened and the shame flooded in again.

I turned my face back to the open air as we bounced past a line of army trucks going the opposite way. The land had flattened out, lying low and covered in a haze of the finest mist. Just enough to set everything shimmering behind a veil of watery grey light. Beneath it the land seemed brown and barren, but as I looked closer I could see little stubs of spring growing up through cracks in the earth – endless rows of green spriggy plants, laid out neatly across fields so wide I could almost see the earth curving off into the distance. A single row of bare-branched trees stood out along the horizon where the sun was beginning its descent, flushing the sky with a faint glimmer of gold.

The truck juddered to a halt outside a wide and very high set of metal gates, which I had caught a glimpse of as we turned off the main road. We had arrived.

The driver left the engine running as he jumped down from the cab. I listened to the uneven crunch of his boots on gravel as he limped to the gate. Words were exchanged with someone on the other side then he limped back and hauled himself up into the cab. A clanging, grating sound announced the opening of the gates, the truck leapt back into life, and we were taken through. I watched as the uniformed guard closed the gates behind us, securing them with three heavy bolts, before returning to a small sentry box to the side. A double wire fence, just as high as the gates, ran to each side of them before disappearing out of sight behind some long buildings. In the half-light of dusk they seemed to rise like shadows out of the flat landscape.

The guards who had accompanied us unhooked their four prisoners from the sides of the truck and jumped down as it came to rest. One grabbed the sleeve of my coat to pull me down after him, and pushed me towards the wall of the building we had stopped outside. He stood just behind, where he could keep an eye on me. A chill crept up my back as I felt his stare go right through me. The three other prisoners were led down the long straight road that divided the two rows of shadowy buildings.

I was stiff and sore from sitting so long on the wooden bench, jolted sideways as the truck careered over potholes and rattled down hills. I felt nauseous, despite having eaten nothing but dry bread all day, or perhaps because of it. I longed for a slice of fresh white bread, soft inside and wrapped in a crisp golden crust, with plenty of butter and plum jam – like we had before the war. For the second time since Trevor had told me the war was about to begin, I felt the full weight of it settle into me. I had arrived at the very heartbeat of the war, closer than I had been before – closer even than during the air raid, when at least Helmut and my friends were there with me. Now I was totally alone. Fear gripped me again, nudging at the sick feeling in my stomach, until I retched onto the bare ground.

It seemed like an eternity before a woman came out of the building behind us, saluted the guard, and he was dismissed. She was tall and thin, with breasts held in and flattened by the tight army uniform – I couldn't make out its colour under the glaring overhead lights that had just been switched on. They cast dazzling beams down from on high, highlighting our sins I supposed, warning us against any attempts at escape. It would be impossible to avoid the long row of white beams that flooded the length of the muddy track that ran through the camp, and also encircled the perimeter fence. There was no way out. Guards were alert at the big metal gates. We would be watched over at every moment, even while we slept.

I looked down the central track where army trucks, motorbikes and officers' black cars came and went. The officer with the flattened breasts gave me a shove to start me walking, and held my arm tightly as she guided me up the row of low buildings on our side of the track. She didn't speak a word until we stopped in front of one of the huts.

It was a long tunnel made of corrugated iron. At the front was a brick wall with a door in the centre. The ordinary wooden door, like any house might have, was strangely at odds with the peculiar nature of the building. It looked like half a building with its other half curving deep underground. Perhaps the under-part was the place where the souls of the dead, or the damned, were sent. An easy journey, straight down from bed to hell.

'This is where you'll stay. The sergeant will show you where to sleep. Come to the office tomorrow and I'll give you your duties.' She spoke curtly, clipping the ends of her words as if she didn't want to waste too much breath on me. I thought of Esther. I thought of Miss Parker. My silence deepened.

She pushed me inside and handed me over to the night guard.

Along each side of the dingy corrugated tunnel was a row of camp beds, canvas stretched on metal frames with fold-up legs. On each bed, the regulation thin pillow and grey blanket that would scratch and itch my skin.

This would be my home for the next two years.

I glanced along the length of the building as I was led towards the far end. Most of the women seemed young but a few looked ancient, with thin wisps of grey hair escaping from headscarves, and old knees, some bony and calloused from too much kneeling, some plump and sagging beneath their nightshirts. They all turned to look at me as I passed them. Pale pools of light circled the oil lamps on the wall, but the corners of the hut were dim and their faces seemed to float like empty haloes in the stale air. No one smiled, not a word was spoken as I was led to an empty bed. I was given a towel, toothbrush, facecloth and hairbrush. These were considered the essential possessions at the camp, but what I was in most urgent need of was some rags, as I could feel the first trickle of my monthly bleed.

Ash had helped me manage all this when it began, just a few months ago. I had felt embarrassed at first, but never the shame that flooded me now. I imagined they could all see my sorry state and were whispering behind flickering fingers, and laughing. But they soon lost interest in the new arrival and returned to their conversations. There was muted laughter. I wasn't sure if it was directed at me, but I was too tired to work it out. I crawled under the prickly blanket with all my clothes on and pretended to sleep.

Once they were all in bed too – the door locked and all but one of the lamps by the entrance of the hut switched off

– I wept silently beneath the blanket. Then I reached into the cabinet by my bed for the facecloth, and wedged it into my knickers to catch the blood.

31

A sound, one long, solitary note, like the first wail of the air raid siren, seared through my sleep, dragging me back to consciousness. The door at the far end of the long hut was flung open and grey morning light seeped in. The sergeant on duty stepped up to the opening, exchanged words with someone outside, saluted briskly then turned to us. Framed against the half-light I could see that she was short and slim with full breasts and pulled back shoulders. Her feet turned out like a ballerina's.

'Everyone up, on the double. Sharp now, ladies,' she bellowed out.

'Got your bleed, love?' A whispered voice startled me from behind as I scrambled out of the awkward bed. I must be showing. Again, the shame. I could feel the heat of it turn my face red.

'Don't worry – we're all cursed here,' she laughed. 'I'll show you where the rags are. Then breakfast, if you can call it that.'

'Hey, Doris, what you got there? Had a baby, or what?'

'Mind your business. Young'uns need a bit of help here. You were new once – remember?'

'Na – can't remember that long ago.' The other woman made a splintering sound that was meant to be a laugh, but it sounded harsh and angry to me.

'Come on, ladies! Hurry up or you'll miss breakfast. One minute to be out of here, and that's it. No more talking now.'

As she marched through the hut, inspecting the women and the beds they had left behind them, I saw that she wore a tight khaki uniform – skirt, jacket and a cap that was much too large for her small head. She tilted her head back to see out from under its rim. 'Harriet! Get back here and make this bed. Laura, tidy up this mess – now!' She poked with a stick at a heap of clothes on one of the beds, and the reluctant Laura flounced back to fold them in the correct way and put them into the cabinet by her bed. 'Now don't let me see you leaving a mess again or you'll get marks.' Marks, I was to learn, was just like at school – if you got enough bad marks you would be punished. As if being here were not punishment enough.

'What's your name then?' the woman behind me whispered.

'Ellen.'

'I'm Doris. Show you the ropes if you like.'

'Thank you,' I whispered back.

She took me to the wash-hut and showed me where to find what the women called the ragbag. A row of sinks stood on one side, toilet cubicles on the other, with no locks on the doors, and showers at the end. I followed Doris's example, stripping off my clothes then running beneath the row of ice-cold sprays, from one end to the other, dodging the freezing water as best we could. Everyone smelt of sweat and other sweet-sour scents, so it didn't matter really if you weren't clean. And everyone was naked together so it didn't matter in the end if you were fat or thin (though most were thin), with plump ripe breasts or withered teats. After my first run through the shower, I felt the shame of my nakedness begin to wash away, even if the dirt did not.

Once all the women from our hut were dressed again, we were marched outside to a tarpaulin canopy where two female soldiers were ladling out breakfast. I queued behind Doris for a bowl of watery gruel. At least it was warm and it was not grey bread.

Doris and I sat at a trestle table with six other women, all

British. I thought Doris might be about forty, quite old, but her face could be haggard beyond her years. She had seen life, I could tell. There were about twenty female prisoners, segregated from the male prisoners by a row of soldiers in khaki who stood, backs to us, eyeing the rabble of sinners at the rows of tables on the other side. Men and women alike were dressed in filthy work clothes – belted shirts and trousers for both, mostly covered in mud stains and hanging too loose. Many wore cloth caps. Some of the women had tied scarves around their heads.

I still wore the skirt and jacket I had on when I left our house in Newcastle to find Ash and Helmut. That felt like weeks ago, but it was only yesterday.

'Where you from, love?' one of the women asked between slurps of tea. The others at the table all stopped talking and turned to look at me.

I just stared at her. I couldn't find my words again.

'Dumb as a doorknob,' muttered another, and turned her attention back to her neighbour. 'Hey, fancy that one with the 'tache – the new one?' She nudged her friend and they both giggled.

'In your dreams, Lil. Soldiers won't look at the likes of you now,' chipped in one of the others.

'Why not? Lady Muck, I am.' At that they all roared with laughter. 'Still got what it takes, y' know.'

'Bet you have,' said Doris, raising her eyebrows. 'Too much for your own good, I'd say.'

The women laughed again, until the petite officer, who it seemed was our special minder, strode over and rapped her stick on the table. 'Enough, ladies. Off to your posts, NOW!' Though she was small her voice was big, and she liked to shout. The women, mumbling under their breaths, stood up one by one and sauntered towards a truck that was waiting near the locked gate. They seemed to know when discipline was required and when it was not.

'Not you, missy.' She tapped my shoulder with her stick as I made to follow them. 'You come with me.'

I was led to the first building, near the gate, where I had waited yesterday evening to be collected. She knocked on the door and after a moment it was opened by the tall one with the tight chest. She seemed to be the senior female officer.

'You'll be with Unit C this week. Ellen Rushton, isn't it?' She looked right over my head as she spoke. I felt invisible. Still without looking directly at me she thrust a pile of old work clothes into my arms. On the top lay a worn army jacket. It looked much too big for me. I noticed a round patch of black cloth stuck on the front, just where the heart would be. The number 254 was branded onto it. 'Go with Sergeant Isherwood to your hut and change into these. Quickly please. Then come back here to join your Unit.' She saluted Sergeant Isherwood and stepped back into the hut. The door banged behind her.

And with that my first day of work began.

Unit C was taken by truck to a farm some miles from the camp. There was nothing else for miles around besides the dilapidated farmhouse with its yard encircled by barns and outhouses. Roofs were tumbling in, wooden doors falling off rusted hinges. The air of neglect was depressing. Flat fields stretched for miles, the broad squares of grass and crops divided up by ditches and straggly hedges. Row after row of fields, ditches and low hedges for as far as you could see. And mud – lots of mud – on the roads, the roadsides, the edges of the fields. In places, a whole field, empty of vegetation, was just a quagmire of black mud and manure. The smell was foul.

We were a team of more than twelve – three other women and the rest were men. We had two guards, whose main job seemed to be making sure the men did not touch the women and the women did not look too invitingly at the male prisoners. They were allowed to let their gazes linger on the guards though. The younger one would wink if he caught a woman staring at him. No one seemed interested in trying to run away – but then, the guards did have guns.

'Know how to use a scythe?' I was startled from my private thoughts by the older one, who didn't wink and suffered no nonsense.

I shook my head.

'Here, stand like this. Now hold the scythe like this – no, not so close – you don't want to chop your legs off.' He adjusted my position, took hold of my elbows from behind, and made a slow sweeping motion. I watched horrified as the sharp blade swung past my left foot, just missing it.

'Good. Just a bit more space, not so near your body. Don't be afraid of it. Now try again, without me.' He watched as I slowly repeated the movement, this time holding the lethal weapon as far away from my legs as I could.

'Hmm. You'll soon get the hang of it. Not too heavy, is it?' He didn't wait for an answer, but I didn't have one anyway. The scythe was heavy in my young hands, but I didn't dare complain. I was here to be punished so I would have to take what came my way from now on. 'Okay, step over there and practise a bit. I'll come back for you when we're all ready.' And with that he turned back to the other prisoners, who were being furnished with scythes and pitchforks.

I practised – step sideways, swing out and up, sweep down low across the body, and a little flick up at the end. I began to enjoy the movement – it became a dance – step, swing, sweep, flick. I remembered the motion of the swing in the back garden, and for a moment there was a tiny flutter of joy, and then sadness, in my heart. It soon passed.

We were ordered to follow the older guard along the edge of a drainage ditch, while the young one took up the rear. The stagnant water smelt rancid for lack of enough rain to make it flow freely. I walked behind a broad-hipped woman who trudged heavily as if her bones could barely carry her weight.

Her boots were worn, the sole of one of them loose and tied on with string, like Helmut's, the boot on his wounded leg. He had tried to stitch it together with some twine I had found in the scullery, but it wouldn't hold and the string was still needed. I wondered where he was now, if he was still alive, if he was thinking of me. I was sure he would be angry with me for leading the soldiers to him. I pushed the thought away and focussed my mind back to the sound of our footsteps squelching along the muddy path.

We arrived at a field that was nearly waist high in weeds and grass, everything sprouting vigorously after the alternating spring rain and sunshine. We were to cut it right back so that it could be ploughed over and planted again. Within half an hour I had got the hang of the scythe. The whish of the blade cutting through the air, the feel of splicing through a bundle of stems, seeing them slowly cascade to the ground in a heap – I found some small satisfaction in the repetitive motion. By the end of the day I felt like an expert. After the distress of the last few days, it was a relief to fall into the rhythm of the work, to let it exhaust my body beyond speech so that my mind finally became quiet too. I slept soundly that night, after a meagre supper of cabbage and potato stew.

32

'She died, y'know – the one who used to sleep there.'

I looked up at the woman who had spoken. I didn't know her name, I didn't really care. I wasn't interested in making new friends, just to lose them again.

'They worked her to the bone and she went and died, she did.' She sat down on the edge of my bed and patted it, making sure I knew that this had been the dead woman's bed before it became mine. 'Not one of us though. Ukrainian, that one was.' She nodded towards the huddle of women from my unit at the far end of the shelter, heads bowed together in furtive conversation. 'There was a right fuss made when they buried her in the local churchyard, mind. The Fenland folk didn't like that one bit. And then the papers got hold of it and started shouting on about slave labour. But that's what we are, y'know – slave labour.'

'Give over, Agnes – you're scaring the poor girl.' Doris tried to protect me, but it would take more than a few words to protect me from what was inside of me. I let Agnes carry on scaring me. I deserved it.

'She's old enough to get herself in trouble, so old enough to know what's what.' Agnes turned back to me. 'What you done, anyway? You didn't say.'

'Can't say,' I muttered, blushing. How could I possibly tell these women what I had done. Or why. Or how I felt about it all.

'Please yourself then, if you want to be like that. Only trying to be friendly.' She got up and continued down the row of beds to her own, where she stretched out with her hands behind her head and stared up at the ceiling.

'I'd give anything for a fag. D'you have one, Agnes?' Doris asked.

'Nope. No chance.'

'Beth?'

'What d'you think?'

'I thought that soldier might have given you some – the one you were chatting with.' Doris winked.

'And if he did?' Beth smiled coyly and batted her lashes. The women laughed. Then Sergeant Isherwood came in and shouted the lights-out orders.

For six days I had scythed the field. My back hurt, my arms ached, my legs were so tired they could barely hold me up anymore. And my hands were covered in blisters that had burst each day and bled, then swollen up with fluid again the next. I didn't care what Agnes and the others thought of me. I just wanted to sleep and forget.

They gave us one free day each week – begrudgingly. It was Sunday and no-one was supposed to work on Sunday, but we had to clean the wash-hut, the kitchen, our sleeping hut and our clothes. At least it was a rest from the farm work.

'Can I ask something?' It was the first time I had been allowed to work with the English women and I felt like talking a bit. Doris was next to me, on our hands and knees in the wash-hut scrubbing the concrete floor of the showers where the rivers of mud had dried up.

'Course. What's up?'

'Nothing. I just wondered what the black patch on the jackets are for?' All the prisoners wore this sign, and as far as I could see they were all branded with the same number.

'Oh that. In case you try to escape – they use the black patch as target practice. Funny, eh?'

I shuddered. 'And the number?'

'Camp 254. Working Camp. That's us.'

'I see.' I turned my attention back to the scrubbing brush and pushed it vigorously round and round, in wide circles, smearing the mud from one place to the next. Trying to get out of my mind the image of prisoners running across the rutted fields, being shot at by hidden soldiers – right in the heart. Bull's eye, and the blood gushing out. The image of the evacuated children being fired out of cannons flashed across my mind again. More blood, spilt guts. My heart began to race and sweat was bursting out on my forehead.

'Hey, you'll finish up like that Ukrainian woman if you go on like that. Take it easy, love. Gentle, like this.' She swept her brush in a slow, sustained arc, side to side, barely touching the concrete or the mud. As if she was spreading the white icing on a Christmas cake into a perfectly flat snow scene. I imagined Doris had done that before. She looked like someone who had made Christmas cakes for a family before the war. 'There you go, easy! Don't strain yourself. It makes no difference anyway. Mud'll be back as thick as anything tomorrow.' She sighed and sat back on her heels to wipe her brow.

'D'you have children?' I felt bold as I asked, but Doris seemed open to questions like this. I was wrong.

'That's my business, ain't it?' She looked at me sharply, her face tightening into a frown.

For a moment I was afraid she might hit me. I mustn't ask personal questions, that was clear. She continued scrubbing the floor. I put my head down and returned to the scrubbing too, following her advice to go gently. I found a nice graceful rhythm and let my whole body sway side to side. In my head I began to play a tune that we had learnt at school, back in Newcastle, before the war. 'My Bonnie lies over the ocean,

My Bonnie lies over the sea ...' It soothed me and helped me forget that I had upset Doris, my only ally in this forsaken place.

'You'll stay with Unit C this week.' Sergeant Isherwood tapped my shoulder with her stick after we had finished breakfast the next morning, tipping her head right back to stop her cap from sliding over her eyes. Unlike most of the women, I was about the same height as Sergeant Isherwood, so it was easier for her to look down at me. Again the others at my table, the women who spoke English, sauntered off to their truck and I was directed to mine. The three other women in Unit C were Ukrainian, like the one who had died in my bed, and spoke no English. They worked closely side by side, seeming to ignore me as I tried to ignore the men who spoke in a gaggle of different accents but seemed to understand each other well enough to get along.

I didn't mind the silence. It helped me to forget, at least for the hours that I worked in the fields. In the evenings my guilt and shame, and all my fears would come rushing back in. All I wanted was to work and sleep. I longed for nothing anymore. I had given up hope of seeing Helmut again. Despair would set in each night as I tossed about on the uncomfortable camp-bed, itching under the coarse wool blanket and waiting for the oblivion of sleep to take me in.

This week we would be digging. We were to turn over the field we had cut back last week, by hand.

'Why not do with tractor?' asked one of the men in a thick and rolling accent.

'The farmer what owns the land has sold his tractor for scrap – scrap'll be made into weapons. Helping the war effort – so no complaining from the likes of you lot, if you please,' the old guard explained. I didn't believe him. He seemed to be someone who liked to punish people and clearly enjoyed making us work to the bone. He never lifted a finger himself.

But we had to obey orders. I was given a rusty spade, too

long for my height. It was a struggle to thrust it deep enough into the earth and stamp down hard with my foot. Hour after hour I struggled with the spade and the hard earth, jolting the handle into my chest as I hit flint in the ground. I had a dark bruise over my breastbone by the end of the day.

By mid afternoon the sun was shining, burning down onto my back. I could feel it through the thin and threadbare shirt, eating away at my skin, tearing off another layer of me when I felt there was nothing left to peel away. I was already stripped raw, right down to my bones. I thought there was no further I could fall, no more misery to descend into, but the unseasonal heat was pulverising me into the soil. I could die here, I thought. A wave of giddiness swept over me. The ground was giving way beneath me, the horizon shifting. I swayed and the rutted earth raced up to meet me as I fell.

The next thing I knew I was lying on my side, my face inches away from the muddy boots of the young guard. He was standing over me, his face haloed by the sun behind him so that I could hardly make out his features.

'You okay, miss?'

I pushed myself up on one elbow and looked about, confused for a moment, unsure where I was. Then I heard the other guard calling over.

'Hey over there – no time for sitting about. Get on with your work.'

The young one reached out a hand to pull me up. 'Ignore him – bark worse than his bite. Sit down for a minute if you need to.'

'I'll be alright, thanks.' I deserve it anyway, I thought but didn't say out loud. I held out my hand and let him help me onto my feet. Still there was a shifting inside my brain, a swirling motion that threatened to loosen my feet from the earth and release me into flight, or drop me back down again. I felt nauseous. The guard held my arm tight for a moment.

'Steady there. Sure you're alright?' He came close and I

could smell his breath – a trace of hours-old nicotine and the sickly odour of someone whose stomach was not in the best of health. I tried to pull away but he held me there, his face close to mine. He had acne marks on his sun-browned skin, which gave a rugged appearance that suggested life experience way beyond his years.

For a moment I was paralysed in his grip. I waited like this until the horizon was no longer shifting in and out of focus, until I could clearly see the row of trees against the cloud-strung sky and knew my feet were firmly on the ground again.

'Thanks. I'm okay now.' I pulled my arm away and picked up the long rusted spade. I didn't want this young man getting ideas about me, so I turned my back on him and resumed my battle with the hard earth. He shrugged and sauntered off towards the Ukrainian women, who stayed at all times in a tight cluster.

As I dug, the words kept repeating inside my head – with each push on the spade, 'I deserve it' – with each turn of the black soil, 'I'm here to be punished'. Again and again I turned over the soil and told myself I deserved what I was getting. Until my mind became numb by the action and the words, repeating endlessly. I was purging my guilt as I laboured. I would dig out the weeds and the stones from my soul, turn over the muck until I uncovered something precious and free again.

But when the day's work was over the battle in my heart would continue. I had betrayed my country by helping Helmut, and now I must suffer for it. But how could I reconcile the need to atone for my sins with the longing to be with him that still ate into my heart at night, when it was dark and only the snores and mutterings of the sleeping women disturbed the silence?

Towards the end of my second week the air battles began in earnest. There had been some distant skirmishes, and practice runs from the nearby training base were a regular sight during the day, but nothing like the hell that was let loose that night. A hoard of German bombers had swarmed in over the North Sea and our planes were streaming out to meet them.

I leapt out of bed, before even the air raid siren began, but there was no siren. I stood on the cold floor by my bed, shaking with fright. They were close. They sounded right above us and there were so many of them I imagined they blotted out the stars and moon.

'Get back to bed,' whispered Doris. She was lying stretched out on her back and rigid, like a corpse, the blanket pulled up under her chin. Her white bony fingers curled over the top of it, pressing against her cheeks. In the dim light she looked like a frightened child, with eyes wide and staring. I thought of Daniel in those dark nights, back in Bellingham.

'Shouldn't we get to the shelter?' I whispered back. Other women were whispering and turning over in their beds, but none of them got up.

'They won't hit us – in case there's any of their own down here. They're careful that way.'

There were no bunkers or air raid shelters for us. I crept back into bed and continued to shiver as the planes roared and rattled through the moonlit world above us. Engines revved, came closer, dived away. An explosion. Another. Three in close succession. The two armies of planes danced across the sky, weaving, ducking, soaring up and spinning down in whirls of fire. Doris was right. They didn't hit us, but they sounded very close by. The metal frame of my bed vibrated each time one crashed to the ground. Sharp pinpricks of fear rushed along my arms and left my fingers tingling and numb.

When it was all over, and what were left of the German planes had retreated back out over the water, I tried to sleep, but I felt as if my own heart was about to burst open. Could Helmut have been in one of those planes? I knew it was unlikely that he'd have returned to Germany, all in one piece, and be flying in the war again. But I couldn't help the thought piercing up from somewhere beneath my consciousness that maybe he had been up there dropping bombs on my country – on me. And then, to confound even this terrible thought, the fear rose up that he could have been one of those blown out of the sky that night, splintered into pieces by a strike from my own side.

I had to move. I slipped out from under the blanket and tiptoed past the women in their beds, some snuffling and snoring, some turning restlessly. The usually vigilant watchwoman was sleeping. I crept past her and pushed open a thin crack in the door. She had forgotten to lock it. As I stepped outside, moonlight washed over me. Full moon. The night world was luminous, peaceful. Out here in the natural world nothing had changed. I sucked in a mouthful of cold air and felt it trickle into the tiny pockets of my lungs, where I had closed down the life since I lost Helmut. My chest filled, and the tears gushed out. Deep wracking tears that wrenched from my belly and brought my body, curled up, to the ground.

Eventually I fell asleep against the side of the hut, my hands gripped tightly over my chest, trying to hold it all together. My hands clasped tight as if I might pray in my sleep, but there was no one to pray to – my angel had gone.

33

I knew he would find me. For the first few weeks I was waiting, as I worked all day in the fields – scything, weeding, digging. Eventually the early summer harvest began. It was on the first day of the harvest that I was called to the office instead of being sent out with Unit C and the hay carts. I knew what it meant.

I entered the office, which was like the other corrugated tunnels only filled with tables, chairs and metal filing cabinets instead of camp beds. He was sitting in the middle of the room with his back to the door. He had lost some weight and looked smaller, shrunken somehow. Or maybe I had grown. Or perhaps I had never noticed that Trevor was quite a short and thin man – not like Mr Dempsey, certainly. Here amongst the strutting sergeants, with their loud abrupt voices and broad muscled shoulders, he looked withered and old. I felt a sliver of pity, wondered if Esther still loved him at all, because if not, perhaps nobody did. I remembered that I had sometimes loved Trevor, but as I watched his rounded back and drooping head, the small hands that gripped the knobbly knees to brace him for what was to come, I felt only pity.

'Hello Trevor.' I announced myself, before the woman officer who had escorted me in could alert him.

He jumped to his feet, dropping his hat and almost toppling the fold-up wooden chair to the floor.

'Ellen, my dear girl.' He reached out his arms to embrace me and I saw that there were tears in his eyes. Then my heart leapt a little and sprung open. I could not shut him out when I saw him like this, so sad and pathetic.

'Oh, Ellen dear. How did you end up here?' He brushed away a tear and stood up straighter. 'But don't worry – I've come to take you home.'

For a moment I glimpsed the strong man I had once looked up to as my father, but he could not sustain the height and sank back into himself as he stepped forward to hug me. I let him. He wept. I felt the tears spring to my own eyes, but I refused to surrender to them. If I did, it would give him the power to take control of my life again, and I was not going to let that happen. I let him hold me and I slipped an arm loosely around his narrow back, feeling where the ribs and shoulder blade poked through the threadbare jacket that hung loosely about him. No one, not even the once wealthy and powerful, were immune to the ravages of this war. And without Esther there to cajole him on, I guessed that Trevor had no reason to keep up his appearance.

'How are you?' he asked, after we disentangled clumsily from our embrace. He was looking directly at me, with so many questions in his eyes, perhaps wondering if it really was me, for I had grown and changed a lot since we last met. I was taller, my breasts had filled out, and I was becoming strong with the labour we had to do each day. For this meeting I wore the red and blue scarf that Doris had given me, tied around my thick hair the way the Landgirls wore them. She had introduced me into the ways of surviving the camp. She had softened the pain of losing Ash.

'I'm okay. I like it here. I like the work,' I declared. This was partly true. I enjoyed being outdoors every day, working on the land. In the harsh and regimented life of the camp with all its rules, I had begun to find small moments of joy amidst the mud and pigswill and the endless square fields with their rotten ditches. Sometimes the sun shone brightly over the flat lands and I could see for so many miles I thought my heart would burst. On days like that I imagined my angel flew by.

'But you can't stay here. It's not right.' Trevor was nervously twisting and untwisting his hat, the way Daniel used to do. I wanted to tell him to stop. It was making me nervous too. 'Maybe you made a – well, a mistake of judgement, let's say – but you are …' I stood up tall and frowned at him. 'You *were* just a child.' Trevor was shrinking again. I waited to see what he proposed, though I knew I would reject it, whatever it was. I knew that being in the camp was the closest to freedom I would find, until I was properly grown up. And it seemed that freedom was the most important thing to me now. Now that I didn't have Helmut by my side.

He paused for a long time, searching for words. I waited.

'It's time for me to go to America, to join Esther.' He rubbed a hand over his now bald head, as if wiping something away, some stray hair that had forgotten to fall out, or some old feeling about living with Esther perhaps. 'Things have not gone well for my business. We were bombed – the main warehouse gone, all the stock burnt up, everything.' I thought he would cry again, but he held his head higher and took a deep breath. 'It's time for me to let the younger men take over. They can get it up and running again. I've done all I can …' He trailed off and his thoughts drifted far away.

I could see he had had a hard time, and again I felt sorry for him. As I took hold of his hand, the way he used to take mine as a small child when I was upset, I felt as if I were now the adult and he the child.

'I'm sorry about your warehouse, the bombing. You should go to America.'

'Come with me, Ellen. I'll be able to get you out of here. They'll listen to me. I'll look after you. Please come – we can start again. We'll live in the country if you like.' If he had been down on his knees he could not have begged me more earnestly. I imagined renewing life with Esther might not appeal to him, and my presence would make it more bearable, but that was not my idea of a future.

I stood firm. 'No. I've made up my mind. I'll stay here and work. Whatever I did wrong before, I'm making up for it now, helping the war effort, growing food for the country. There's nothing else I want to do.' And in the moment I said this I realised it was the truth.

'But you're a child still. You should be at school, out playing, doing things children do.'

'I've grown up. The war has changed me and I can't go back.'

I think he saw then that I was determined to stay. He pleaded a bit more, but as he did, he seemed to grow weaker and I felt more sure and strong. I thought of myself as a Landgirl now, not a prisoner, and that made me happy. I would not go back to being Esther and Trevor's daughter. With the help of Doris and the others in the camp, I would become a woman.

Once Trevor left for America my status changed. According to the camp officials, I was now an orphan and the question of moving me anywhere else simply disappeared. I stopped waiting and settled into the daily routine of the camp.

After saying no to Trevor I felt a strength begin to grow inside me, like a tree taking root. I knew now that I could manage by myself. I would make my life work out, somehow, without Esther and Trevor controlling me. I was free to be myself, Ellen. That was all – just Ellen – I belonged to no other name.

I kept hoping I would meet Helmut again after the war – I kept hoping he was still alive. I would look for him when it was all over.

I thought of him every time the planes flew over, which they did often, and we huddled in our beds in the dark as the two armies danced in the night dark skies above us, sweeping and ducking as each side showered the other with fire. Now that I knew they would not bomb the camp I wanted to creep out and watch. But after the night I had been found curled up in the dirt beside the hut, between the rubbish bins, the sergeant had been reprimanded and made to keep a closer guard over me.

There weren't any Germans with us though. There were Italians, Irish, Ukrainians and others of complicated origin – those who had been captured by the Germans and forced to fight on their side, against their own countrymen. Then captured again by the British. We – Doris, Agnes, Beth and the others – were Fifth Columnists. I didn't ask what crimes had been committed and no one asked me that question again.

I thought of my angel at night, when the day's work was done and I lay on my cold bed feeling lonely. I wished Humphrey was here to hug close to my chest, but I knew all that was far behind me now. He would be sitting on the windowsill of my room in Bellingham, waiting for me to return, but I never would. Instead I imagined I was wrapped in the glimmering white wing, curled up in its softness beneath the tree where I had first seen it, and then I could fall asleep.

<h1 style="text-align:center">34</h1>

The familiar tap on my shoulder came as we were finishing our morning porridge – more water than oats these days, as rationing steadily increased. Even though we grew all these crops to feed the country there was never much left for us.

'You're to join Unit G this week. Follow the others please – and mind you behave. They're a bad influence, this lot.' Sergeant Isherwood glanced around the table from under the peak of her cap, attempting to assert her authority over her unruly charge of British women. They were the worst, she kept telling them.

Doris patted my other shoulder. Agnes winked at me.

'You'll be alright with us. Don't believe a word that one says,' Doris whispered, nodding towards the sergeant.

'Quiet! I heard that,' bellowed the sergeant, raising her stick as if she might strike Doris. Doris stood up to her full height and looked down at the sergeant then, without another word, she turned her back and began walking slowly towards the gate, humming beneath her breath.

I followed the women from my table towards the truck that stood idling by the open gate. A corner of the tarpaulin that served as a roof flapped in the wind, where the rope had come loose from one of the eyelets.

'That means you're here to stay a while.' Agnes turned and winked again as she hauled herself up onto the back of the truck. 'They always put the new ones in Unit C – and the ones they don't know want to do with. Get the hardest jobs, they do. To see what they're made of.' She edged along the bench to make room for me. 'Glad I never was one of them. They decided from day one I'd be here a long time. A very long time …' She let her breath dwindle out between her teeth into a sighing, whistling sound.

'Yep, they do that,' chipped in Beth. 'Like that poor Ukrainian woman – gave her the worst time and then she went and died on them. Good you're with us now, love. We have a bit of fun, we do.' She nudged my arm and grinned at me. I forced a smile back. I couldn't imagine where fun was to be found here.

As well as the eight of us, nine or so Italian women crowded into the truck. They were beautiful, every one of them – even the older ones had a glamour about them. Some wore lipstick, and locks of shiny dark hair sprung from under elaborately knotted headscarves. Their eyes were dark and bright. They hadn't lost their spirit like the sad Ukrainian women had.

One of them began to sing as the truck bucked into motion. Soon they had all joined in and were bellowing out their song from the tops of their lungs, heads thrown back and arms waving in time with the tune. At the end of each chorus they burst out laughing. We assumed it was something dirty and some of our gang laughed too. It was infectious. By the third verse everyone was la-la-ing along, out of tune and as loud as they could make it, banging out the rhythm with their feet on the wooden floor of the truck. Tentatively I joined in, but soon I was hollering with the rest of them. We linked arms and lurched from side to side, until the truck swerved sharply round a bend and half of us landed on the floor in a heap of sprawling laughing sweaty bodies.

We arrived soon after that, some of the women still breathless and laughing on the floor, legs splayed out and fingers reaching for a hold on one of the benches as the truck jerked to a stop. We clambered down and the guards marched us into a field of cabbages – row after row of them.

They hadn't said a word about the raucous singing – in fact I thought they were trying to hide smiles, so I guess it was allowed. Even enjoyed.

Spread out in a long line across the width of the field, we each had a row of our own to pick. I stared at the shiny green globes that had been slowly poking up out of the earth through the spring, and wanted to laugh. What I saw was a row of green footballs and the urge to kick every one of them was almost irresistible. Doris must have sensed the tide of energy in me, my foot getting ready to strike.

'Now, we take it easy, love. It's a slow race to not be the first to finish. You don't want ever to be the first,' she warned.

'Why not? What'll happen?'

'Those guards, they'll give you another lot to pick and you'll be here all day.'

'But someone has to be first.'

'Just make sure it's not you. We have a system, so just go slow. Follow Agnes and me – we set the pace.'

So we all went slow, and we spent all morning on this one field, everyone finishing at almost the same moment in the end. The quick ones waited for us who were lagging behind. The pace gave me lots of time to enjoy the sun and the birds flying by.

All the stooping was hard on my back, but not nearly as hard as scything and digging had been. The two groups of women batted songs back and forth – a competition, a battle that temporarily dispersed any hostility there was between our countries.

> *Ma n'atu sole cchiù bello, oi ne',*
>
> *'o sole mio sta nfronte a te!*
>
> *'o sole, 'o sole mio*
>
> *sta nfronte a te, sta nfronte a te!* they sang.

It really didn't matter too much that they were enemies once you got to know them. I liked the Italian women, and we laughed a lot.

That evening Sofia sat on the edge of my bed with her legs crossed, the toes of her left foot barely reaching the floor. She was short, plump, and very shapely – rationing had barely touched her. Doris leaned over to look at the photograph in her hand.

'Nice, very nice. What's he called?'

'Enrico. He my lover,' Sofia announced proudly.

I could feel the hot blood creep up my face, I don't know why, and quickly turned my head to hide, but Beth, quick as a spitfire, had seen me blush.

'What's up, Ellen? You gone all red, love?'

'Nothing.' I coughed, trying to camouflage my embarrassment.

'Ah, let her be. She's young yet – she'll learn about things in time.' Doris, always the one to come to my rescue.

'Yeah – in quick time, in here,' quipped Agnes. 'Anyway, tell us about this Enrico – is he in the army? Or is he here, maybe? I wouldn't mind meeting him – wouldn't you, Beth?' She nudged Beth, a crooked grin spreading across her face that made her look quite mean.

'Oh yes! He's a dish.'

'Well he is mine!' Sofia laughed, her face lighting up and her eyes bright with pleasure as she tucked the photo back inside her bra.

'You got a secret lover then, Ellen?' Beth wasn't going to let it go.

'No – I mean, no – I haven't – not a lover.'

'Is that no, or no – or maybe yes.' She was snuggling up behind me on the bed and I could feel her warm breath on my neck, teasing me. The smell of stale sweat was sweet in her hair. 'I think there's some lucky boy back home – yes? A nice young boy.' She pinched my cheek, very light – it didn't hurt but inside I was smarting. The memory of Helmut was rearing up and if I wasn't careful I might blurt out something without even meaning to.

'No! Leave me alone.' I pushed Beth off my back and stood up.

'Hey love, it's okay. We all had a sweetheart when we were your age. Nothing to be ashamed of.' Doris again.

For a moment I wished I could tell them about Helmut, but I didn't want them spoiling him with their smutty jokes, their winks and nudges. I decided not to. He would stay my secret.

I shook my head and stepped out of the circle of women, almost running along the length of the hut and out into the warm evening air. I took some deep breaths. They must never know. I would bury Helmut deep in my heart and never tell a soul.

We had stopped for lunch, all of us sitting in a long row along the edge of the field, sitting in the dirt with our legs stretched out in a manly way. There was no need for decorum here. The old guards were used to us and just smirked when we got too rowdy. Now, they enjoyed their little moment of power as they distributed small packs of meat paste sandwiches. Again. It was all we had had for lunch all week, and the next week would be the same, no doubt.

'My grandmother said you should always sit with your legs crossed if you wanted to catch a *nice* man.' Beth laughed. 'Can't see how you'd catch a man like that – quite the opposite I'd think.' She jigged her legs in and out.

'Now what would you want to catch a man for – really?' asked Doris. 'More trouble than they're worth, in my opinion.' I thought Doris must have had a bad time with men. She looked cross and wasn't joining in with Beth's joke.

'Come on, y' know, Doris! But you're right though – sometimes they're not worth the trouble.' Beth lay back on the prickly verge of the field, where stubble from last year's harvest had not been turned back into the soil. 'Can't ever trust a man for long, can you.' She closed her eyes and let the sun play over her already weathered skin.

'I guess what really matters is how they treat you – are they kind – do they respect you? Doesn't matter how handsome, if a man doesn't respect you, it's not worth it in the end.'

Doris was right. I was thinking of Helmut and how kind he had always been to me – even if he was dependent on me for his life. I suppose that made a difference, but it was more than that too. And then there was Esther, who I didn't think respected Trevor very much – it worked both ways between men and women.

'What d'you think, Ellen?' Doris looked me right in the eye, her gaze open and sincere, as if she really wanted my opinion. No one had ever asked my opinion like this before.

'I think you're right – he has to be kind and respect you, or it's not going to work out well. And when he's grateful to you for the things you do, then it makes you want to do more for him.'

'Oh Ellen, you sly one. I think you do have a young man. That's exactly right – you know what you're talking about, my girl.' She patted me on the hand and smiled. 'You'll make someone a good wife one day – if you want to, that is. You don't have to, you know. Agnes there, she never was married, and she's okay – well, sort of.' We both looked at Agnes who was, at that very moment, biting into her bread and meat paste, and batting a wasp away with the other hand.

'Flippin – bugger them,' she muttered, as the wasp kept circling around her, ambushing her and the sandwich.

Doris and I laughed – out of affection for Agnes really.

The days and weeks dragged by, each one much like the other. Harvesting apples in the autumn was my favourite time – it was easy to slip an apple or two into your trouser pockets for later. No one minded, if they noticed at all.

Then December came and something extraordinary was about to happen. There would be a Christmas party for all the prisoners – the men and the women together. After a whole year of being prized apart by the guards – those brave souls who transgressed being put on toilet cleaning duties for a week – no one could talk about anything but the Christmas party now. There was to be music and dancing, and a cup of beer for everyone.

The afternoon of the party came at last. Sofia and her friend Francesca were doing up my hair, tying it into elaborate knots and wisps and curls. I couldn't imagine what it looked like, and there was no mirror to look into, but they kept crying, 'Bella, Bella!' so I surrendered to their nimble fingers as they tugged and twisted my thick gaggle of hair into shape.

'Now, eyes. Must have eyes.' Francesca dug into a grimy toilet bag and fished out a stick of black kohl. Sofia smeared it around my eyes.

'Steady on,' called Doris from her bed. She was painting the inevitable black line up the back of each leg, but keeping half an eye on what was happening to me. 'Don't want the girl looking like a trollop.'

'She is fine, very beautiful. Men will like.' Sofia laughed. She found fun in every little corner of life, prized out the joy where no one else would have dreamt of looking for it.

I touched my hair gingerly. I couldn't work out what form they had woven it into, but I was happy to trust Sofia's words. Maybe I did look beautiful and maybe men would like me. Why not?

There were no party dresses for us, though a few women had a skirt tucked away – perhaps they had persuaded one of the guards to find one for them. Favours could always be exchanged if you were pretty – and smart enough – or so Beth had told me.

When evening came Sergeant Isherwood ushered us out of the hut.

'Walk in single file so I can see you all,' she yelled from the back, but we were already hurrying in clusters towards the long hut that served as the officers' mess. A string of light bulbs hung over the doorway where a group of men lounged against the wall, talking and laughing as they passed around a cigarette. Vera Lynn's voice came crackling through the air – 'There'll be bluebirds over The white cliffs of Dover …'

Isherwood was clearly nervous at the task ahead of her. How on earth would she keep control of twenty women in a herd of cooped-up men. But she wasn't alone. Reinforcements had been brought in. As we approached the mess and stepped into the dull wash of greenish light that spilled out from the open door, we saw that the lounging men were soldiers, brought in to reinforce the regular guards.

'Hello, Soldier!' called Beth.

'Hi, Honey.' He doffed his hat as she passed.

'Ooh, he's handsome,' she whispered behind her hand. 'Bet you I can get him behind the mess by the end of the night.' We laughed. She probably could. I thought of Ash behind the cowshed, but somehow it felt different with Beth, more fun, a game. With Ash, I had always sensed a kind of desperation in her furtive meetings with the village boys.

The hall was teeming with men. Some stood in groups and passed around a cigarette. Others leaned against the walls, watching warily, their grey unshaven faces hovering in the half-light. Who knew what friendships and hostilities had developed between the prisoners. The soldiers and camp guards wandered amongst them, some exchanging a word or two with the prisoners – others ignoring the men in ragged clothes. A hubbub of voices, foreign accents, the smell of soap washed over sweat. Across the ceiling two strings of paper decorations had been hung, corner to corner, crossing in the middle of the hall. At least here was some colour amidst the browns, greys and khakis of prison life.

As we swept in with our lipstick and fancy Italian hair-dos, a hush rippled through the hall. A hundred or more pairs of eyes turned towards us and someone whistled under his breath. I hung back, watching as Beth and the Italian girls sashayed towards the centre of the crowd. The men parted like the Red Sea to let the girls through. I had to admire them as they chatted and giggled, sent glances towards the younger men whilst pretending to ignore their hungry looks.

Doris hooked my arm in a motherly way.

'Now you stay close to me if you want. You don't have to dance with anyone unless you like him enough. Okay?'

I nodded. I was both scared and excited by all the attention we were getting.

At that moment a lively dance tune came on the gramophone – big band jazz music was all the rage, and everyone seemed to know this tune. The conversations started up again and the room was full to the brim with noise. A bold young man came towards us and, after a brief word in her ear, swept one of the young Italian women into his arms. Others followed, swinging the women around the room. I feared for Sofia's safety as she was thrown in the air by a hefty man with the muscles of a wrestler.

Unsure whether I wanted to be part of this, I gripped Doris's arm tighter. I could fight off a boy with a stick and a pudding basin haircut, but I wasn't so sure about these men. We made our way through the writhing crowd towards one side of the room. Some of the men were dancing together, others stayed in huddles around the edges watching, like us – afraid or envious, or quite simply not interested after a wartime full of hard labour and fear.

We were into the third tune when a young man came up to Doris and me. He looked at her shyly, then at me. Doris was imposing with her height, her angular face and long nose, hair pulled back sternly from her brow. He might have thought she actually was my mother, and directed his question to her.

'Do you mind if I dance with the young lady, ma'am?' Doris raised her eyebrows at his polite request.

'D'you want to dance, Ellen? Go on, have a bit of fun if you want.' She released my arm and the young man, hardly more than a boy really, took my other hand and led me into the middle of the room. He put his free arm stiffly around my waist and kept holding my hand, gripping it tight. I could feel the sweat on his palm. He was nervous too.

As we began to sway, unsteadily but keeping more or less in time with the music, all I could think about was Helmut. This young prisoner was about the same age. Probably from some place on the eastern edge of Europe, judging from his accent.

'You English?' he asked me after a while. He had to shout to be heard over the music and the shouting that was coming from the back of the mess.

'Yes.'

'Oh.' He seemed disappointed. ' Me, Wasyl.'

'Me, Ellen.' I couldn't think what else to say so we swayed on in silence, carried by the mass of dancers, jolted and swivelled as couples came careering wildly into us, then squeezed close together as the crowd swelled. We did our best to avoid eye contact. I began to feel nauseous with all the turning and swinging. I loved to dance, but not like this. I longed to break out of the stifling throng of hot bodies.

Finally the record came to an end and there was a pause while a new one was put on the turntable. I quickly said thank you to Wasyl and made my way towards the exit. The music began again as I was halfway across the hall, faster and louder than before, a lift in the beat you could not resist. I was spun and caught by whirling couples as I fought my way to the fresh air. The swing – whoosh, up and down, arcing over – my head was spinning, my heart pumping so fast I thought it would burst. Joy began to fill me even as I battled to escape the heaving mass. Then the door was there and I tumbled out.

I whirled out into the freezing night air. The shock of the cold bit my skin but I kept dancing. The music was inside me now and the energy of it was spilling up through me, up like a fountain from deep in my belly. For a brief moment I was free, doing what I loved to do, letting my body take me. My arms open wide, my head flung back, I was drinking in starlight as I spun out into the night. Pools of light were filling my body, awakening every cell. I was carried by the pure joy of the movement.

The tune came to an end and I collapsed on the ground, rolling onto my back with my arms and legs spread wide. I let my body yield into the cold earth and laughed with the sheer pleasure of feeling so alive.

Out of the darkness came a chorus of cheers and I heard someone clapping.

'Bella, bella,' shouted one man.

'C'mon love, give me a dance,' called another, but he tripped over, drunk, as he stepped towards me.

I was mortified. My dance was not meant for them to see, not even the nice-looking Italian who was coming towards me with a hand stretched out to help me up.

'You like to dance with me?' he asked. He looked kind, with eyes that were dark and shining, a spray of crinkled lines at the corners.

He didn't wait for an answer, just took my hand and ran back into the hall with me following. He swirled me back into the surge of bodies. Men dancing with men were hurling around, some on the floor wrestling now. Those lucky enough to have a woman to dance with were jiving with gusto. The women looked beautiful as they spun and jigged their hips. Doris was dancing now, and even Agnes had found a partner, an older man with a limp, but that seemed to please her. She was smiling as he tugged her across the floor with a certain kind of grace that comes with age.

Without more words, the Italian swept me up and we were jiving with the best of them. My body knew just what to do. I had been dancing like this all my life, but alone. As he swung me up into the air, then down on the floor between his legs, and up again, I was back on the swing in our garden – up and over, down, round – whoosh – back, forwards. I had been rehearsing this dance all those years ago, but now, here was someone to join me. Our dancing became wilder. I was spun and tipped and thrown into the air. I was flying. We swung into each other's arms, then were flung apart, gripping each other's hand tightly and laughing with joy. The crowd moved aside to give us more room. As I turned and turned, a circle of happy faces flashed by.

Later, when the music had finished and we had been ordered back to our huts, I walked outside with my dance partner, my arm linked over his. We turned to say goodnight, and I thought he looked a little sad. Probably he had a sweetheart back home and he was remembering her now. I had forgotten about Helmut for the first time in months. He took my hand and kissed my fingers as he looked deeply into my eyes.

'Thank you, beautiful English girl. I am happy to meet you.' He kissed my fingers again, and might have kissed all the way up my arm, but the guards were watching and shouted for us to go back to our own huts.

'Ah well. The war. I will see you another time.' He gave me such a charming smile that my own face melted into a big smile too. All my shyness had fallen away with the dancing.

'And thank you. I'm Ellen, by the way.' I wanted to throw my arms around his neck and give him a kiss but I knew that was not allowed. We stepped away from each other and I joined the women who were traipsing back to the hut, laughing as they chatted about their conquests of the night. He hadn't even told me his name.

'Happy Christmas,' one of the men shouted to us.

'Happy Christmas,' we shouted back in one voice, and the whole place erupted in a chorus of greetings.

In the midst of it, one lone voice began to sing, 'Silent night, holy night …' In a moment everyone was quiet, listening, caught in the spell. One by one we all began to sing, softly, tenderly. Many voices singing in their own language to the same beautiful tune. Everyone knew this tune. There was frost and starlight, and around us the night was still. Even the old guards and the soldiers stopped and listened, some joined in. I noticed Sergeant Isherwood singing. Tears were running down her cheeks. I wanted to cry too. I wanted Helmut to be standing there beside me on that cold Christmas night. I wanted to enjoy this moment with him. I wished he could be here to enjoy the moment with me. I wondered if he was safe, if he was thinking of me, wherever he was.

Whenever I passed by the Italian dancer in the camp, we would smile at each other, but I knew that was all it would ever be – a nod and a smile, a friendly hello. He had a sweetheart, maybe a wife, somewhere else in the world, and so did I. He was my dancing partner for just one night, and yet I would remember that night as a special moment in my growing up. I learnt from him that it was possible to dance with another – not always to dance alone.

<h1 style="text-align:center">35</h1>

'So you're sixteen now, I believe?' The tall and thin officer was even thinner now, and her face looked pale in the greenish lamplight of the office. Her mouth was pursed tightly as if this fact was somehow distasteful to her.

'Yes, I am – since two weeks ago.'

'It's time for you to go back to civilian life. You've done your time here and I don't think you'll be getting any more ideas of aiding the enemy. Will you now?' She glared right into my eyes, her eyebrows raised as if warning me not to answer that question. I kept silent.

'Will you now?' she repeated, more loudly this time. I *was* meant to answer.

'No.'

'Good.' She rummaged in a drawer and drew out a small brown paper packet. 'You've worked hard enough and Sergeant Isherwood believes you've earned your camp money. So here.' She passed the packet to me quickly, again giving me the feeling that she found something distasteful about this encounter. 'When you get back to Newcastle, take this to a bank and they'll convert it for you.' I knew this transaction would mark me in the eyes of the bank clerks as a traitor. It would be hard to leave the humiliation of this judgement behind.

For our work we earned one shilling a day (the men earned two) – in camp money. What we didn't need while we were there they saved up until we left, but we all knew that they deducted most of it for various alleged misdemeanours or expenses they had on our behalf. Still, there would be a few shillings, maybe even a few pounds to help me get by till I received my first real wages. A thrill of excitement ran through me. I was to be given a grown-up job in the city, and a small room to live in – all of my own, no one to share it with.

It was my final evening at the camp and I returned to the hut to find a small group of women huddled around Doris's bed, arguing.

'Let me see,' demanded Beth.

'My turn.' Agnes snatched something from Doris's hand. I caught a glimpse of brightness, a flash of light reflected up into the roof. 'Oh my God! What a sight!' She clutched her face in horror.

'Now you know what we have to look at every day.' Doris laughed and reached over to take the object back. 'Here, let Ellen have a look. She's the pretty one now.'

She beckoned me over, hiding the small object behind her back.

'Now close your eyes and hold out your hands. Don't peep.'

I did as I was told and felt a thin object, something cold and hard, being pressed between my fingers. Its surface was smooth and the edges sharp.

'Don't look yet.' The others giggled but didn't interrupt as Doris adjusted the small rectangular object in my hand until I was holding it up in front of my face.

'Okay, now you can open your eyes.' She clapped her hands as she spoke, as if pleased with what she had done.

'I gasped as my gaze fell on the object I was holding up. Not at the thing itself, but at what it was revealing. A plain rectangular mirror, tarnished around the edges, the glass scratched and silvered – and in the centre a face looked back at me. My own face – but I hardly recognised myself from the young girl I had last seen in Pet-dear's bathroom mirror.

There was no spare flesh on my cheeks, but the bones were wide and the skin reddish-brown from all the sun and wind that had touched it – they gave my face a full and confident look. My brown eyes sat deeply in their sockets and shone there, bright from the effort of the day's work. From under the scarf I had tied around my head, curls of auburn hair had loosened themselves free.

'Here, put some of this on.' Doris pulled out of her pocket a stub of red lipstick and carefully painted my lips. 'Now look!'

'Isn't she pretty?' said Beth, with just a hint of envy. Despite her brave talk, she was not young anymore and her face had become lined and grey from the austerity of camp life.

'Yes – you're a woman now, Ellen. They'll love you back in the city, you'll see.' Agnes nudged me. A nudge was her way of showing everything – in this moment, it was meant to convey affection.

'Here, you keep this, love. You'll need it where you're going.' Doris pressed the lipstick into my palm and gave me a quick hug. I caught a hint of sadness in her eyes before she turned away and handed the precious mirror to Beth.

Tears welled up in the back of my eyes too. Doris had been a real friend, a support through two hard and dreary years, and like others before, she was about to disappear from my life forever. I knew we wouldn't meet again – outside the camp there would be nothing to draw us together, no paths that would cross. She would go back to London eventually, I to Newcastle. But at least this time I could say goodbye.

'Thank you, Doris. You've been really kind and I won't ever forget you.' The words stumbled out, trying to cover all the sadness that was lying underneath.

'Ah, get away with you girl.' Doris tried to cast my words aside but I saw her smile as she glanced back at me. She reached over and squeezed my hand. 'You'll be alright, love. Just remember – a person must treat you with respect and kindness, otherwise you walk right away. You deserve that much.'

The tears spilt over my eyelids and I could only nod my agreement and smile at Doris.

The next morning I returned from the office with the bundle of clothes I had been given. I stood in the doorway of the hut, the light behind me and the dark space of the dormitory in front. With the neatly folded clothes laid over my arms, I suddenly had a memory of Esther carrying her freshly washed and ironed laundry, folded neatly and laid out over her arms in just the same way. Like a cold baby offering.

She had called out to me from the hallway. She was hidden behind her masked face, allowing only her disapproval to show. But now, in a flash of recognition, I saw her as she really was then. Grieving. In that moment I realised that Esther was someone who had carried a dead baby in her arms, and in her heart. Her own baby had died. Or maybe been born dead – gone, right at the very beginning of its tiny life. And she hated me for being so alive, taking up all the space in her pristine home with my running and dancing. All she could do to protect herself from the pain of it was try to control everything – herself, her home, Trevor, and especially me. In that moment I could feel sorry for Esther. There was no point in continuing with my anger. She was to be pitied, not hated.

A dark blot fell away from my heart, just as the black circle on my jacket would very soon, as I took off the prison uniform for the last time.

I was glad the women had already left for their day's work. On my bed lay a large canvas rucksack, the familiar khaki showing signs of battle-wear, stains and discolouration creating a mottled effect. I wondered what had been spilt there. Blood? Or just rain and mud? Numerous pockets with small leather fastenings covered the outside. A piece of thin rope threaded the eyelets around the top to keep it closed, with a flap of canvas buckled over the opening.

Placing the clothes on the bed, I picked up the rucksack to feel its weight. The steel frame was heavy. To test the size I swung it onto my back, but it dwarfed me, coming down past my hips. The straps that were there to tie it tight around the waist dangled past my knees. I hoped I wouldn't have to walk too far with this on my back.

I put it back on the bed and began to separate my small pile of belongings, lining them up in a row next to the rucksack. At the bottom of the pile were my old clothes. I picked up the grey wool skirt and held it against me. It was too short now, coming down not even to my knees, though I had lost so much weight that I thought it might still fit around me. Make do and mend – I was sure I would find some use for it. I tucked it into the bottom of the rucksack, and on top of it the dark green cardigan that Esther had given me on the first Christmas of the war. There were holes in the elbows, which I didn't remember being there, or had simply not noticed before. I could probably still squeeze into the cardigan, and could darn the bare patches. The blouse was clearly too small for me now, but I would find a use for the cotton. A girl could always find a use for more rags. I rolled the blouse up and dropped it into the bag. My jacket was missing but I knew it would no longer fit me anyway, and I had been given a new one big enough to grow into.

One by one I picked up the new garments and held them against me, before stripping out of my filthy work trousers, shirt, and army jacket with the black target practice patch over the heart. I let them drop onto the floor around me. I would let them lie there – a last small act of rebellion. I smiled as I imagined an irritated Sergeant Isherwood finding them there, maybe even having to pick them up herself. Serve her right.

I put on the new brown wool skirt, voluminous khaki blouse, and dark grey jacket.

As well as these clothes (which made me smell like boiled wool), I had been given a spare blouse – the cotton was stiff and not as thick as my old one, but it would do for this time of year. A spare set of underwear – old ladies' bloomers large enough to take two of me, and a scratchy vest. And an extra pair of knee-length grey woollen socks – no stockings – still there were no stockings for people like me. I would have to paint black lines up the backs of my legs when I reached the city, as Ash had done, as all the women did now. I allowed myself a moment to wonder what had happened to Ash, whether I might meet her again. I was no longer sure that I wanted to. I had grown beyond my need for Ash. I had met others who had shown me there were many different ways to become a woman and helped me to find my own particular way.

I laid the new clothes carefully on top of the old. Together they barely lined the bottom of the rucksack. The space of it was dark and cavernous. It smelt of stale sweaty socks and rain.

On top of the bundle I had been given were a towel, facecloth, toothbrush and hairbrush. Once the towel would have been white but it had been laundered over time to a greyish colour. The toothbrush, hairbrush and facecloth all looked new. I picked them up one by one and smelt their freshness, then put them into the pockets of the rucksack – the hairbrush in one, the toothbrush in another and the facecloth in a third pocket. The pockets still hung off the sack like empty pouches, my paltry possessions having little impact on them. The bag itself had a robust presence, but my belongings were of little significance in the face of whatever it had contained before.

The hut was still empty. Keeping an eye on the entrance, I slid my hand under the thin pillow. My camp-issue flannel nightshirt was still there, worn thin now, its faint blue and grey stripes running into each other from being boiled then bleached in the sun too many times. I glanced over my shoulder to check that no one was watching me, then sneaked it quickly into the bag, not sure if I was meant to take this too, but knowing I would need it when the colder nights came.

Finally I opened the drawer of the cabinet beside my bed. There was the stub of red lipstick that Doris had slipped into my hand the night before – her parting gift. I gave the lipstick its own pocket in the rucksack, dropping the slender stick of gooey stuff into the darkness and buckling up the small flap again.

My bag was packed. All of my worldly possessions were there. I tied the thin piece of rope at the top, pulled over the main flap, and hoisted it onto my back again. It felt hardly an ounce heavier than when it had been empty. But I felt glad.

I stepped out into the morning light. I was free. My new life was about to begin, and this time it would be my own life. There was no one to control me now.

Act Three

36

I feel your hand holding my hand, your fingers cold as they stroke mine.

'Don't try to talk. You must keep very still now, try to rest.'

'But I must tell you what happened, how I met James. I want you to meet him one day.' Your hand is slipping away. I try to hold onto it – my mother's hand, it must be – but I can't. 'I never did find Helmut, though I tried – after the war – I wrote to the British army and the German air force, to Muenster. They didn't reply. I guess there were just too many missing people once the war ended.' My hand is tingling, where it remembers your touch. 'I didn't find Ash either, but I'm sure she would have made a life for herself in the city. She always found a way to survive. And Daniel – he was sent back to Mrs Grainger after Mrs Dempsey had found him all alone in the house and taken him in until Trevor returned. In the end it worked out alright for him – he was bright and got a scholarship to Durham. I saw him after the war – he was still angry with me for leaving him behind, but eventually he grew up and probably forgot about it.'

I reach out for you again but I can't find your hand. I feel your breath close by though.

In Newcastle I was given a room in a house with others like me – poor people, homeless people, people with no family to turn to. We were given jobs to pay for our meagre keep. It was a life of drudgery, working in the munitions factory twelve hours a day, too exhausted to do much else. I didn't want to make another friend, only to lose them again.

The air raid saved me.

It was two in the morning and the house had been sleeping when the sirens wailed out, rising like the cry of a giant mechanical baby into our dreams, prizing us out of whatever comfort or fear we had found there. Up and down the mechanical scale went the siren, so utterly bleak and haunting. It tore at the sinews of your heart and you knew it meant that lives would likely be lost in the night. Always hoping it would not be your life, or your friend's or a loved one's.

My head still thick with sleep, I slipped into my coat and shoes, gathered up a blanket, and followed the others down stairs and onto the street. With fear spurring us on, we began running to the public shelter, joining the streams of people who flocked from all directions towards the big doors of the Municipal Hall.

The siren wailed out through the night skies once more. Someone stumbled in front of me and fell to the ground. I almost fell on top of her as the crowd rushed past, bumping into me in their haste. Bending down to help her up, I saw an old and lined face, eyes as pale as clouds, hardly seeing. She waved a gnarled hand as if to shoo me away, but I held her arm and tugged at it.

'Get away with you girl. A'll be fine,' she said, trying to shake off my hand.

I bent down to get a firmer grip. With both hands under her shoulders, I managed to pull her to her feet. The crowd was thinning now. The sirens blared out again as the stragglers reached the open door and descended, one by one, into the underground rooms that would shelter them for the night. The rattling of the planes was getting louder. The first explosion erupted further down the river, setting a tremor of fear through the earth and lighting up the sky down by the docks.

'Put your arm round my neck.' I tried to pull her up, but the arm was limp, as if it didn't want to be lifted to safety, and hung heavily across my shoulder. I held her hand tightly and her body trailed behind, would not walk.

'Come on,' I panted, 'you must try to walk.'

'Let me be,' she whispered. I wondered if she was dying and it no longer mattered to her if she was left out in the street for the bombs to find her unprotected corpse. I would not give her up though, as if my own life depended on getting this frail old woman safely to the shelter, as if every wrong I had done could be righted by this one act, even if it was my last.

Bending low, I squirmed beneath her ribs and scooped her onto my shoulder, to carry her, like a stack of hay to the cart. I was grateful for the two long years of labour now, how strong they had grown me, but she was not slight and I was struggling to hold her there.

I thought of you. I thought – this could be my own mother. I cannot let her die out here in the road, like helpless prey left there for the planes to swoop down on and demolish in one fierce strike. But they were getting close now, engines coughing and whirring across the sky, explosions searing the night, leaving a stream of fireballs in their wake.

'Here, let me help.' A man's voice shouted above the din, right behind me. As I turned I almost dropped my heavy bundle, but he caught her and swept her into his arms. 'Come on – run!'

We ran. We reached the shelter just in time to see a blaze of fire erupt across the square, the boom of the explosion following right behind the light. Flames and smoke. The crash of walls collapsing, the suck of the underdraft.

'Get inside!' He pulled me from the entrance where I stood, transfixed by the fire as it took hold, licking and sweeping through the building, walls becoming translucent in the heat before they fell. We were the last to arrive. He banged the door shut behind us and we descended the dark stairway into the bowels of the building, the hollow cracking noise still throbbing in my ears.

'That was a close shave,' the young man said as we arrived at the bottom of the long flight of stairs into a labyrinth of cellar rooms, lit by paraffin lamps and smelling of fear. I followed him as he found a place to lie the woman down. 'Can you stay with her while I get help?'

'Of course.'

Only after he had returned with a nurse, and given over his charge, did he turn to me and ask, 'A relative?'

'No, she just fell in the road in front of me.' I was shaking, now that we had arrived in the damp safety of the shelter – from the effort of carrying her weight, or the cold, or fear – I was not sure which.

'You're brave – well done. You should join the Wardens. We need more strong young women like you.'

'I might do that.'

Beneath the soot and grime I could see he was handsome and I guessed that his hair was a sandy brown colour, though in the dimness it was hard to tell. Light danced in his eyes, reflected from the lamp that hung from a hook on the wall above us. He smiled. 'Hello. I'm James.'

'I'm Ellen,' I said, feeling shy and young again, as I had not felt for a long time. I took his outstretched hand and it felt warm and strong, like Helmut's had felt. I wanted to melt into him, but he was a stranger so I took back my hand and dropped my gaze. We sat side by side as bombs exploded up above us, sometimes close enough to set the building trembling. The cups of tea we had been given were stirred into waves and eddies of chaotic motion. The dark tunnels of the shelter vibrated with the sounds of children crying out and babies screaming. Mothers soothed and scolded in turn, old men threw dice or rustled newspapers, some discussed and argued about the outcomes of the war. No one slept.

James and I did not speak much, but I was glad to have him sitting by my side. When the air raid was over and he was called back to duties he asked if he could see me again. I said yes.

And that's how Act Three of my life began. My life with James.

37

'Darling, it's me. I'm here now.'

It takes great effort to open my eyes. My eyelids feel heavy, like mud sliding over my cheeks, an avalanche of mud and scree. I struggle to pull myself back. His voice is thick and warm. His fingers are playing with mine.

'You're going to be alright,' he tells me. 'I came as quickly as I could.'

Now I see him. His eyes are red and there are tears brimming over. 'Dear James, don't cry, don't be sad. I'll take care of you.'

I'm not sure if I said that out loud. He doesn't seem to hear but he sees me open my eyes and he smiles. More tears, big tears roll down his face, like rain, like a river.

'We sat by the Coquet River, watching the children play in the water, catching tadpoles in a net. Do you remember? The sun was shining, it was warm. Anita in the red shorts she wouldn't take off all summer. Martin as brown as a berry and happy as could be. You played football with them on the river meadow while I pretended to sleep, but I was watching you. Do you remember that day, James?'

'Shh, don't tire yourself out, love. You need to rest — the doctor says.'

'But I must tell you about my angel. I never told you about him. I want you to know …' He doesn't hear me. He is picking up each of my fingers in turn, as if counting them. Have I lost one?

'Please James – I must tell you – I found an angel.'

'Oh that's good, darling. An angel.' Then the tears spring from the corners of his eyes again and he pulls my hand up to his cheek. It takes so long to arrive there. The cheek is wet. Beneath the wetness I feel the soft, rough skin I know so well, and the sharp stubble where he hasn't shaved. I can smell him now. James, my love. You are here now and I feel safe.

'Then I found you, James. And with you, I found everything I had been searching for. In the end it was you.'

I close my eyes and I am sinking back, sliding down the avalanche, rolling with the mud and scree. 'I must go now, James. Tell Martin and Anita I love them. Please tell Anita – when she's older – to look for Liza – if I can't find her, she must try. She must meet Liza one day. Will you promise me that?' Again, I don't know if he hears me.

Another voice arrives, a woman this time. Is it you, Liza? He drops my fingers as he turns towards the voice, and I slide away. With the mud, into the dark.

And then I see him. Approaching through the darkness, Helmut holds a hand out towards me. 'Come, Ellen. Come now – it is time.'

There's a soft glow, a darkness that shines – light and dark at the same time. Like my heart, full of shadows and joy. He is here, my angel. The wing of white silk wraps around me, and he draws me to him.

Acknowledgments

My thanks to Chris Snape and the writing group for their support and enthusiasm; the tutors and participants on the CBC writing course for their creative ideas and very generous and encouraging feedback; and to my dear friend and fellow writer Liz McCormick for being there at every step of the way.

I am indebted to authors Juliet Gardiner, Mike Brown, Derek E Johnson, Midge Gillies, James Marsh and Wasyl Nimenko, whose work has helped enormously in my research of Britain during the second world war, and especially the experience of children.

Thank you as always to friends and family and, in particular, to my mother Audrey Lily Farrow, whose experience as an evacuee during WW2 was one of the inspirations for this story.

About the author

Linda Hartley studied dance and creative writing at Dartington College of Arts, UK, then went on to train as a somatic movement therapist and psychotherapist. She has worked in these fields for many years as a therapist and teacher, developing professional training programmes in Germany, the UK, Lithuania and Russia. She has offered workshops and retreats that explore the relationship between movement, image and words, and currently leads retreats in the Discipline of Authentic Movement in her Norfolk studio. Writing has always woven through her practice.

the broken line is her first novel, and *angel wing* is its prequel.

Linda lives in England, near the North Norfolk coast.
www.lindahartley.co.uk

www.ingramcontent.com/pod-product-compliance
Lightning Source LLC
Chambersburg PA
CBHW061118100726
47911CB00013B/597